HALF A FAERIE
FAERIES OF DOOR COUNTY

TONI CABELL

I0769999

Copyright © 2024 by Toni Cabell

All rights reserved.

The characters and events in this book are fictitious. Any similarity to real persons, living or dead, is coincidental and not intended by the author.

No part of this book may be reproduced in any form or by any electronic or mechanical means, including information storage and retrieval systems, without written permission from the author, except for the use of brief quotations in a book review.

Edited by MK Editing

Cover Design and Character Art by BookDesignCompany

Published by Endwood Press LLC

 Formatted with Vellum

Drakus–Chen Wedding

Mr. and Mrs. Everild Leopold Drakus
request the pleasure of your presence
at the marriage of their daughter

Estella Viktoria
to
Sammy Lee Chen

Saturday, the eighth of December
At half past five in the afternoon

Mooncrest Inn
Door County, Wisconsin

Reception to follow

CHAPTER 1
PARANORMAL WEDDING PLANNER

CASSIA

Friday, December 7

I take another sip of my spicy, chili-pepper-infused hot mocha and stare out the picture window of the Sit for a Spell Café. Nine inches of snow glistens on the sidewalks, the cars parked along Main Street, and the roof of the Rhyme 'N Riddle Bakeshop across the street. Fluffy, white flakes swirl in front of the window, pommeling the frosted glass and piling up on the sills. With another foot expected by morning, I'm growing more anxious by the minute. Will everyone make it to the wedding?

I clamp a hand over my mouth, which suddenly feels like I'm drinking sawdust instead of mocha. With my free hand, I reach up and touch the top of my left ear, and then my right. The tips of both are *pointy*. No, no, no... this is *not* happening right now!

I rummage through my handbag until I find my bright pink compact case. I don't bother opening my mouth and peering inside because I know why my tongue is stuck fast to the roof of my mouth. I suffer from anxiety-induced xerostomia, a fancy term for dry mouth.

Instead, I push my long, blonde bangs back from my face and lift up a chunk of hair. My safe, normal human-girl ears now rise upward into dramatic faerie-girl points. And the ends of my eyebrows are slanting upward too. My bangs are a bit longer than fashionable, and my hair always covers my ears, precisely for this sort of accidental faerie breakout.

At least I'm not feeling any wing-stumps forming beneath my top, but this is bad enough, since I have zero control over my faerie nature. I let my hair fall back into place and drop my head in my hands with a groan.

"Sweet moonglow, what's wrong?" Aunt Phoebe slides into the bench seat across from me. We're sitting in one of the antique oak booths rimming the front of the café beneath the plate glass windows.

Like me, my aunt is wearing jeans, a long-sleeved sweater, and a black apron with Sit for a Spell embroidered in golden thread across the top. She's using a glamour to mask her faerie features: tipped up eyebrows, pointy ears, and furled, gold-and-black wings. Phoebe, like every other faerie in Riddle Hill, has hidden slits in the backs of her tops so she can stretch out her wings after hours, or while she's baking in the kitchen.

Supers can see through any glamour, but our human customers are none the wiser. However, there's one more thing about my aunt that only I can see: the way her magic twinkles and swirls around her in a continuous spray of golden sparkles. Phoebe can *see the results* of her magic, but I can *see the thing itself.* I could sit and watch her magic all day.

"Is it Olivia?" asks Phoebe, sounding worried. "She's not hurt, is she?"

I mumble into my hands. "Olivia'sth justh fine! An' sthee adoresth th' sthsnow."

"Cassia Tinker Bell Spellman, stop muttering and tell me what's going on!"

I cringe when I hear my middle names spoken aloud. I can still recall the snickers at the start of every school year, when my teachers called out my legal name for their attendance records. Even other faerie kids made fun of me: the half-human, half-faerie crossbreed without any magic of her own, named after the sassiest faerie in fiction. What were my parents thinking?

Fortunately, my aunt rarely uses my full name, and then only in the company of other supers.

My head snaps up. What if one of our non-supernatural regulars has stopped by for a late afternoon carryout? Aunt Phoebe never turns away a customer, and I'm clueless when it comes to casting a glamour.

I quickly scan the cheery, sunshine-yellow restaurant, decorated for Christmas with fresh greens, red bows and berries, and white-tipped pinecones draping walls and windows. My eyes go directly to the massive stone counter running along the back wall. Five gargoyles, one per carved corbel, give me a cheeky wink. I ignore them; gargoyles are nothing but trouble, and the café's little monsters are no exception.

A glass-domed display case filled with Phoebe's cakes and pies sits at one end of the long counter, and I can see my aunt's gold faerie dust twirling inside. My mouth starts to water just looking at the dessert case, and my tongue loosens a little bit. Since it's well past three in the afternoon, the last of our lunch-time customers are gone. We're alone, except for Uncle Nash cleaning pots in the kitchen.

I reach up and push my hair back from my face and ears. Phoebe's gray eyes blink and then narrow. "Are you going through the change?"

I let out an exasperated sigh. I've been waiting two decades for my wings and faerie magic to manifest. All my sweaters have hidden slits just like everyone else, but I've never needed them.

I take several sips of my mocha to completely unstick my tongue. "I'm twenty-nine years old. If I were going to transform, don't you think it would have happened by now? This is what it always is for me—a panic attack!"

My mom was a human who believed in magic, and my dad was Phoebe's twin brother. And while supers cross-mate more often than you might think, human-super matches are far less common. Anything can happen. Take my half-brother, Jake, who was adopted by my dad after he married my mom. Jake's birth father was a werewolf, and so is Jake; he shifted for the first time when he was a toddler.

"What were you thinking about when your, ah—" Phoebe waves her hand in the air "—when your symp-toms started?"

"Weddings, snowy weather, and what could go wrong." I'm planning a different supernatural wedding each weekend until Christmas—three in all—including my cousin Sophie's wedding on December twenty-second. "I'm not anxious about Sophie's, at least not yet, but I'm starting to worry about how the weather will affect Estee's tomorrow."

Sophie and Estee are my two best friends. It's purely coincidental they're getting married a few weeks apart, and it's only natural they wanted me to plan their weddings, since that's my side gig. I'm a full-time server at my aunt and uncle's café, and a part-time wedding planner for the supernatural community.

Estee, my gorgeous vampire chum, is finally marrying her nemesis at the Riddle Hill Police Department, Sam Chen, a dashing faerie from Nashville who moved into town last year. Sam immediately started issuing Estee tickets for the merest infractions, such as double parking her car for twenty minutes in front of Vlad's Victuals, or turning left at a red light at night when no one else was around—except, apparently, for Sam. After the seventh ticket Estee ripped up in his face, Sam worked up enough nerve to ask her out. By the fifteenth ticket, they were engaged.

Phoebe smooths back her auburn bob, even though not a strand is out of place. It never is; my aunt works fourteen hours a day, but she always looks fresh and put together. Unlike me, with my too-long bangs, sloppy ponytail, and dark circles under my eyes that I camouflage with makeup. Working two jobs and raising Olivia on my own gives me very little time to actually sleep.

"Have you reconfirmed the details?" asks Phoebe, who knows the best way for me to manage my anxiety is to unpack whatever triggered it in the first place.

"I spoke with Mona at the inn just an hour ago," I tell her, "and with Mrs. Drakus, Estee's mom, last night. I can't think of anything major that could go wrong at this point. On the other hand, this is a lot of snow, and the wedding is tomorrow."

I pull out my tablet and run through Estee's reception checklist once more, just to be sure. Double-checking everything helps me feel a little more in control. "Let's see. Open bar, sit-down dinner, and a vampire band from Kewaunee, so they'll make it despite the snow. Plus, we'll have a games corner with pick-a-duck, bean bag toss, mustache props, and an old-timey photo booth, all set up and run by Granny Catbeam." I recommended the carnival-themed reception, since Sam took Estee to the state fair for their first date.

"What about flowers?" asks Phoebe.

"Designed by Mrs. Drakus."

"Then I think you're worrying needlessly. This is northern Wisconsin; everyone expects snow this time of year."

My phone vibrates on the table. Phoebe and I both glance down at the caller: *Mooncrest Inn.*

"Oh dear," murmurs my aunt. "I hope I didn't speak too soon."

I shrug, trying to tamp down my unease. "Maybe it's a prospective client staying at Riddle Hill's finest resort." I take a deep breath before answering the call. "Cassia Spellman, the Wedding Wizard. How may I help you?"

"We're taking on water, Cassia!" whines Mona Lisa DeMaris, who spent the past decade as a cruise director.

She uses seafaring similes when she's stressed. "Hang on tight because the surf's rough!"

"Whoa, skipper, slow down and fill me in."

"Don your life vest and dive right in," Mona groans into the phone. "There's nothing left but to swim for it!

"Go on, I'm listening."

"My supplier just called me. Apparently, this snowstorm is wreaking havoc with his deliveries. He can't fulfill my food order for tomorrow. I won't have enough chicken for the reception. I won't even have enough for the head table. I'm so sorry. I don't see how I can save this ship!"

The snowfall isn't enough to disrupt work or school for Wisconsin natives, at least not yet, but the heaviest band of snow is passing south of us. The storm's already caused traffic pileups and flight cancelations.

I hear Mona's fingernails tapping on her keyboard, searching in vain for a food supplier able to deliver dinner to a ballroom full of wedding guests, in a snowstorm, on extremely short notice. Unless we can find a supplier who managed to get out ahead of the storm—which the inn's supernatural vendor failed to do—according to Mona, we're adrift without a paddle.

I clutch a fistful of my hair, and my ponytail comes completely undone. "Tell me what you have on hand." Mona and I go through the menu together. With strategic substitutions, Mona can swing appetizers, soup, and salad. She has plenty of wine and spirits in the inn's extensive cellar and always keeps a ready supply of tart Door County cherry juice on hand for vampire guests.

Dessert is also covered, since I hired Sophie to bake the wedding cake. The Rhyme 'N Riddle Bakeshop will be delivering the cake and several trays of cookies and pastries tomorrow afternoon.

Mona tries to put a positive spin on the missing main course. "It could be worse. At least we'll have appetizers and dessert. Maybe with an extra case of prosecco, we can sail through after all."

I gaze out the café's windows, wondering how I'm going to rescue Estee and Sam's reception from turning into one of those wedding horror stories that guests will gossip about for years to come. Mona sighs into my phone. We both know the laws of physics apply to natural and supernatural phenomena alike. While a bit of magic might improve a dish's taste—my aunt Phoebe's café is living proof of that—no amount of magic can make *something* out of *nothing*.

"Even if we have to buy every frozen chicken nugget between here and Sturgeon Bay, we're going to cobble together something for a main course," I say firmly.

"Yuck. I hate those little breaded bits of maybe-protein. We've got to come up with something better." I hear Mona snap her fingers through the phone. "Oh, one more thing. The organist we hired for the ceremony passed out while practicing in the inn's chapel today. Turns out she has the flu. I didn't want to toss this in your lap too, so I called Sophie and begged her to fill in tomorrow. She said yes, but you owe her big time. And to make sure this didn't happen at *her* wedding. I'm glad you have a cousin who can bake *and* play the organ."

I roll my eyes. Poor Sophie's going to be almost as

busy as me tomorrow, between putting the finishing touches on the cake, catering the dessert trays, and then playing for the wedding ceremony.

"Look, let me talk to Phoebe and Nash, and I'll call you back." A soft, mournful whimper escapes from my lips as I hang up.

"You're not really going to serve reheated chicken nuggets, are you?" asks Phoebe, who was listening to the one-sided conversation. "It won't be just the vegetarians who'll be complaining."

My temples start to throb, so I massage them with my fingers. "The inn's supplier is snowed in, which means we have no main course for a hundred and fifty guests tomorrow."

Phoebe hops up from her seat. "Let's talk to Nash and see what we can come up with in a pinch."

I shake my head. "This is a bigger disaster than even Uncle Nash's kitchen magic can fix!"

"Come on." Phoebe drags me out of the booth. As we skirt around the freestanding tables and chairs jammed between the oak booths up front and stone counter in back, I notice Phoebe's tacked up two new posters on the community bulletin board near the entrance. One advertises our town's Holly Festival the week before Christmas; the other is a real estate ad listing properties for sale.

We breeze past paintings of ancestors hanging on the walls, dressed in Renaissance-Faire-type garb. They all have upturned eyebrows and pointy ears, and a few show a bit of fang, or tail, or fin, depending on their parentage. Since it's after-hours for the café, they're free to be themselves. Most of them nod and wave as we pass by, and I wave back.

Cousin Heliotrope adjusts her flowing purple scarf and plays us a few chords on her harp. Captain Killian, my grandfather's grandfather, strikes a commanding pose in his navy uniform. Killian lost an eye and a hand defending Queen Victoria from a goblin attack when she visited our shores. A black patch covers his missing eye, and his metal hook glints as he salutes us.

Unlike the gargoyles, who've gone from winking to blowing raspberries at me, our family members are well behaved. They even pass for human around non-supers, who don't seem to notice their eyes, ears, or other oddities. The gargoyles, on the other hand, are constantly rude, especially to non-supers, who assume they're animated and love to snap photos of them on their phones.

We pass through the swinging doors in the back. Here, the cafe's vintage, Euro-cottage vibe disappears, replaced by Phoebe and Nash's shiny, stainless-steel commercial kitchen.

Riddle Hill's supernatural community knows Phoebe Spellman and Nash Brownlee are faeries, and our human patrons strongly suspect there's *something different* about the café and its owners.

Phoebe has an uncanny ability to connect with her customers and discern exactly what foods and dishes will please them most. She's also an amazing pastry chef who passed along her baking magic to her daughter, Sophie.

Nash descended from a long line of Irish kitchen

faeries also known as brownies—not the girl scout kind, nor the fabled wee folk in fiction, but the big, burly, bald-headed, amazing-at-cooking kind—and he's got a magic touch when it comes to food prep.

We interrupt Nash as he's reviewing his menu for the following day. Phoebe explains the problem to Nash, who whistles and draws his dark eyebrows together. Then he and Phoebe open the doors to their coolers and pantries, peer at the tops of the kitchen shelves, and even look underneath the cabinets, mumbling in a special language all their own. I follow them around the kitchen, becoming more nervous by the minute.

Finally they turn to me, and Nash gives me two thumbs ups. "We can do chicken limone with scalloped potatoes and grilled root vegetables. For vegetarians and vegans, we can do pasta primavera with an EVOO sauce base. Will that work?"

My mouth drops open. "That's amazing... and perfect! But are you sure it's not too much? I don't want to overtax you."

My uncle smiles. "It's all good. You worry about everything else, and let us worry about the food."

"Rescued again by my amazing faerie godparents!" I give Nash and Phoebe a quick hug. My phone vibrates in my back pocket, and I pull it out to scan the message: a question mark followed by a crying emoji.

"What now?" asks Phoebe.

"It's Mona." I smile and text the new menu details. Mona replies with a thank-you and multiple sparkly hearts. Returning my phone to my jeans pocket, I untie my black apron. "Olivia's school bus is running late with all this snow, and now I'm running late for Estee and Sam's rehearsal. I'm going to change into a skirt and head over to the chapel. I'll swing by your house and pick up Olivia after I'm finished."

"Ah... you may want to wait a few more minutes before you head out." Phoebe points at my ears.

"Oh no, I completely forgot!"

All the other faeries in the family, including Olivia, have enough natural magic to mask their pointy ears, tipped-up eyebrows, and other supernatural features in public. And my werewolf brother only shifts during the full moon, or when his supernatural strength is required, like at his job with the Riddle Hill Fire Department.

I'm the only family member who has no control over my quasi-faerie nature—and no magical abilities— except for my useless gift of being able to see everyone else's magic.

"One 'shocktail' coming right up." Nash chuckles at his own joke as he pulls out his blender. He adds almond milk, coffee, malt, and then a pinch of several spices, including cinnamon, nutmeg, and allspice. Pressing the button to stir up the beverage, he utters the words to a spell under his breath.

I watch as Nash's magic spirals around him, a swirl of faerie dust the color of burnished copper, which twinkles brightly before winking out. "Your brown magic has hints of red today," I tell him.

"Does it now?" replies Nash with a grin. "You must be picking up on my Christmas spirit."

As I drink my uncle's concoction, my eyebrows and

ears return to non-supernatural normal. "I think I'll need some more before this month is out."

"You'll need some more Christmas spirit?" asks Nash.

I shake my head. "I have a feeling I'll need more of your 'shocktails' to help me get through three weddings in December."

"My dear Cassia," says Phoebe gently, "you can *see magic*. That's a unique gift and one hundred percent faerie. If you could lean into your faerie nature a little bit more, it would truly shine. And then you wouldn't have to worry about managing your symptoms when you're stressed. In fact, I think you'd find you'll be less anxious overall."

I shake my head. "I need to learn how to *mask* my faerie nature, not *lean* into it. Otherwise, I may really humiliate myself someday."

I ARRIVE at the old chapel adjoining the inn and pull open the heavy door, painted a cheery lake blue. I pause on the threshold, scanning the white-washed walls and dark wooden pews. I think I detect a hint of unfamiliar magic but see nothing out of the ordinary. Perhaps I'm experiencing a magical hangover from Nash's spell. I know my own errant magic can't be the cause.

I set up a portable speaker on a table inside the chapel and attach my phone. I downloaded the music for the wedding ceremony last week and congratulate myself on my forethought, or perhaps premonition, that I'd be short one organist for the rehearsal. I've had a funny feeling about this wedding, and so I over-prepared, although Sophie would say I over-prepare for everything.

Despite the snowfall, everyone arrives for the rehearsal on time, except the best man. Estee told me that Sam and the best man used to play in a garage band in high school and are close as brothers, except of course for the secret. The one secret all supernaturals observe: don't tell a human, unless you obtain special permission from the elder council, which rarely happens.

Elders are not prone to trusting humans with supernatural secrets, even though we've come a long way since the Salem Witch Trials. Supers live longer than non-supers and consequently have very long memories.

Sam's best man has no idea he's attending a supernatural wedding in a community populated by faeries, elves, gnomes, werewolves, vampires, and a handful of witches who got kicked out of their coven.

"Will's flight landed this morning, before they closed O'Hare." Sam runs a hand through his short, black hair. "He rented an SUV large enough to plow through the snow and should be here any minute."

Estee rolls her large, amber eyes and tosses her head, her light-brown hair brushing her shoulders. "You've been saying that for the past two hours. You know Will... he's definitely disorganized... and he's *always late.*"

Before the bride and groom get into a tiff over the best man's tardy habits, I whisper, "I don't think the flower girl and ring bearer are going to last much longer, and the minister has another commitment tonight. Besides, your rehearsal dinner is starting in forty minutes, and you need to be there. Let's rehearse now, and I'll run through the best man's duties later when he arrives." I tap my phone and turn up the volume as the opening chords of *Moon River* fill the chapel.

We're halfway through the minister's instructions when the blue door swings wide open, sending a blast of frigid air across the pews. "Sorry to be so late. I can't recall the last time I drove through this much snow—I'm out of practice!"

I turn toward the chapel entrance, curious about the owner of the deep baritone voice with the slight country twang. Estee and Sam hurry over to greet the newcomer. They shake hands, and then the best man pulls them both into a quick bear hug before the three of them head back down the aisle to rejoin the group.

The best man is tall and well-built, with black, wavy, slightly damp hair—he's gone hatless despite the blizzard conditions—and a week's worth of stubble on his square jawline. His designer leather jacket is suitable for an October stroll in New York but not nearly warm enough for a December snowstorm in the Midwest.

When Sam introduces his best friend, and the man trains his velvety-brown eyes on mine, I have trouble concentrating. I wonder whether Nash's shocktail gave me partial amnesia, because even though I personally designed and double-checked the wedding program listing every member of the bridal party, *I immediately forget the best man's name*, which has never happened before.

Mr. Friend-of-Sam is the best-looking man ever to set foot in Riddle Hill... and yet, *I'm sure I've seen him somewhere before.* As the man reaches out to shake my hand, he gives me a high-wattage grin that makes my knees wobble like a bowl of Nash's cherry jelly. A warm flush spreads through me, and I can feel my face turning pink.

My mouth forms an *O*. Of course I know who he is—I should have recognized him immediately!

Countless images of this guy, some with his ex-wife, others with his famous red guitar, have been plastered across social media and on every celebrity magazine sold at Vlad's Victuals for months. I even own an old, over-sized t-shirt with his handsome face displayed on the front.

I clear my throat, stammer a welcome, and finally manage to withdraw my hand from his. I reposition the bridal party, show the best man where to stand, and ask the minister to resume the rehearsal. My head spinning, I retreat to one of the pews.

Will Rossi, of Roxie and Rossi, was the male half of the most popular singing-songwriting team in the country, until Roxie struck out on her own, splitting up their act and their marriage for good. Will Rossi has been in hiding ever since, running from the paparazzi, from his fans, even from his creditors, according to the articles.

I groan softly under my breath.

I really, truly hate surprises—almost as much as I hate unnecessary drama—and with hunky, human Will Rossi in Riddle Hill for the wedding, there's no doubt about it.

I'm going to have my hands full, dealing with plenty of both.

CHAPTER 2
ESTEE AND SAM'S REHEARSAL

WILL

Later Friday

I'm still thawing out as I listen to the minister run through our instructions for tomorrow's ceremony. Despite the hefty fee I paid at O'Hare for my rental SUV, the heater isn't working properly, and my feet feel like two blocks of ice encased in Italian leather. I'm definitely underdressed for winter in Wisconsin.

I've never understood why Sam decided to relocate to Riddle Hill last year. Sure, he finally landed his dream job—Sam's always wanted to be a cop—but *why here*? He tells me the department is selective, modern, and has the kind of benefits package you can only find in the bigger cities. I'm happy for Sam, but it strikes me as odd. Why would you need such a well-trained police force in a quaint little village?

Here's another thing that's kind of weird. I tried researching Riddle Hill before I left New York. I found very little online, just a page of local businesses with some peculiar names: Sit for a Spell Café, Rhyme 'N Riddle Bakeshop, Sage Mage Supper Club, Howling Shores Pub. Oh, and a grocery store called Vlad's Victuals, which sounds like it belongs in Transylvania rather than northern Wisconsin. Maybe this place wants to become the Salem of the Midwest.

I'll admit it feels good to be on the road again. I haven't traveled since... well, since the news broke a few months back. You can have anything you want delivered in the city, and that's what I've been doing—lying low and not giving those paparazzi pests anything new to write about.

At least I have decent digs with a good view of Central Park. My newfound solitude hasn't been all bad; I installed a gym inside my second bedroom, something Roxie would never have sanctioned, and I've been using it too. I've also started working on some new material that draws from my country-rock roots. It feels really good to be composing again.

As the minister drones on, my eyes wander over to the second pew, where the wedding planner—Cassia Spellman—is reading something on her tablet. She's pretty, very pretty actually: slender figure, honey-blonde hair, green eyes, and full lips that are slightly parted right now. Sam says she's well-organized, a real pro at wedding planning. Even so, I managed to surprise her tonight, when she finally realized who I am. Which is kind of funny when you think about it. After all, Sam told her my name months ago, so I'm not sure why she was so shocked when we finally met.

I'm still staring at Cassia when someone—one of the groomsmen—asks her a question about the check-in process. The entire bridal party is staying at the inn for the next two nights. Cassia glances up, catches me gazing at her, and turns a rosy shade of pink. I obviously just made her blush again, and I'm starting to feel guilty. She's not some flirty, flighty, fangirl, the kind who used to bang on my door in the dead of night. I should stop staring, but there's something so earnest, so genuine about this woman that I'm having trouble taking my eyes off her.

Cassia proceeds to answer the other guy with all the seriousness of a newscaster. I'm so busy watching her, I don't even realize she's asked *me* a question.

"Mr. Rossi?" Cassia repeats herself. "How about you?"

"How about me… what?" I hear Sam snickering behind my back, but I ignore him.

"I know you just arrived. Would you like me to get you checked into the inn while you head over to the rehearsal dinner? I can get one of the doormen to carry your luggage upstairs."

"That would be great." I smile, perhaps a bit too brightly, because her green eyes widen, like a deer in headlights. "Thanks," I add. "I really appreciate it."

I reach out to give her my keys. My hand touches hers for the second time this evening, and I'm jolted by a charge of static electricity that makes me drop the keys on the floor. We both bend down to retrieve them and bump heads.

I hear an "oof" and place my hand on her shoulder to steady her. Cassia's face turns flaming red.

"I'm so sorry. Are you alright?" I say as we both rise. She's managed to grab my keys and is gripping them so tightly her knuckles are turning white.

"I'm just fine, Mr. Rossi." Cassia pivots on her bootheels, thanks everyone for attending the rehearsal, and gives us a few last-minute reminders before heading out into the cold.

Cassia Spellman never once glances back at me.

I'm surprised to discover that bothers me more than it should.

"Come on, let's grab a beer at the bar," suggests Sam. "Estee's going back to the inn with the bridesmaids."

We're sitting at a table in a private dining room at the Sage Mage Supper Club. The restaurant looks like an old medieval castle, complete with an oversized statue of a knight and horse, clad in bright silver armor, mounted on a pedestal in the lobby. The room we're in has stone floors, black iron chandeliers and sconces, lots of ivory linens, antique china, and faded tapestries covering the walls. The whole effect is so Old World I almost think I'm on tour in Eastern Europe.

But I had a surprisingly good meal, paired with an excellent red wine: beef tenderloin, garlic mashed potatoes, balsamic-drizzled Brussel sprouts, crisp greens with a creamy vinaigrette, and several kinds of pies for dessert. I noticed Estee's family drank red punch rather than the sparkling water, which I figure is a local tradition.

"What about the other guys? Should we invite them?" I ask.

"Nah." Sam shakes his head. "They're locals—Estee's brothers and a couple of friends from the department—I see them all the time. Besides, we wound up getting pretty smashed last night, and I promised Estee I'd be on my best behavior tonight."

After Sam kisses Estee goodnight, I follow him out of the room. We walk down a dark, paneled passageway, descend a flight of stairs, and enter a dungeon-like room. Groups of guys and gals are gathered around plank tables or seated at the bar. Mounted animal heads hang on rough-hewn, stone walls above us. But there's something off about those heads. If I look at them out of the corner of my eye, they sort of shimmer.

I know I'm not plastered; I've only had two glasses of wine with dinner. Maybe my eyes are just tired from the long drive. What should have taken me four and a half hours took eight because of the snow. Sam and I head over to the massive teakwood bar with brushed nickel footrails, pull up a pair of stools covered in fur that I hope is fake, and order two Ghastly Ales from a local brewery.

"You promised to be on your best behavior with *me*?" I tease Sam. The two of us got into all kinds of mischief as teens growing up in Nashville.

Sam chuckles, his dark eyes glinting. "Yeah. Which means you're accountable to Estee if anything happens."

I raise my hands, palms up. "Hey, I'd never tussle

with your soon-to-be-wife. She's beautiful *and* formidable."

"I'll drink to that!" Sam and I clink our mugs and each take a long swallow. Then my best friend shifts around on the stool and pins me with a thoughtful stare. "How are you *really* doing, Will? The stuff I'm reading... I know it's not *you*."

I glance down at the wooden countertop, which is polished to such a high sheen I can see my blurry reflection. I take my time, staring into my beer before drinking it partway down. "I've stopped reading all that drivel. What's the latest gossip?"

"That there's another woman who was behind your breakup. Apparently Roxie got fed up with your 'philandering ways' and finally asked for a divorce."

I snort. "Sounds like Junior's been spinning again." A year ago, Junior Jennings was managing the Roxie and Rossi band; now he's promoting Roxie's new solo career, which I fully support. I want to see Roxie continue to soar—but I didn't expect her success to come at my expense.

I know this isn't my ex-wife's doing. Roxie's not vindictive, just very, very driven. Although Roxie and I parted amicably, that's not the case with Junior. I've never felt I could trust him. I suppose the feeling's mutual, because he's been planting some unflattering and totally untrue stories that are making it hard for me to find work. I've had to hire a lawyer to deal with Junior, but all that takes time. Meanwhile, my bank account's dwindling, and my career's in freefall.

Sam sighs into his mug. "Look, I don't mean to pry… it's just…"

"It's Estee, isn't it?"

Sam nods. "Estee keeps pressing me for the truth, because she wants to believe in you as much as I do." Sam punches me lightly on the shoulder. "But it's kind of hard when you're such a tightlipped country boy."

I have to laugh. Despite the fact we've been friends since grammar school, Sam and I are about as different as two guys can be. He's outgoing and lively, almost too chatty at times, while I'm more like my dad; I don't open up easily. That's why the only person who knows the truth about my divorce is my sister, Maggie, who keeps secrets better than the CIA.

I decide it's time I tell Sam the full story. "I asked Roxie for the divorce last December."

"*What?*" Sam gasps, choking on his beer. "But that's not…"

I squint at the boar's head hanging behind the bar. I rub my eyes because I swear *it has three horns*. But when I look again the horns are gone. This is more than eye fatigue; I make a mental note to see my ophthalmologist when I'm back in New York.

"You know we'd been drifting apart for years, as husband and wife, and as partners in a business I no longer even like. I never wanted to live in New York. And I hate all the social climbing that Roxie excels at. So after we wrapped up our last album, I told her it was time we go our separate ways."

"Wow." Sam runs a hand through his hair. "Was Roxie surprised?"

"Nope." I shake my head. "I think she was relieved and probably a little miffed that I pulled the plug first, instead of her. Roxie wanted to be the one to make the media announcement, and I agreed. I figured I had nothing to lose, and I wanted to go out like a gentleman."

"Like a chump, you mean," grumped my best friend. "So Roxie waits eight months to announce your breakup, and then she lets Junior run the narrative—and run your reputation into the ground."

"Pretty much." The original announcement implied I was holding Roxie back from bigger and better things; she's the star and I'm something of a hanger-on. Now Junior is claiming another woman led to my breakup with Roxie. I stopped caring what the media thinks about me a long time ago, which might explain why every tabloid in the country claims my music career is over.

Sam claps his hand on my shoulder, orders us another round, and hops off his stool, his mug raised in the air. He tells me to stand up; I arch my eyebrows at him, but I follow his lead. A few people glance over at us, and then a few more. Sam raises his voice and shouts, "Here's to Will Rossi, who's finally come out of his self-imposed exile. Rossi is moving on, to bigger, better things, and you heard it here first!"

I groan at Sam's corniness and drink a toast to my future success, whatever it may look like. The bartender asks for my autograph on a napkin, and a few other folks wander over, asking for autographs and snapping selfies with me. A couple of attractive women pull up stools on either side of us. It's getting late, and my best friend's getting married tomorrow. Sam glances over at me, to see whether I want to linger at the bar after he leaves, but I shake my head.

I zip up my leather jacket and follow Sam up the stairs. As we pass the ridiculous knight in shining armor in the lobby and step outside into the bitter cold, I realize there *is* a woman who's occupying my thoughts.

Cassia Spellman.

And I make a decision right then and there: I'm going to find out everything I can about her.

CHAPTER 3

THE WORST BEST MAN

CASSIA

Saturday, December 8

The full moon is shining so brightly through the slats of my bedroom blinds I can't fall back to sleep. I push myself out of bed, thinking of my werewolf brother. Jake and his pack are running along the frozen shoreline tonight, howling, brawling, and having a grand old time. Come dawn, they'll be battered and bruised, but curiously content. They'll return to the fire station, where they'll consume a massive breakfast prepared by my uncle Nash.

The moon affects me too, but in less dramatic fashion. I snatch my tablet from the nightstand and stumble into my darkened living room. I don't turn on any lights to avoid waking Olivia, but I know where the sofa is, so I grope my way toward it. Grabbing a wooly throw, I sink down onto the sofa with a low sigh. My only cure for insomnia is to review my wedding checklists, adding

26

notations whenever a fresh idea or anxious thought rouses me from sleep.

Although I've already double- and triple-checked my list for Estee and Sam's wedding, I'm wondering how to manage a celebrity of Will Rossi's stature—and fallen reputation. He's been hiding out for months, finally choosing to emerge from his New York City apartment this weekend. If word gets out he's here, our town will be swarmed by paparazzi—the icky, nasty, supernatural kind, who're much more aggressive than their human counterparts. They won't hesitate to use their snooping skills to make Will Rossi regret ever coming to Door County.

I have to find a way to limit any potential fallout from his visit.

I begin with the photographer, one of Estee's vampire cousins, who lives and works in Riddle Hill. Julien Drakus would sooner destroy his camera equipment than sell his photos to the tabloids. On the other hand, wedding guests love to snap photos on their phones and post them to social media—and supernatural wedding guests are no different. There's nothing I can do to prevent it, but maybe I can encourage Will Rossi to maintain a low profile while he's here for the weekend. How hard can that be?

Then I smack my head with the heel of my palm.

Will Rossi is giving the best man's toast at the reception! Given his very public break-up with Roxie, can I trust him to deliver anything remotely appropriate? Even his former manager said Will Rossi is jealous of his ex-wife's success and bitter over how things ended.

I get up and try pacing around my living room in the dark, but I stub my toe on the driftwood coffee table Jake made for me. Stifling a yelp, I sit back down.

Okay... I can't prevent Will Rossi from delivering his speech... but maybe I can do the next best thing. I'll compose a nice, safe, little toast and hand it to him. If he reads that toast, then I can avert at least one potential disaster. I yawn and decide to go back to bed; I'll work on the script later, after I get some more rest.

Instead, I forget to set my alarm and oversleep.

"Mommy, wake up!" I hear Olivia in my dream, which has something to do with Will Rossi's keys on the floor. I mumble in my sleep, telling Olivia she's too young to drive.

Will Rossi's shaking my shoulder; how rude! I slap the hand away, and Olivia shouts, "Mommy! Jenna's here. Don't you have to go to work?"

I open my eyes with a start. I'm lying in my pearl-gray bedroom as bright sunlight dances around the edges of my drawn blinds. Olivia's leaning over me, her blonde hair tickling my face.

I draw my seven-year-old daughter into a hug. She's still warm from tumbling out of her bed, and I kiss the top of her head. "Thanks for waking me up! Please go ask Jenna to fix you some breakfast."

After I'm dressed, I pop into my tiny kitchen, which I've painted bright pink, to give Olivia's babysitter last-minute instructions. I plant a kiss on Olivia's soft cheek, praise the picture she's carefully coloring, and head out to work.

The café is packed, which is great for the family business but hard on my feet. The gargoyles roll their eyes at me all morning, as if the full house is keeping them from something important. Our customers keep Phoebe and me scrambling until it's time for me to leave for the inn.

Sophie arrives at the inn's parking lot the same time as me. The two of us wrestle the three-tiered cake, decorated with flowers, balloons, and little red and white carnival flags, from the back of Sophie's white van onto a cart. We slowly wheel the cake-and-cart over to the inn's delivery entrance. Guiding it through the kitchen, past the lobby with the fire crackling in the grate, and into the ballroom, we transfer the cake to a skirted table.

"The cake's gorgeous, Soph!" I pause to snap a few photos on my phone. "This may be your best one yet."

"You're great for my ego." Sophie chuckles, her eyes twinkling. "And you say that every time."

My phone buzzes with a text from Estee: "Will forgot his tie and vest. HELP!"

I stifle a groan and then cast my cousin a saccharin-sweet smile. Sophie tucks a lock of curly brown hair behind her ear and eyes me suspiciously. "I'm almost afraid to ask... what's up?"

"The best man left his vest and tie in New York, and the wedding's in less than two hours."

"Unbelievable." Sophie shakes her head. "I suppose you want me to run to Malaki's Menswear and rustle something up?"

I bring my hands together in a prayerful pose. "Yes, please?"

"Fine. What color was his vest and tie?"

"Red, but frankly, I could work with white, ivory, or any shade of green."

My cousin grabs her car keys and calls over her shoulder, "Your IOU list is getting pretty long, cuz."

"I'll make it up to you," I say, grinning. "You'll have the perfect wedding... I promise!"

Sophie returns thirty minutes later and hands me an ivory tie and vest. "Gotta run—my part-timer at the bakery needs to leave early. I'll be back in time to play the organ for the ceremony."

I blow her a thank-you kiss before entering the inn's main lobby, decorated for a Victorian-style Christmas, with a twelve-foot tree covered in antique ornaments and white faerie lights. Boughs of greens are draped across the curved staircase, polished wooden desk, and mantel above the fireplace. I dash up the stairs to the third-floor rooms, where the groom, best man, and groomsmen are staying.

I pause before the dark oak door. I absolutely refuse to blush again in front of Will Rossi, who rattles me in a way I can't comprehend. Sure, I own every one of his albums, and I secretly crushed on him in high school, but that was years ago. It's not his rockstar status; I deal with powerful supernaturals all the time. I even planned a wedding for a Romanian vampire prince whose fiancé had grown up in Riddle Hill.

But Will Rossi is different from the vampire prince. For starters, he's human. His superpower is his music, and as a human-faerie girl with no natural magic, I really respect that. For another, he's hit rock-bottom, personally and professionally, yet he doesn't seem to be devastated like I'd be—like I was when Derek and I split up. I don't understand how Will Rossi can be so calm in the face of so much negative press and future uncertainty. I'd be an absolute train wreck.

If I'm being completely honest with myself, which three years of therapy has taught me to be, there's one thing about Will Rossi that does unnerve me. Somehow, the man is even better looking today than a decade ago. Strands of silver now thread through his wavy, black hair, and when he grins, little crows' feet gather at the corners of his velvety eyes. Add his wide shoulders, narrow waist, and country drawl to the mix... and he's every girl's heartthrob.

Bottom line, Will Rossi is ridiculously attractive. Fortunately, Derek cured me for good. I'm never falling in love again with a drop-dead gorgeous performer. Nope. Not happening.

I slowly inhale and exhale three times before knocking on the door, which Will Rossi opens. He greets me with a friendly nod and takes the vest and tie from my outstretched hand. I feel cool and in control.

"I told Estee you'd figure something out," he says. "That's what wedding planners do, right?" Looking down at the vest and tie, he shrugs. "Though it's not red. Guess it'll have to do."

Not even a thank-you! Now I'm annoyed, which helps me stay focused on the task at hand: making sure Estee and Sam's wedding goes as smoothly as possible. "Please remind Sam and the others you need to be at the chapel by four."

"Sure thing, darlin'." He winks and closes the door.

How dare Will Rossi wink at me after arriving late for the rehearsal, forgetting important items, and expecting me to fix it all for him? I stomp back down the stairs, fuming.

I always handle a dozen tiny details in the hour leading up to the actual wedding ceremony. The maid of honor loses an earring; the bride starts to cry because she's happy, nervous, scared, or sad; the groom needs ibuprofen for a hangover; the flower girl has to go to the bathroom and no one can find the child's mother. Estee and Sam's wedding is no different. When Mr. Drakus finally walks Estee down the aisle, I expel a sigh of relief. My work isn't over, not by a long shot, but getting the bride and groom to the altar is a major step.

As I watch the ceremony unfold from the rear of the chapel, I glance down at the program in my hand, spot Will Rossi's name, and gulp. In a little while, he'll be giving the toast that I forgot to write. I grab a pen from my purse and jot down a few lines on the back of the program.

It's okay. I'll wait for an opportune time, when Will Rossi is alone, to provide him with the scripted toast.

After the ceremony, the wedding party remains in the chapel with Julien Drakus to pose for photos. Meanwhile, I send the guests next door to the inn for cocktails and appetizers. When Julien wraps up the chapel photos, Estee, Sam, and the rest of the party use the covered sidewalk, cleared of snow, which connects the chapel to the inn. It's bitterly cold, so no one lingers, except for the best man, walking behind the rest of the party, shoulders hunched forward inside his tux, checking his phone.

I'm nervous about confronting Will Rossi, but I have to do whatever I can to protect him—and Riddle Hill—from a paparazzi onslaught. As Will steps into the vestibule, I catch up with him and hand him the program. I'm about to show him the toast I've written when he asks to borrow my pen. He scrawls his name across the front of the program. "There you go." He winks again.

I look down at the program Will Rossi just autographed and clear my throat, aggravated he's managed to rattle me again. At least I'm not blushing this time. "Wait a minute, please, Mr. Rossi."

We're hovering in the entrance to the inn's side lobby. Along one long wall stands a highly polished mahogany bar, reputed to be a gift from Queen Victoria to her faerie godmother, who owned the inn at the time. Servers in crisp black uniforms wander through the crowded room with appetizer trays. Although sometimes tempted, I never eat or drink at the weddings I plan. I figure I'm on the clock and should exhibit professional restraint.

Will tents his eyebrows. "You want me to autograph all those other programs?" He points at the extras I grabbed on the way out of the chapel.

"Ah... no, not exactly." I hesitate.

"Then how can I help you?" Will gives me the same gorgeous smile I've seen on albums, posters, and magazine covers through the years. I find myself growing warm beneath my dark green wool dress. I inhale through my nose and exhale slowly through my mouth, visualizing myself remaining calm, unflustered, with a clear, non-blushing complexion.

Flipping over the program he autographed, I tap what I've written in my neatest block letters on the back. I clear my throat again and explain, "Here, I've composed the best man's toast for you."

Will's brilliant smile fades. He skims the short speech and hands the program back to me with a scowl. "I don't need anyone scripting my lines." Pausing, he adds, "Besides, that's just plain embarrassing. You make me sound like some old mother hen, reflecting back on a few fond memories."

"Under the circumstances, Mr. Rossi, I thought you might want to keep it simple."

Will's scowl deepens. "Under the circumstances? You mean because of my split with Roxie? And all the negative press?" Will runs a hand through his longish, wavy hair, which grazes the collar of black tux. "I get it now. You think I can't be trusted to give my old buddy Sam a normal, happy toast on his wedding day. You figure I must be jaded or something."

I stammer, "I thought I'd make it easier for you—"

"My glory days are still ahead of me, darlin'!" He gives me a mock salute and heads to the bar.

Phoebe sidles up next to me, staring at Will's retreating back. "Who is that fine-looking young man? He looks vaguely familiar."

"Will Rossi," I whisper.

"You mean from Roxie and Rossi?" Phoebe lowers her voice. "I read all about their break-up. Poor man." Then my aunt glances over at me. "What's wrong with you?"

I shake my head. "I really upset him just now. I tried to script his best-man's toast."

Phoebe's eyes twinkle. Putting a hand on my shoulder, she says, "Honey, you can't manage every last detail, not in weddings and not in life. Stop trying to do the impossible."

I nod at my aunt, who gives my shoulder a motherly squeeze and goes to help Nash with the food.

Derek always called me a micromanager, although he didn't mind when I was the one worrying about how we'd pay our rent or purchase groceries. As an often-unemployed actor, he relied on me to pick up the slack while he pursued whatever acting role piqued his interest, in whatever city we happened to live in at the time.

I worked two, sometimes three jobs, even after Olivia was born. But when Derek used our rent money to buy a plane ticket to LA for an audition—"his big break"—I returned home to Riddle Hill with Olivia. Three years later, I'm still a careful planner and budgeter, and Derek still hasn't found his big break.

I square my shoulders. Time to stop thinking about irresponsible Derek and ensure Estee and Sam's special day goes off without any major hitches, or at least any hitches I can prevent.

TOASTING THE BRIDE AND GROOM

WILL

Later Saturday

I tip the bartender, take my bourbon and ginger, and step away from the line at the bar, searching for an exit out of the crowd. I don't want to backtrack to the side door where Cassia Spellman is speaking with another woman, probably relaying how I gave her an autograph she didn't want. I snake my way around the servers and guests and wander into the ballroom next door.

I take a step back, surprised by the red and white striped carnival tent in one corner, where several games and a photo booth are set up. Round tables covered with red tablecloths and topped with lacey snowflakes dot the room. Miniature Norfolk pines, festooned with tiny ornaments, decorate the center of every table.

I'm impressed; Cassia Spellman is beautiful *and* talented. Exiting the ballroom, I cross the inn's main lobby, where a cheerful blaze is crackling in the wood-burning fireplace. I slip out of the inn's front doors and almost turn right around. The frigid temperature nearly freezes the breath in my lungs. I exhale a frosty puff of air and take a long swallow of bourbon.

I think about Cassia, and the air of vulnerability behind all her checklists. I can't shake off the hurt look in her eyes that I put there.

It was bad enough I missed half the rehearsal the day before. Sam called to warn me about the weather forecast and urged me to fly out a day early, which I could have done if I'd just gotten my act together.

And of course, I packed at the last minute, forgetting my vest and tie and forcing Cassia to find me another set. Then I signed the program she handed me, although she didn't ask for my autograph. Finally, I insulted the toast she'd written, which wasn't as awful as I pretended.

Through it all, Cassia was polite, professional, and pretty adorable, while I was an arrogant jerk.

I shake my head and finish my drink, stomping my feet to stay warm. The bitter cold drives me back into the lobby.

I place my empty glass on a side table and stand in front of the fire, rubbing my hands together to get the feeling back in my fingers. I inhale the woodsy scent, bringing back memories of winters growing up in Tennessee, where folks chopped wood and used real, honest-to-goodness fireplaces. None of those fake, gas-burning logs like you see all over New York, like I have in my own apartment.

How did I become so citified I forgot how much I

enjoy the crackle of burning wood and the warmth of an actual fire?

I know the answer to that question—Roxie, who never liked our home town of Nashville, always wanting something more, bigger, better—and I hitched my wagon to her star, never looking back until the past few years.

The celebrity magazines claim that without Roxie, my career is over, while hers is just getting started. They quote Junior, who says Roxie can focus on her solo career now and take her music in a new direction.

That last part probably is true, since I composed all our music. And while Roxie is listed as the lyricist on our songs, I also wrote all the lyrics. What can I say?

Sam was right last night when he called me a chump.

"Excuse me, Mr. Rossi." Cassia comes up behind me. "We're about to take our seats."

I turn away from the fireplace, glad for the interruption. I can't fail to notice how perfectly her wool dress hugs her curves, and how the green shade picks up the color of her eyes, which are reflecting the fire's glow. "Please, call me Will. And I owe you an apology."

"Not at all." Cassia shakes her head. "I'm the one who should apologize to you. I have an unfortunate tendency to want to manage every last detail. I'm sorry for trying to script your toast."

"I would have done the same in your shoes. And I appreciate a good manager—mine is permanently indisposed, since he's working exclusively for my ex these days—but I do miss his organizational skills, which as you can tell I'm sadly lacking."

Cassia laughs, a hearty, country-girl kind of a laugh. Still chuckling, she guides me to the head table, pulls out my chair, and waits for me to sit down like an obedient child.

Then she leans over and whispers, her breath tickling my ear, "Just make sure your toast is rated G and has a happy ending, Mr. Rossi."

My pulse races wildly at her nearness, but then she's gone, walking away in her spiky heels. Staring after her, I'm struck by a longing so fierce it takes my breath away. I *will* get to know this woman—I *must*.

When it's my turn to deliver the toast, I reminisce about my friendship with Sam and repeat some of our funnier mishaps growing up. (Since Sam is now a cop in this town, I steer clear of the illegal drag racing and underage drinking.) I conclude with how happy Estee has made my best friend and then raise my glass of prosecco.

When I sit back down, I catch Cassia's eye. She gives me a warm smile and a thumbs-up.

My heart turns over like the old engine on my grand-dad's tractor, and then the strangest thing happens. I feel myself growing warm inside my tux, and my face flushes pink. I don't think I've blushed since high school.

Cassia's smile. It's like entering a place of warmth and welcome after stumbling around outside in stormy weather. I have to see that smile again... I have to see her again... But how can I get Cassia to see the *real me*, Will from Nashville, who's actually a pretty decent guy, and not Rossi the Rocker, who's been accused of stuff that would make my old pastor blush?

I have to do something tonight to show her who I really am. But what?

I wait until after the band (which isn't half bad) plays a few sets. During a break, I seek out the lead guitarist, a very tall guy with blond dreads and dark red lips. Maybe he's related to Estee's side, since her family all seem really partial to the fruit punch that stains their lips red. As I approach him, I could swear *the dude's got fangs*, which he quickly tucks away inside his mouth. I vow not to touch another drop of alcohol for the rest of the night.

I introduce myself, explaining what I want, and this guy's eyes pop a bit. Despite his possibly fanged mouth, Kozani's an agreeable fellow. He takes me over to meet the rest of the band, all of whom have offbeat names (Maggard, Norrix, Serbius, Obsidian, and Zegrath). I wonder if these guys are part of some Harry Potter fandom club. We shake hands and confer, selecting one of my older ballads to perform. The song was a big hit five summers ago, which feels like half a lifetime now; in the music business it is.

The band troops back onto the dais, located across the room from the striped carnival tent. I stand off to the side, waiting for my cue as Kozani goes to the mic. "We have a special treat in store tonight! The best man, Will Rossi, formerly of the Roxie and Rossi band, is going to help us out with the next number!"

The ballroom erupts in applause, and everyone under eighty crams onto the dance floor. Kozani hands me his guitar, and I step up to the mic. As I strum the opening chords to *Paradise Smile*, a hush falls over the crowd.

I haven't performed publicly in a year. Although I'm

jittery, almost like it's my first concert and not my thousandth-plus, I feel good. I enjoy performing, especially in smaller venues like this one. And I need this right now —I need to sing this song—and I need that pretty, honey-blonde woman standing by the carnival tent to hear me.

Kozani's band does a great job following my lead. I lean into the notes and lyrics, crooning as if my life depends on it. Maybe it does; all I know is it's time for me to make some music. Wedding guests are snapping photos on their phones, and I'd not be surprised if a few of them post their photos before the night's over. Like Sam said last night at the dungeon bar inside the Sage Mage, I'm ready to emerge from hiding and start something new.

When I finish the song, everyone's clapping and cheering, including the servers and bartenders. Even Cassia, who's left the carnival tent and is standing at the edge of the dance floor. I grin, bow deeply, and pass the guitar back to Kozani.

Estee gives me a hug; Sam shakes my hand, and then I'm surrounded by folks clapping me on the shoulder and taking selfies with me. A few of the guests hand me their programs to autograph, which is kind of ironic. I wait until the crowd thins out, then I make my way over to Cassia.

"Did I acquit myself tonight, Miss Cassia?"

"Absolutely!" Cassia smiles. My heart leaps at full throttle, just like that old tractor engine after a good oiling. My temperature starts rising again too. "Your toast was pitch-perfect, and that song happens to be a personal favorite. Thank you for making this a special night for Estee and Sam."

I'm feeling happy for the first time in a long time. I'm convinced the rest of the evening is going to go my way. "Would you care to dance?"

"I'm sorry, Mr. Rossi, but I'm still working."

I wonder if I've misunderstood. That's not what I thought she'd say, and I really want this woman in my arms. "You mean you can't dance at all tonight?"

"Unfortunately, no." Cassia purses her mouth slightly.

"Maybe some other time, then." I gaze at her full lips, wondering what it would be like to kiss them, and I find myself leaning toward her. Fortunately my brain reengages just in time, and I stop myself from invading her personal space.

"Of course," Cassia murmurs. Then one of the bridesmaids taps her on the shoulder to ask her something. She turns her head, and the two women drift away.

I start to follow Cassia, like a moth to flame, but I stop abruptly when I realize I've lost her. She's melted into the crowd, and I'm reeling.

Who is Cassia Spellman?

Does she have some secret, magical superpower?

All I know is I've fallen under her spell.

SIT FOR A SPELL CAFÉ

CASSIA

Sunday, December 9

I arrive at the café before the doors open, when it's just me, Phoebe, Nash, and Olivia. I guide my daughter into Phoebe's small office off the kitchen, where she promptly falls back asleep on the couch. Then I return to the dining area, quietly slip past our ancestors dozing in their picture frames, and ignore the five gargoyles wiggling their large ears at me beneath the stone counter.

After I got home last night, paid the babysitter, and looked in on Olivia, I sat at my kitchen table with a mug of warm milk and thought about Will Rossi. I can still remember which Roxie and Rossi songs I listened to at various stages of my life—the love songs, the break-up songs, the sassy-fun songs, and the sad songs.

When Will started singing *Paradise Smile* last night, I dropped the rubber ducks I was sorting for Granny

Catbeam and moved toward the edge of the dance floor, drawn by the poignancy I heard in Will's voice. His performance was nothing short of mesmerizing.

Then that very same man, who'd just crooned an old love song in such a new, tender way, asked me for one dance. And what did I do?

I turned him down because I was still on the clock.

But Estee and Sam wouldn't have cared if I'd danced with Will Rossi last night. In fact, they probably would have encouraged me. *What was I thinking?*

Now, I'll never have another chance to dance with Will Rossi—with the man who can sing as if he's buried his heart in every chord. I find myself whimpering every so often just thinking about it.

Aunt Phoebe unlocks the front door, flips the sign to Open, and our regulars begin trickling in. I'm grateful for the distraction because it takes my mind off my own stupidity.

Before long I'm topping up mugs and chatting with customers, most of whom I've known all my life. While Riddle Hill's main industry is tourism directed at the discerning traveler, the café's early Sunday crowd is mostly local. As I make my rounds, I carry a carafe of tart Door County cherry juice in one hand—for the vampires because they need it, and for the humans because they like it—and a pot of fresh-brewed coffee in the other.

I approach a man sitting in one of the window booths from behind; even though I can't see his face, I'm sure he's not a local. His ball cap is pulled down low, and his dark hair curls over the back of his turtleneck sweater. He's studying the menu with such intensity I suspect he may be a restaurant inspector.

Since we serve both humans and supernaturals, we're subject to both sets of laws, inspections, and customs. I don't see any swirls of magic or evidence of a glamour about him, so I assume the man is from the Department of Agriculture, Trade, and Consumer Protection, and not the Food, Potions, Magic, and Monsters Authority, which regulates supernatural businesses everywhere, not just in Wisconsin.

I pause in front of his booth, holding up both the carafe and pot. "Juice? Coffee? Or both?"

Will Rossi glances up from the menu, removes his ball cap, and gives me a smile so dazzling I have to blink. Twice.

Will Rossi is here! He hasn't left Riddle Hill!

"Coffee please." He pushes his cup toward me. "Second job?"

Small shockwaves rattle my insides. I'm floored by a range of conflicting emotions: relief Will hasn't left yet, curiosity over why, delight at the way he's smiling at me, and irritation for feeling relieved, curious, and delighted.

Having Will Rossi sitting here in my family's restaurant is doing a head number on me. Pouring out his coffee feels different, more intimate somehow, than seeing him at Estee and Sam's wedding.

Will is still waiting for me to reply.

"Main job, actually. Weddings are my side gig." I tilt my head to indicate the picture window where we can see cars driving past on Main Street. "Are you heading back to O'Hare today? The highways should be plowed by now."

Will shakes his head. "I'm dog-sitting for Sam and Estee. While they spend two weeks in sunny Spain, I'll be living with two yellow labs named Sleepy and Dopey, and a barky miniature schnauzer named Grumpy. As far as I can tell, they've been aptly named."

I laugh. "Yep, I know them all." I wonder why Estee and Sam asked Will to watch their dogs. Estee has a huge extended family who could have done it while she and Sam honeymoon. It's also a bit risky, since Will has no idea his best friend is a faerie or Riddle Hill is a supernatural community.

I set the juice carafe and coffeepot down and pull out my old-fashioned ticket pad, which Phoebe and Nash prefer over digital point-of-sale devices, claiming they might interfere with Nash's kitchen magic. I think they simply don't want to bother learning the newer tech. "Are you ready to order?"

Will closes the menu and nods. "Grapefruit juice. Scrambled egg whites. Whole-wheat toast. No butter."

"Is that *all*?"

"Why, isn't that enough?"

I shrug. "Sounds like a typical breakfast, if you're from New York or LA. Very healthy and not very much fun. No bacon or sausage or hash browns. No pancakes smothered in butter, or waffles with strawberries and whipped cream."

"Sounds delicious, but my personal trainer has me keeping a food journal."

"A food journal, huh? Okay, I'll get this order right in, but don't be surprised if Phoebe changes it."

"What?" Will's brow creases.

I never try explaining my aunt's special brand of magic ahead of time. How can you tell someone who hasn't grown up in Riddle Hill that Phoebe Spellman knows exactly what food her customers need when they walk into the café, and if they don't order it themselves, she'll take matters into her own hands?

The locals all know that at the Sit for a Spell Café, you get what Phoebe decides you need, not necessarily what you order, and they consider it one of the perks of eating here. It's a bit more difficult explaining that to out-of-towners—whether human or supernatural.

I return with the daily special: a frittata with goat cheese, spinach, tomatoes, and caramelized onions, with a side of cottage fries, country ham, and homemade raisin toast.

Will's mouth gapes open. "This isn't even remotely what I ordered."

I point to a disclaimer at the bottom of the menu. "*At the Sit for a Spell Café, there's Magic in every Morsel. We Promise to Serve What You Need... Not Necessarily What You Order.*"

"I thought that was just a marketing gimmick! You mean it's for real?"

"Of course it's for real. Now before you send that food back and upset my aunt, why don't you try a few mouthfuls? If you really hate it, I'll take it back and get you those egg whites and dry toast you think you want."

"And what do I tell my personal trainer?" Will

doesn't sound especially concerned about disappointing his trainer.

"Tell him to take it up with Phoebe Spellman at the Sit for a Spell Café," I reply. Will's eyebrows shoot up. I top up his coffee and move on to the next table.

I keep an eye on Will's plate as I serve my other customers. After he plows through all the ham and about half of the frittata, I stop by with his grapefruit juice. "Well, what do you think?"

Will puts down his fork. "Reminds me of my mother's cooking. And I can't recall the last time I tasted ham this good, maybe on my granddad's farm back home." He glances at the grapefruit juice. "I think I'll be scrapping that whole food journal idea while I'm staying here."

"Glad you like your breakfast."

"Does anyone *not* like it?" he asks.

"Some customers complain when their food arrives, but once they have a few bites, their whole mood changes, like they found something they hadn't realized they'd lost."

"Sounds a bit like *Peter Pan*."

I nod. "It's interesting you made that connection to my aunt Phoebe. Peter was her grandfather."

Will chuckles. "Now I know you're joshing me."

I grin and then head over to the table beneath Captain Killian's painting in the darkest section of the café, where Julien Drakus and several of Estee's other cousins are sitting. Despite all the misdirection in films and books about vampires catching fire or blistering or whatever in direct sunlight, the simple truth is they just don't like it. Direct sunlight hurts their highly sensitive eyes, which is why they avoid the sun.

It's obvious Estee's relatives have been up all night at some after-party, and I know what they want: a tart cherry juice pick-me-up and some of Nash's good cooking before they head home to crash.

At some point, while I'm scurrying between the tables, booths, and counter, Olivia wakes up and wanders in from the back office. A bright faerie child who takes after her father, Olivia is outgoing, charming, and loves an audience. All the regulars know her, and she's quite comfortable joining a customer at their table if invited. Most of the time she winds up on a stool at the counter, waiting for Nash to cook her breakfast.

But not today... Somehow, while I'm busy serving everyone else, Olivia takes a seat across from Will Rossi.

My daughter's faerie magic hasn't emerged yet, other than her ability to cast a glamour, so I'm not worried about any wayward spells around Will.

As a general rule, faeries manifest their gifts when they're between eight and ten years old, so Olivia's totally normal. However, she's also one-quarter human, so it's possible her magic might come in a bit late. Knowing Olivia, though, I doubt it. She's been precocious in everything else, and I don't expect her magic will be any different. She's been able to maintain a glamour since age three, so she's got me beat.

Since I'm preoccupied with taking orders for a table of jolly Christmas elves taking a much-needed break during the busiest season of the year, all I can do for now is keep an eye on her. I notice Olivia snacking on a piece of Will's raisin toast, which he has obligingly cut into four squares. At some point I signal to Phoebe, hoping she'll go retrieve my daughter and avert any potential mortification on my part. Instead my aunt chuckles and tells Nash to get some blueberry pancakes started for Olivia.

Finally, I make my way over to Will's booth and arrive just in time to overhear Olivia. "My mommy doesn't cry as much now, except when my daddy upsets her. But some songs still make her cry."

Sweet moonglow, why are Will and Olivia discussing me and my tears? And Derek?

How dare Will pump a seven-year-old child for information! I'm fuming and want to wring the man's neck, but I remind myself he's also a customer.

"I see you've met my daughter." I can't meet Will's eyes, so instead I stare down at the table.

Will puts down his coffee cup. "I hope you don't mind; I invited Olivia to join me. I noticed her chatting with a lot of the customers and assumed she was the café's official greeter."

Olivia giggles, and I turn to her. "Uncle Nash is making blueberry pancakes for you." She scoots off her seat, thanks Will for the toast—I'm pleased with her manners—and dashes over to the counter.

I wait until she's out of earshot and then look directly at Will. He's obviously waiting for me to say something, and I get the impression he's somewhat embarrassed I overheard that snippet of conversation.

"I'd appreciate it if you wouldn't ask Olivia about her

father." I bite my bottom lip. "He's let her down a lot over the years."

"I'm sorry," says Will softly. He sounds like he means it, but I'm still furious. "I didn't mean to pry."

"Uh-huh." I'm skeptical, but I remember my training. The customer is always, or almost always, right.

I hold up the coffee pot, and Will shakes his head. "It's time for me to take Sleepy, Dopey, and Grumpy out for their walk." Will pays his bill and leaves a good tip but doesn't overdo it, for which I'm grateful.

We work straight through until our official closing time at two-thirty-two p.m. Unofficial closing time is whenever the last of our customers has left the premises, which most days, including today, is closer to three.

Olivia's in the kitchen "helping" Uncle Nash wash the pots, so my aunt and I are alone. Phoebe pours me a cup of coffee and points to one of the stools at the counter. As I sit down, the gargoyles roll their eyes at me. I'm so annoyed that I return the favor, which makes them vibrate with excitement. The little fiends stand on their heads and kick up their heels, so I go back to ignoring them.

"You look tired," says Phoebe. Cousin Heliotrope must have overheard her, because she starts to play a soothing melody on her harp.

"I didn't sleep very well last night," I admit, stifling a yawn.

"What's bothering you?" asks Phoebe, who knows me better than anyone. After Jake and I lost our parents in a car accident twenty years ago, my aunt and uncle stepped in and raised us along with Sophie. I can't imagine what it was like for Phoebe, who'd just lost her brother and sister-in-law, to become a mother overnight to her niece and nephew.

Phoebe seems to worry about me more than she ever worries about Sophie or Jake, which makes no sense. After all, I'm the serious, cautious one, afraid of making any mistakes. I've become even more careful after my unhappy marriage to Derek, probably the one time I led with my heart and not at all with my head.

I lift my shoulders in a half-shrug. "Nothing's bothering me."

Phoebe draws her shapely eyebrows together. "What's not bothering you wouldn't happen to be six feet tall, with dark, wavy hair, dreamy brown eyes, and a country drawl?"

"Not exactly." After I relay what I overheard Olivia telling Will, I say, "He shouldn't have asked Olivia about me. And I had no idea Olivia remembers all my tears over Derek."

"You don't know for sure what he asked Olivia. Children that age volunteer all sorts of information. And there's nothing wrong with Olivia recalling you cried when you were sad. It's a perfectly normal reaction. You can't shield her from life."

I give Phoebe a sheepish smile. "I know you're right. I wish I could, though. Shield Olivia from getting hurt, I mean."

I finish my coffee, hop off the stool, and stick my tongue out at the cheeky gargoyles, which I know is immature but makes me feel marginally better.

CHAPTER 6

DOPEY, GRUMPY, AND SLEEPY

WILL

MONDAY, DECEMBER 10

I'm back at the café for breakfast this morning and wind up sitting in the same booth under the front window. Across from me is a long, stone counter supported by a row of carved, animated gargoyles that somehow I missed yesterday, probably because the place was so jammed. Right now they're puckering up their lips and blowing kisses at everyone who walks past.

I spent ten years traveling and performing, and I never encountered animation this good. I shake my head in wonder. Riddle Hill is full of surprises.

Phoebe Spellman, who looks like a middle-aged, redheaded version of her niece, stops over to introduce herself. She pours my coffee and asks me a few questions about my food preferences, but I explain I'm not picky. I'll eat anything so long as it's as good as yesterday's meal. That gets her chuckling, and she leaves to put in my food order.

Cassia's young daughter is just finishing breakfast at the counter. Olivia hops off her stool and bends down to pat each gargoyle on the head, which makes them appear to quiver with excitement. The child spots me and waves. Then Cassia helps her into a jacket, slips a backpack onto her shoulders, and the two of them jog out front so Olivia can catch her school bus.

Cassia hasn't glanced my way once since I entered the café, so I assume she's still miffed at me. Honestly, I didn't intend to learn quite so much about her—or her extensive Roxie and Rossi music collection—or her unhappy divorce.

Kids are so transparent; I almost felt guilty yesterday, listening to Olivia talk about her mom. I say *almost* because if Cassia's daughter hadn't been so forthcoming, I would have asked a few questions, just to get the ball rolling.

I'm wildly attracted to Cassia—if anything, my yearning seems to be growing with every encounter— but I can see I have to slow my roll. This lovely woman, who used to cry at my break-up songs, has been badly hurt. I could scare her away if I'm not careful.

The problem is I'm out of practice; I haven't dated in over a decade. I'm as rusty as my granddad's old pickup, which he refuses to replace because it's still running.

I even offered to buy him a new one, but Gramps said, "My dear boy, I appreciate the offer. But I cain't see spending money on a new truck when my old'un is working jest fine. Besides, yer still mighty young and should be savin' up fer a rainy day yerself—'cause sure as the sun rises in the east 'n sets in the west—those rainy days come fer us all."

Boy, was that prophetic. That's all I've been dealing with lately—between my breakup with Roxie, my career's downward spiral, and my mom's cancer—it's been nothing but stormy skies for the past year.

Until three days ago, when I arrived (late and missing half my gear) in Riddle Hill and met Cassia. I felt like a ray of warm, yellow sunshine was finally peeking through all my gray rain clouds. I know I sound corny, but that's the truth.

After breakfast (as good as yesterday's), I drive my rental SUV to Sam and Estee's house. They own a charming blue cottage tucked down a side street about half a mile west of the downtown area. Normally, I'd walk to the café and back, but there are piles of snow everywhere, and the sidewalks are barely passable unless you're prepared, which I'm not. I seriously under packed for this trip. I'm borrowing what I can from Sam, but I'm bigger than he is, so everything is tight and somewhat uncomfortable. I need some winter clothes and a pair of tall snow boots that actually fit.

As soon as I enter the garage, I hear Grumpy's piercing bark. The barking grows louder as I push open the door leading into the all-white kitchen, and the clicking of dog paws on the tiled floor makes me grin. Grumpy's hopping around, yipping, and even Sleepy's roused himself enough to greet me with a *woof*. But I don't see Dopey, who never fails to join the rest of his pack for a round of barking.

Dopey's appetite was off this morning too. Should I be worried? I'm not sure, but I go in search of the big yellow lab anyway. I find Dopey in the grayish-blue great room off the kitchen. He's lying in front of the stone fireplace, panting and whining.

This isn't good. I have a dog in distress and no idea what to do or where to take him.

I jog back into the kitchen and try to find the instructions Estee meticulously wrote out for me. I know they were on the kitchen table two days ago, and I remember moving them somewhere, but I don't see them. Dopey whines again, and I have to do *something*.

I run out to the garage, climb into my SUV, and retrace my route to the café. I find parking half a block away, skirt around a dirty pile of snow, and dash through the door.

I see Cassia in the back, standing in front of the counter, speaking with her aunt. She's wearing jeans and a black sweater beneath her Sit for a Spell apron. Her long, honey-blonde hair is held back by a large clip that my fingers itch to undo, because Cassia's hair should be free to tumble down her shoulders.

Yes, I know, she works in a restaurant and needs to follow the rules, but it's a crime to incarcerate those tresses behind a metal clip.

The gargoyles all start wagging their heads from side to side when I come through the door, like they're saying, "What, you again?" The tech behind them is truly remarkable, but I don't have time to appreciate it right now.

Skirting around the tables, I head directly for Cassia. "I'm sorry to bother you at work," I blurt out, "but Dopey hasn't been eating well, and now he's started panting and whining. I want to take him to the vet, but I don't know where to go."

Cassia's jade-green eyes widen at my less-than-graceful entrance. She looks a little shocked, like she can't imagine me worrying about the dogs. (In fact, I have a soft spot for anything with fur, scales, or feathers.)

"I could run you and Dopey to the animal clinic where Estee takes the dogs." Cassia glances at Phoebe, who waves her hand, telling her to get going. After removing her apron, she grabs her coat and purse and follows me out the door.

Cassia's car is parked behind the café, so she tells me to meet her back at the house. I nod, jog back to my vehicle, and arrive at the blue cottage the same time as Cassia. We access the garage, pass through Estee's gleaming white kitchen, and enter the great room.

Sleepy is sprawled out on the large, gray, *U*-shaped sofa that takes up half the room. He opens one eye and rolls over onto his side. Grumpy runs a circuit around the perimeter, barking furiously until he realizes it's me. Dopey is where I left him, lying on the rug in front of the fireplace. He whines, pants, and whines again.

Cassia drops to her knees beside Dopey and scratches behind his ears. "You're right, he doesn't look like himself at all. Poor fellow."

I clip the leash on Dopey's collar, and the other two dogs stand up, tails wagging, expecting to go along. Shooing them away from the door, I lead Dopey outside. Cassia opens the hatch to her silver Honda CRV; I encourage Dopey to hop inside, and then slide into the passenger seat up front. I can hear Grumpy's sharp barking as we pull away.

We head south on Highway 42, passing stone cottages with smoke curling from chimneys, and thick stands of evergreen trees, their branches laden with snow. Now that I'm sitting in such close proximity to Cassia, I can't think of anything to say.

I'm like a pimply kid with braces on his teeth and cowlicks in his hair... totally awkward. I glance over at Cassia, who's focused on the road. I'm glad one of us is, because I'm having trouble concentrating on anything other than her.

Cassia is more than pretty; she possesses the classic beauty of an old-time movie star. There is something almost ethereal about her. I force myself to look away, staring through the windshield. "Thanks for doing this. And for your hospitality in general."

"I'm always happy to help a dog in need," says Cassia with a smile. "And hospitality is pretty much our family business."

"I like your family. Your aunt's uncanny; your uncle's cooking is amazing, and your daughter is sweet and smart."

Cassia slows down as she rounds a bend, where the view of Green Bay disappears for a bit, hidden by the tree-covered bluffs. "Thanks. Of course, you haven't met my entire family, but I have to agree they're a pretty special bunch."

"Do you have other relatives in Riddle Hill?"

"There's my cousin Sophie, who's a pastry chef. She made Sam and Estee's wedding cake. And my brother, Jake, is the fire chief and also the mayor—he's the over-achiever of the family. My grandmother owns Catbeam's Comics 'N Games. You probably saw her running the games corner at the wedding. Pretty much any Spellman or Brownlee you meet up here is related to me somehow."

As we clear the next bend in the road, the bay comes back into view, frozen solid near the shore, its frosty gray-white color reflecting the weak December sun.

"It sounds like nearly everyone has two jobs around here, even Sam, who moonlights occasionally as a security guard. Why is that?"

"Most folks can't make ends meet with just one job, especially since tourism is our main industry, and the season runs from June through October. Our winters can be long if you're not used to the cold."

"I've noticed; I've resorted to borrowing from Sam's closet. I don't know that I could ever get accustomed to the cold."

"It gets pretty cold in New York, doesn't it?"

I nod. "But it doesn't last; neither does the snow. Up here, I feel like I've stepped into a snow globe."

Cassia looks over at me, her lips parted slightly in surprise.

"What?" I ask. What did I just say that makes her look at me with something like interest? Like maybe she's seeing me—the *real* Will Rossi—for the first time?

She shakes her head and looks back at the winding road. "Nothing. Just that's how I've always described Riddle Hill in the winter, like living inside a giant snow globe. Newlyweds must like it. December weddings are becoming more popular."

"Do you have another wedding later this month? I think Olivia mentioned something."

"Two more, actually. One this coming weekend and one the following weekend, three days before Christmas. The last one will be my cousin Sophie's wedding, so that'll be a true family affair. Olivia is thrilled she'll be the flower girl."

I whistle. "I don't know how you keep it all straight. I struggle to manage myself most days."

Cassia casts me a quick glance but doesn't say anything. I notice her hesitation and ask, "What's on your mind that you're too polite to say out loud?"

She concentrates on the twisting two-lane highway. "You've had other people managing your life for so long, it's no wonder you find it difficult to stay organized. No judgment here. I'm simply stating the facts."

Cassia deftly manages a hairpin curve. As we round another bend, the sun peeks out from the clouds, glinting off the snow-topped trees and icy bay. Cassia whips on a pair of sunglasses stashed in the car's side pocket.

I blink, temporarily blinded by the bright sunshine. "You'll get no argument from me. I didn't realize how out of touch I've become with the way most people live. I feel like I'm re-learning the basics. It's kind of humbling."

Cassia seems to be struggling to suppress a smile.

Does she think I'm some stuck-up, out-of-touch rockstar? Have I made that bad of a first impression? Or is this my second... no wait, third impression now? Well, whatever. I need to up my game.

"A dose of humility isn't all bad," she replies. "Most artists feel the need to be grounded from time to time. Who knows? Getting in touch with real folks might be good for your music." Cassia must be worried she sounds critical, because she quickly adds, "Not that your music isn't already really good. Amazing, even. I've been a fan for a long time."

"How big a fan? And for how long?" I ask, beaming at her. "Are any of my songs a top five favorite?"

Cassia rolls her eyes. "What were we just saying about humility?"

We both laugh, and I sense the ice thawing between us.

Cassia pulls into a parking lot in front of what appears to be a log cabin, tucked inside a stand of towering, snow-dusted, pine trees. The sign out front says, "Doc Demetrius, Serving Your Pets Since 1898."

"Huh," I say, pointing at the sign. "That's some typo! I think your local vet means '1998.' "

"Oh..." Cassia purses her lips. "You must be right. I've never noticed that before."

I shrug, hop out of the Honda, and unload an unhappy Dopey. I lead him into a deep red waiting room, which strikes me as an odd color choice for a veterinarian's office.

It's dark inside; the lights are dimmed, and heavy brocade drapes cover the only window. There's a desk, half a dozen plush velvet chairs, and photos of various pets arrayed on the walls—dogs, cats, rabbits, parakeets, parrots, turtles, snakes, gerbils, hamsters, ferrets, and even some bats—all probably patients of the clinic through the years.

Then I observe a little shimmering on some of the photos. For just a moment, I spot what appears to be a two-headed serpent, a scaly dragon, and a phoenix rising from the ashes. But when I blink they're gone.

Cassia doesn't seem to notice anything amiss, so I assume it's eye strain again. Or maybe some of my neurons aren't firing properly because it's so danged cold up here.

A tall, thin, silver-haired man with gold-framed spectacles is sitting behind the desk reading a newspaper by candlelight. What century is this guy living in? Maybe the sign out front isn't so off after all.

When Dopey whimpers, the old man neatly folds his paper and glances up at us. Cassia introduces me to Doc Demetrius, who leads us back into a more updated examining room. It's not exactly state-of-the-art, but there's an electric light fixture overhead, a stainless-steel examining table, an X-ray machine, and some metal cabinets along the wall.

We've advanced from 1898 to 1972, give or take. I lift the yellow lab onto the table and hope the dog doesn't have anything requiring emergency surgery, because I don't think this fellow is capable.

"What have we here?" Doc asks. As I hastily outline Dopey's symptoms, the vet checks his eyes, mouth, and ears before pulling out his stethoscope and listening to the dog's heart, lungs, and stomach.

The doctor holds his stethoscope over the lab's abdomen and asks a few questions about Dopey's bathroom routines. I have trouble recollecting Dopey's specifics because I'm caring for three dogs at once.

As Doc Demetrius palpitates Dopey's belly, the dog grunts. Nodding, Doc gives Dopey a chewable tablet and then hands a bottle of them to me. I try shoving the bottle into the pocket of Sam's green parka, because I'm going to need two hands to wrestle Dopey into Cassia's Honda.

But Sam's coat is too small for me, and the jar is too big. Cassia sees my dilemma, plucks the pill jar out of my hand, and drops it into her purse.

Gah! How embarrassing! There's no way I'm going to be able to impress Cassia wearing clothes that don't even fit.

I need a whole new winter wardrobe, and I need it fast. But I nearly always shop online at a few favorite (and I'll admit, fairly exclusive) menswear stores. The prospect of trawling through some backwoods store in Riddle Hill fills me with dread. Maybe I can still shop online and get everything shipped to me overnight? It's worth a try.

Doc Demetrius pets Dopey and then helps him down

off the table. "Give one of those pills to Dopey twice a day to help him with his flatulence."

"Huh?" I ask, clipping on the dog's leash. Did I hear the doctor correctly?

"I expect Estee might have forgotten to tell you in the excitement of the wedding, but Dopey needs a regular dose of digestive enzymes to keep things running smoothly through his pipes. He'll be fine once the enzymes kick in."

"Thank you, Doc," says Cassia.

Now I'm downright mortified. I dragged Cassia away from her job because Dopey has excess gas.

"Happy to help!" Doc Demetrius smiles, and I take a step back.

What appears to be a tiny bit of fang catches on his lower lip. I can't tell whether Cassia notices because she's standing in front of me. She clears her throat loudly, and the old man rolls his lips together. The fang —if that's what it was—disappears or recedes or whatever.

Doc ushers us into his deep red, candlelit waiting room again. He grabs a liter bottle of tart cherry juice from his desk and takes a long swallow. Even though I'm itching to go back outside into the sunshine, I'm suddenly very curious. I have to ask about the juice, which coincidentally is the same color as the clinic's walls.

"What is it with all the cherry juice up here? I know Door County has a lot of orchards, but I've never seen so many people drinking cherry juice like it's water. Estee and Sam have gallons of it stored in their pantry."

Doc Demetrius looks at Cassia, who explains, "It's rich in oxidants, and some people praise its medicinal properties."

"Quite so." Doc nods gravely. "There's nothing like imbibing rich, sweet, dark, red juice first thing in the morning. Better than caffeine for me."

"Is that so?" I shrug. "Maybe I'll give it a try."

"You may find you can't live without it." Doc grins at me with his red-stained lips. I recall the possible fang I spotted earlier and suppress a titter. If I didn't know better, I'd think Doc was an old vampire.

We thank him again and head outside, which seems overly bright after spending time in the clinic. Cassia starts the car while I get Dopey loaded into the back. Another awkward silence descends as she pulls onto the highway. I'm embarrassed about Dopey's flatulence-related emergency, and I figure Cassia is too polite to remark on it.

We don't go far when Dopey's digestive system begins working overtime. Little popping sounds start coming from the back of Cassia's Honda. Soon the entire car reeks of Dopey's emissions. Cassia opens her window to let in some fresh but frigid air.

"I think Dopey's system is working again," I say, lowering my window.

Cassia snorts and then giggles, and I burst out laughing. We're still chuckling when Cassia pulls into Sam and Estee's driveway. I get Dopey out of the rear of the car and walk around to Cassia's side. She glances up at me through her half-opened window. Her green eyes are shining with humor, and her cheeks are flushed from the cold.

As I lean down to say goodbye, I can't take my eyes off Cassia's full, pink lips. I drop my head lower, so that my breath is fogging up the bottom part of her window. I want to kiss her more than anything I've wanted in a very long time. But the small part of my brain that's still capable of reason knows that would be highly inappropriate and would scare her off for good.

Instead I ask, "Do you ever get a day off?"

"Single mom, two jobs, three weddings in a row... not much in the way of downtime," Cassia says and then starts fumbling in her purse. Before I know it, she's handing me the bottle of enzymes through the window. She's obviously ready to leave.

I feel myself rapidly deflate.

I need to backtrack, fast, before Cassia thinks I'm asking her on a real date—which I am—but now I'm not. "Well, I'm asking because I could use a tour of the area, if you happen to find yourself with some spare time." There, that doesn't sound like a date at all, but an act of mercy to a clueless out-of-towner.

Cassia seems to agree, because she says, "Sure... If you don't mind coming along on some of my errands, I can show you around a bit. Being a self-employed wedding planner and working for family does have its perks." She smiles shyly at me, and I think, or hope, maybe she likes me a little.

"That would be great." I start to flash her my most winsome celebrity grin, but I tone it down in the nick of time to a mere smile. "I don't think I'll survive until Sam and Estee return if I stay cooped up in the house with three dogs."

Her mouth turns up at the corners. I've won her over!

"I have some local stops to make tomorrow. How about meeting me at the café after the lunch rush, say around one-thirty?"

"See you then," I drawl casually, trying not to sound like I'm about to fist-bump the inflatable snowman in Sam's front yard.

After Cassia drives away, I drop to one knee, hug an eighty-pound yellow lab with flatulence problems, and whisper, "I have a date with Cassia Spellman!"

CHAPTER 7
COSTUME MALFUNCTION

CASSIA

Monday Afternoon

"It's definitely *not* a date," I tell myself as I pull away, "but an act of kindness to Sam's best friend."

I catch a glimpse of Will in my rearview mirror, standing with Dopey in the plowed driveway, piles of snow on either side of him. The cuffs of his red sweater droop from the sleeves of Sam's too-small, green parka. Will has forgotten or misplaced his hat and gloves in this frigid cold, and his tooled-leather cowboy boots have zero traction on the ice.

Will Rossi, the famous rockstar with the swoon-worthy smile, looks almost... vulnerable.

The icy chill around my heart, which I've guarded so carefully since my split with Derek, begins to thaw.

No, no, no! I shout inside my head. I refuse to enter the danger zone with Will Rossi. I remind myself of all the reasons why he's off limits.

First, he's in the entertainment business, same as Derek, and I've sworn off performers for good. Will may be unemployed at the moment, but he has too much talent to stay down for long. He'll be on stage again very soon, mark my words.

Second, he lives halfway across the country. Will is going back to New York in two weeks, and I'm staying here, in Wisconsin. Successful long-distance relationships are rare; if I'm going to date again, I need the odds firmly in my favor.

Finally, and most importantly, Will is human and we are not. I say "we" because Olivia and I are a package deal. My daughter is three-quarters faerie. There's no way a non-super boyfriend could possibly cope. Besides which, I'd need special dispensation from the elder council—every supernatural village has one—to tell Will the truth about us.

They do make exceptions, like they did for my human mother, who believed in magic and all sorts of impossible things. Mom vacationed in Riddle Hill the summer she turned nineteen, and she never left. She married Jake's werewolf dad, and two years after he died, she married my faerie father.

But Will Rossi is not my mother; he's in a category all his own. Our village elders might like his music, but there's no way they'd ever welcome a human of Will's celebrity status and poor reputation into our tight-knit, secretive, supernatural community.

Will Rossi and I are absolutely, positively, never going to date.

Now that I've reminded myself of that fact, I feel

better. Meanwhile, I've been driving without any destination in mind. I find myself in front of a stone cottage with cobalt-blue shutters, tucked down a small lane near the town's harbor. Phoebe and Nash's house, where I grew up, and where I return over and over, whenever I need to feel welcomed and safe and loved. I love their old place, with its scraped wood floors and shabby-chic décor.

I check the time. It's after four and getting dark. My brain's autopilot steered me right; Nash and Phoebe should be home by now with Olivia.

I'm barely out of the car when the front door opens. Phoebe steps onto her stoop. Now that she's at her own house, she's dropped her glamour. Her reddish-brown eyebrows tip upward, and the long points of her ears poke through her smooth auburn bob. Tiny flecks of black dot the golden-yellow of her wings, which she wraps around herself to stay warm, like a soft, feathery shawl. When completely unfurled, Phoebe's wingspan stretches twelve feet across.

My aunt is magnificent in her full faerie form. "How's Dopey?"

"He's fine now."

"What was the problem?" she asks as I enter the foyer, remove my boots, and place them on the boot tray. I hang my fuchsia puffer coat in the crowded hall closet, stuffed with coats, scarves, mittens, and an assortment of hats and caps. I grab a pair of wooly slippers from the bottom of a pile.

As I slip my feet inside, I take a moment to inhale the aroma—a mixture of the cinnamon sticks, pine boughs, and twigs of berries that Phoebe places in vases and urns throughout her home—plus one more ingredient that I can only describe as *anticipation*. If you could bottle it up all the other months and unleash it during the holidays, along with cinnamon, pine, and berries, that's the Christmassy scent in Phoebe's house every December.

I suppose it must have something to do with my aunt's magic, and how she's able to recognize what foods her customers need. Phoebe must know instinctively what *I* need around this time of year too. Even so, she's always a bit confused when I ask her about the scent of anticipation.

I tell her about Dopey's flatulence issues, and Phoebe and I both start chortling as we enter the family room. Two large, yellow sofas, anchored by a blue, oval, braided rug, take up half the floor space. Nash's bentwood rocking chair sits in a corner near the large fireplace, constructed of the same gray, gold, and brown stones as the house's exterior. A seven-foot Christmas tree stands before the large bay window, making the room seem even cozier than usual.

"I imagine Will was a bit embarrassed," says Phoebe.

"A little," I smile, remembering the awkward silence inside the car until Dopey's digestive enzymes kicked into gear. "But I'm sure Will was relieved it wasn't anything more serious. I also think he was a little freaked out by Doc Demetrius's clinic; he seemed antsy to leave."

Phoebe winces. "Oh, I'd forgotten about Doc's decorating choices. Very nineteenth century."

"Doc also showed some fang—by accident, of course—which I hope Will didn't catch."

Phoebe winces a second time. "Sweet moonglow."

"And then when we were leaving, Doc took a big swig from his liter bottle of tart cherry juice, and Will asked why folks around here drink so much of it."

Phoebe's faerie eyebrows rise even higher on her forehead. "What did Doc say?"

"Doc looked at me for an answer, so I told Will the non-super version of the truth, just like we do when our human customers at the café ask about the juice."

While it's true that tart cherry juice is rich in oxidants, the real reason why supers, especially vampires, consume so much of it is *not* for public consumption. Vampires long ago discovered the many health benefits of the beverage, including the most important: the juice satisfies their craving for that other red liquid, which is much more problematic to source and serve.

"Good thinking," says Phoebe. "Having Will living in Riddle Hill for a couple of weeks is going to be tricky, but at the same time, he's such a breath of fresh air. He's not at all what I expected."

"How so?" My aunt has good instincts, and I'm curious to hear her take on Will Rossi.

"For someone who's been through what he's been through—publicly dumped by his wife and betrayed by his manager, his career falling apart, and all sorts of rumors about his financial woes—he seems surprisingly normal. More bemused than bitter by the way things have turned out."

My antenna goes up when I hear Phoebe's pronouncement that Will isn't bitter. It sounds almost the reverse of a conversation we had after my divorce; my aunt warned me to let go of my hurt and anger before they made me bitter.

Pretty soon Phoebe will be suggesting that maybe I could learn something from Will, about how to get on with my life, and all the while Phoebe's real motive will be matchmaking.

"Before you start down your matchmaking path—"

"Matchmaking?" Phoebe casts me a wide-eyed, innocent look. "I haven't tried setting you up with a nice young man in years."

"You mean months, not years," I say, shaking my head at Phoebe's convenient loss of memory. The woman never forgets anything. She greets visitors by name, even if they've only breakfasted at the café a few times through the years. "You set me up with Rob Wolferman this past October, when he needed a date for his and Jake's fifteenth high-school reunion. Remember?"

Phoebe waves her hand. "Oh, Rob doesn't count. He's been your brother's best friend since preschool."

Before I can answer, we both hear Olivia's high-pitched voice coming from the kitchen. "These are the best cookies I've ever had in my whole life!"

Phoebe and I chuckle as we enter the warm, inviting space. With its white-and-gray marble countertops, Aga oven in the corner, and dried herbs hanging over the center island, it's my favorite room in the house. The walls and antique cabinets are painted the same sunshiny yellow as the café, but instead of being greeted by five rude gargoyles, a pair of nine-tailed, miniature white foxes scurry over to me. When I bend down to run my hands over their sleek fur, they purr contentedly.

Like Phoebe, Olivia and Nash have dropped their glamours. My daughter's ears now form cute points at their tips, her delicate blonde eyebrows angle upward, and her purple-and-silver wings peek through the slits in her lavender sweater. Olivia's child-sized wings flutter when she sees me, and she dashes over to give me a sugar-coated kiss.

Nash's faerie form is what you'd expect, pointy ears, angled eyebrows, and enormous wings the color of burnished copper, which he carries furled against his back while cooking so as not to start a fire. But then there's Nash's facial hair; like all other male brownies, his dark beard is thick, bushy, and extends halfway to his waist. Although my uncle trims off a foot every morning, by nightfall, it's grown back.

Once, when he and Phoebe were first married, Nash caught faerie flu, which kept him in bed for over a week. His beard grew so long and heavy that Phoebe had trouble opening the bedroom door after three days. She had to use garden shears to hack off the excess.

I tousle Olivia's hair. "I think you've sampled enough cookies. Let's save some for *after* dinner.

Phoebe points to a satchel by the back door. "Olivia, why don't you take your costume into the family room and try it on? Let's see if it needs any alteration. Your mom and I will be out in a few minutes."

Olivia's wings droop. "Okay." She drags the sack containing her costume across the scraped wooden floor and through the arched doorway.

Phoebe turns to me and whispers, "She left that satchel on the school bus and Elvira swung by after her route to drop it off. I'm not sure what's going on, but Olivia pouts every time I bring up her role in the Children's Pageant."

"Oh no. I wonder what happened... She was really looking forward to the pageant this year."

Since miracles, mystery, and love—the oldest magic of all—figure prominently in the holiday season, the supernatural population of Riddle Hill adores Christmas. Everyone turns out for the annual Children's Pageant on Christmas Eve; even the Grinchiest, grouchiest supers make it a point to attend.

Olivia is standing on the blue oval rug with an oversized, gray, donkey's costume forming a furry puddle around her ankles. Two large ears droop into her face.

"This isn't going to work." Phoebe shakes her head.

"I look ridiculous!" Olivia sulks. "I want to be an angel on Christmas Eve. They get to wear fluffy, pink dresses, extend their wings, and sing one song in the chorus. But I got the talking-donkey part, which comes with this yucky costume and a long speech. I'll never be ready in time!"

I press my lips together to keep from chuckling at the rolls of fur sagging around Olivia. "You're going to be a wonderful talking donkey! They must have selected you for the part because you're so good at memorizing lines. Remember last year? You were amazing as the innkeeper. But we're definitely going to need Aunt Phoebe's help with your costume."

Using a sewing machine, her imagination, and a bit

of faerie dust, Phoebe's made every one of Olivia's Halloween costumes.

My aunt grabs her sewing kit from a cabinet and proceeds to pin and tuck the whole fuzzy mess. "I'm going to shorten the ears and perk up this whole costume. Add a patch of white fur in front and maybe a little red bow tie."

While Phoebe and Olivia chat about angels and donkeys, I start thinking about the tour I agreed to give Will.

Everyone, including Sophie and Jake, has been asking for an introduction, a selfie, or an autograph. Or all three.

They're falling all over themselves to become acquainted with the human rockstar in our midst.

And I'm doing everything I can to keep him at a safe distance.

It's the only way to prevent myself from falling into unsafe territory with Will Rossi.

CHAPTER 8
DRACULA AND A BIT OF TAIL

WILL

Tuesday, December 11

I'm sitting in my SUV, parked in front of the only shop in town that sells clothes for men, Malaki's Menswear. It's not a name that inspires confidence, but a peek inside the shop window confirms I should be able to rustle up some decent alternatives to Sam's closet.

I skipped breakfast at the café this morning because I refuse to show up one more time in borrowed, under-sized clothing. I want Cassia Spellman to see I'm more than a disorganized, disheveled songwriter. I aim to pursue that woman until she can't help herself, until she falls for me like I'm falling for her.

Which means it's also time for me to kickstart my faltering career. I need to focus on composing again, find myself a new gig, and move out of New York, which I can no longer afford.

Before I can do more than daydream about my future

self—strong, confident, secure, and once more successful —a lanky man with a widow's peak that would make Dracula proud shows up in front of the shop. His black hair has dramatic streaks of silver, and his camel hair coat drapes impeccably over his lean frame.

If this is Malaki, the man knows his designers. I own a sport coat with the same label, and it cost more than what I earned from my first concert. I wait until he unlocks the door and flips his sign to *Open* before leaving my vehicle and entering the store.

I feel like I've stepped into a swanky boutique on one of the coasts and not some obscure shop in flyover country. The lighting is dim, the walls are papered in a black-and-ivory geometric print and topped with gilded crown molding. Malaki removes his overcoat to reveal a midnight blue suit from a Milan designer, leather boots so shiny they reflect the lights, and a fawn-colored ascot at his throat. He looks ready to greet royalty.

"Velcome to my storrah," says Malaki, his accent as thick as Bela Lugosi's. "How may I help you, Meester R-rossi?"

He says my name with a rolling *R*, and I notice his lips are stained red, just like Estee's relatives at the wedding and Doc Demetrius in his log cabin from 1898. I'm beginning to feel as if I've entered some alternate universe, like I've passed through a portal and now reside in Transylvania.

But it's cool. I'm not weirded out or anything.

Okay, maybe a little.

"I under packed for my trip and need a new wardrobe for my stay in Riddle Hill."

"Vhat, you need new coat? New boots?"

"New everything. Coat, hat, boots, gloves, and that's just the outerwear. I also need a blazer, some slacks, extra jeans, definitely some sweaters—it's mighty cold up here—and a good suit, just in case."

Malaki's eyes, which are the color of Spanish olives, widen in anticipation of the fat paycheck he'll be getting from my stay in this charmingly odd village. "Jest in case?"

"In case a certain woman gives me a second glance… or maybe it's a third glance? I'm not sure… let's just say I've neither wowed her yet nor wooed her, and I intend to do both."

One of Malaki's thick, black eyebrows arches dramatically. "Veech voman?"

I hesitate, and Malaki chortles. "Come now, Meester R-rossi. I know vat vomen like da men to vare. Tell me, maybe I can help you make good impression."

I take a deep breath. "Cassia Spellman."

Malaki's face turns stony, like I've just asked to borrow his new Tesla to transport Sam's three dogs to the clinic. "Cassia like daughter to me, Meester R-rossi. She verra special."

"We're in complete agreement. Cassia is a very special lady."

Malaki narrows his eyes at me; he's definitely sizing me up. He finally nods his head. "Okie. I help you vis your vardrobe eef you be kind to Cassia. She vas hurt bad by dat last fool."

"Cross my heart," I say, "I promise.

"Ve dr-rink to seal vow." Malaki waves his hand. I

notice his well-manicured fingernails are filed to long points and buffed to a high sheen. Gold rings encrusted with jewels decorate both his hands. The largest gemstone, a ruby the size of my guitar pick, gleams on his right forefinger.

"Okay," I shrug, thinking this is the strangest shopping experience ever. It even beats the haberdasher in Hoboken who keeps chickens in back. One of the hens pecked my leg while I was trying on hats.

Malaki goes behind a black velvet curtain in the back and returns moments later. He's carrying a crystal carafe containing dark red liquid—I'm guessing a tart cherry juice cocktail—and two tumblers. He pours us each a glass. We clink glasses, and I drink.

The taste is not sweet like I'm expecting but has a salty, metallic tang that gives me instant acid reflux. My mouth burns; my eyes water, and my throat feels like I've imbibed lava. I think of Cassia and force myself to swallow the disgusting brew.

I'm still wheezing when Malaki says, somewhat apologetically, "Eets strong to seal vow."

I make a mental note to never accept another drink from Malaki. Now I'm nauseous, but I'm determined to let this crazy Dracula wannabe outfit me with a new wardrobe. The man may have terrible taste in beverages, but he's got style.

By the time we're finished, it's nearly noon. I've spent more than I earned in my entire first concert tour. Malaki helps me load my purchases into the back of my SUV and promises the new blazer, slacks, and suit will be ready the day after tomorrow. He gives me a jaunty wave, and I rush home to change.

It's twelve-forty when I walk through the doors of the Sit for a Spell Café. I pause for a moment to scour the real estate listings on the bulletin board near the entrance, a little hobby of mine picked up from my years on the road. There are some homes for sale, plus a property with nothing but a large barn outfitted like an auditorium inside, which strikes me as a strange use for a farm building.

As I take a seat at my regular booth, which is conveniently vacant, the gargoyles stick their fingers inside their mouths and start gagging at me. I should be insulted but instead I laugh, amazed yet again at the tech involved.

Those robots seem to be making fun of my new wardrobe. I'm wearing a chestnut-brown parka, a darker brown wool cap, a plaid scarf in shades of gold, brown, and gray, and a thick pair of leather gloves. Oh, and fleece-lined boots beneath new designer jeans and a gray cashmere sweater. I feel like a new man.

Cassia is busy behind the counter serving a row of big, burly workers on lunch break. She barely looks up when I enter, but I remind myself she's working and I'm not. I have to respect that her attention is naturally divided, even though I wish it weren't. After Phoebe takes my order, I can't help myself; I keep peeking over at Cassia. I want her to train her lovely jade-green eyes on me.

I hear Cassia laugh at something one of the guys tells her, and I feel instantly jealous. Phoebe emerges from the kitchen and joins in the laughter. Now I feel just plain lonely.

While my family has been very supportive, and Sam is squarely in my corner, a lot of my so-called friends have abandoned me. Not many folks in the industry want to be seen with a has-been; a precious few have reached out privately to offer advice. Most of the time I'm alone in my New York apartment with my guitars and my goldfish, which the old lady across the hall is feeding while I'm away.

I'm still savoring the café's daily lunch special—fish chowder; thinly sliced roast beef on a homemade pretzel bun with arugula, tomato, and horseradish mayonnaise dressing; and side of sweet potato fries—when Cassia swings by with the check.

I raise my eyebrows. "What's the hurry?"

"It's one-twenty-five. Your tour of downtown Riddle Hill departs in five minutes."

I check my smartwatch to confirm the time. "You're pretty prompt, aren't you?"

The corners of Cassia's mouth turn up. She replies with mock sternness, "I'm a wedding planner. A single mom. And a server who works multiple shifts. Being prompt goes with the territory."

I raise my hands in surrender. "You'll get no argument from me. You're an extraordinary time manager." Holding out my cup, I ask with the sweetness of Oliver Twist, drawing out the last word for emphasis, "Please, Miss Cassia, may I have some more?"

Cassia rolls her eyes. "I'll get you some coffee to go. Speaking of going, it's about that time. I'll grab my coat."

Cassia walks over to the hooks near the back entrance, hangs up her apron, and slips her fuchsia puffer coat over her pink sweater. She winds a soft gray-and-pink plaid scarf around her neck, pops a gray wool cap on her head, and pulls on a pair of matching gloves. She looks positively adorable.

We step outside, and Cassia hands me a to-go cup filled with coffee. I take a few sips before realizing Cassia has walked six paces ahead of me. I catch up in a few strides. "Aren't we driving?"

She shakes her head. "All my errands are within easy walking distance. Besides, we're having a warm spell."

I hand Cassia my coffee so I can zip up my new parka, which she has failed to notice. "It's twenty-nine degrees! You call this warm?" I retrieve my cup and take a long swallow.

Cassia waves her gloved hands. "The sun's shining, there isn't a cloud in the sky, and we had a dusting of snow last night. Everywhere you look, you see signs of Christmas. Lights and wreaths decorate doors and lamp posts; shop windows are full of holiday merchandise, and the Norfolk pine in front of village hall is covered with sparkly ornaments. It all makes me feel warm inside."

"I prefer roasted chestnuts, hot cocoa with marsh-mallows, a stuffed turkey in the oven, and a roaring fire. That's Christmas to me. Notice all of that happens *indoors*, where it's warm and cozy."

Cassia shakes her head. "You can't possibly be that much of a couch potato, Will Rossi."

"How would you know?"

"I've seen your music videos. You have some real moves, and that doesn't happen without a lot of practice."

I chuckle. "Well, you got me there. I guess I used to spend so much time rehearsing, performing, and traveling, that when I wrapped up a tour and went home for Christmas, all I wanted was to sit and relax. Used to drive Roxie up the wall."

"Oh, I'm sorry." Cassia looks chagrined, probably worried she's taken her teasing too far.

"No need to apologize. Roxie and I were about as incompatible as two people could be, except when we were performing together. Music was our only common language."

Cassia switches to another subject. "Would you rather stop first at the fire station or the bakery?"

"Fire station, hands down. I'm too full to taste any samples at the bakery right now. Plus, any guy who was once a little boy can't resist a shiny, red fire engine."

"Just remember, you asked for it."

"What's that supposed to mean?" I ask.

Cassia and I walk three blocks to the fire station, which is constructed of the same gray and beige stone as most of the buildings in this town. On the right side of the station are three red, oversized doors leading into the garage. Cassia opens the people-sized door on the left. We step into a lobby painted a soothing shade of blue. Posters about fire safety, training classes, and community events are tacked onto the walls. Straight ahead is a carpeted hallway leading into the administrative area and living quarters.

Cupping her hands over her mouth, Cassia hollers, "Jake, it's Cassia. I have a special treat for you."

I glance over, my eyebrows peaked. Cassia whispers, "My brother is a huge fan."

The first door on the right opens, and a large, muscular man I assume is Jake Spellman walks out with his hand extended. "Pleasure to meet you, Mr. Rossi, and to officially welcome you to Riddle Hill."

I shake Jake's hand and thank him, surprised the fire chief is giving me such a formal welcome, until I recall Cassia's brother is also the mayor. I don't see any resemblance between the siblings; where Cassia is slender, fine-boned, and blonde, her brother is a massive guy a couple of inches taller than me, with brown hair and a thick, well-trimmed beard.

When Jake asks if I'd like a tour of the station, I say, "Absolutely, and please call me Will. Only my accountant calls me Mr. Rossi, and that's right before he delivers especially bad news."

Cassia and Jake chuckle at my sadly true joke, and then Jake claps me on the shoulder. "Why don't you toss your parka on a chair in my office, and then I'll show you around." He turns to his sister. "Are you coming along, or do you have to rescue some bride in distress?"

Cassia rolls her eyes. "I have calls to return, so you go on and enjoy yourselves. I'll be in the training room across the hall."

Jake starts my tour in the garage, where the ambulance, fire truck, and fire engine are stored. I ask a few questions about the apparatus, which he's happy to answer. Then Jakes shows me the personal protective gear and maintenance bay before we head into the living quarters containing dorms, lockers, fitness room, and kitchen, with its stainless-steel appliances, cherry cabinets, granite countertops, and lots of natural light.

I'm impressed with the entire setup, which reminds me of Sam's remarks about the police department; Riddle Hill is a well-resourced village that seems ready for just about anything.

Jake introduces me to the firefighters currently on duty, who are seated at the kitchen table playing cards. Two guys almost as big as Jake, and a gal who stands as tall as me, want me to pose for selfies and then ask for autographs.

As we leave the kitchen, I glance behind me and do a double take. I blink several times and rub my eyes. Whatever I drank at Malaki's must be affecting my eyesight, because all three of those firefighters have long, furry tails sticking out of the backs of their dark blue pants!

My mouth is still hanging open as one of the guys turns around and gives me a sheepish grin, like maybe I caught him in *flagrante delicto*. Jake returns to my side, a bemused expression on his face, and I follow him out of the kitchen.

But I'm beginning to wonder whether there's something wrong with me... or with this town. Because until I set foot in Riddle Hill I never had vision issues, or drank weird red cocktails, or saw tails or fangs on anyone.

Then I think about Cassia and Sam, two very normal people who live and work in Riddle Hill. Whatever I'm experiencing must be related to my prolonged isolation in Manhattan and all the stress of the past year finally catching up with me.

Jake tells me we have one more stop, and I get the sense he's saving the best for last. Although what can top a fire engine?

Or firefighters with tails?

Then he opens a door and takes me into a small, boxy room with gray carpet, dark blue walls, and… a drum set, several guitars, and a keyboard set up on a wooden platform.

I shake my head. "This is a first. Do you need to be able to play an instrument to be a firefighter in this town?"

Jake laughs. "It's not required, but most of the crew enjoys playing. In fact, we perform at some of the local festivals during the summer and fall, which helps us raise funds for the department."

We talk about music, guitars, and favorite bands until Cassia tracks us down. "From fire engines to guitars? What's next?"

Jake says, "Beer, football, and women."

Cassia snorts. "Men are so predictable."

"And women aren't?" asks Jake. "Let's see, there's romance, marriage, kids, mortgages, second honeymoons. I think that about sums it up."

I'm waiting for Cassia's reaction, because I can't believe she's going to let that remark slide. I know Maggie would tear into me if I made such a blanket statement. I'm happy to see Cassia cross her arms and take on her big brother. "Jake Spellman, you're hopeless. No wonder you're still a bachelor."

"Better a bachelor than a hen-pecked husband," Jake quips.

Cassia arches an eyebrow, and I think she's maybe feeling sorry for me and my high-profile marriage, divorce, and fall from grace.

Jake must have picked up on her non-verbal cue, because he adds, "I'm not against all marriages, just the ones that hurt the people I care about." Jake looks pointedly at his sister, and I'm more curious than ever about Cassia and the man who broke her heart.

"Well, this is one wedding planner who has errands to run so her clients' special day goes off without a hitch. What happens after their special day is up to them!" Cassia zips up her coat while I shake Jake's hand and thank him for the tour.

Once we're outside, I say, "Your brother really cares about you. I take it he wasn't too fond of your ex."

Cassia frowns slightly, like she's trying to decide how much to tell me. "Jake begged me not to marry Derek. The two were in the same high school class, seniors when I was a lowly freshman. Jake was probably more opposed than my aunt and uncle. He's never told me why, but I think he must have known Derek was too self-centered and irresponsible to care about anyone other than himself."

"Ouch. How long have you and Olivia been on your own?"

"We moved back to Riddle Hill when Olivia was four." Cassia explains that Derek is an actor solely focused on his career and continually hunting for his "big break."

"I'd say his big break was marrying you and having Olivia."

She smiles wistfully. "Thanks, but Derek probably thinks his big break is still out there waiting for him."

Derek must be a self-absorbed idiot to walk away from Cassia and Olivia. "Some men are just fools," I say with feeling.

Cassia pauses and looks at me. "True enough." She adds softly, "And some women are just as foolish."

My heart starts beating out a staccato rhythm inside my parka-covered chest. I consider taking Cassia in my arms right there on the sidewalk and telling her I'd never, ever leave her. I've seen enough, been through enough, to know it's not fame or fortune that sustains you, but it's the people you love—and who love you back—that gets you through.

Cassia is still gazing up at me, her kissable pink lips slightly parted, obviously waiting for me to respond. The words are forming in the back of my head but none of them seem quite right. I'm still trying to find a way to say something profound, to reassure her I'm not another flighty Derek, when someone flings open a door behind us.

I flinch as a woman shouts, "Welcome to the Rhyme 'N Riddle Bakeshop!"

And my magic moment with Cassia is gone.

CHAPTER 9
RHYME 'N RIDDLE
BAKESHOP

CASSIA

Tuesday Afternoon

Will jumps a foot, startled by Sophie's loud greeting. I stifle a groan at my cousin's poor timing, which couldn't be worse if she tried.

Poor Will looks crestfallen.

I just know he was about to say something really important... or do something really sweet... like kiss me.

Which of course would have been a bad idea. Terrible, in fact.

I mean, out here on Main Street, with the cars going past and shoppers on the sidewalks?

In front of my cousin, who'd never let me live it down? And across the street from my aunt and uncle's café?

But here's the truth... just now, before Sophie barged in and ruined the perfect moment, I really wanted Will Rossi to kiss me.

There, I've admitted it. This man, who's more gorgeous than ever in his new chestnut parka and designer jeans, is breaking down my defenses, one wall at a time.

Will Rossi is all the things I shouldn't want—an unemployed singer-songwriter who's in town for a short while—and who's one hundred percent human. But I'm finding him hard to resist.

And I'm absolutely terrified.

"What are you waiting for? Come on inside!" cries Sophie. That's my cousin; lively, outgoing, kind to a fault, and a decibel louder than necessary. She's a bit much sometimes, but I love her to pieces.

A blast of warm, yeasty air washes over us as we enter the bakeshop.

Sophie holds up her phone. "Ooh! Stay right there. I'm going to snap a few photos of the two of you for the bakery's new promo campaign." She pauses, probably because it's just occurred to her Will might not want the extra publicity. "Is that okay with you, Mr. Rossi?"

Will is about to answer, but then Sophie interrupts him. "Oh, what's wrong with me? We haven't been introduced yet! I'm Sophie Brownlee, Cassia's cousin." Then she flings her hand toward Will, who shakes it, looking slightly dazed at my cousin's zigzagging, one-sided conversation.

"Pleased to make your acquaintance," he drawls. "And it's fine with me if you want to share some photos online."

Will naturally assumes Sophie will be posting to the social media apps he's familiar with. But we use Super-

Suite, an app followed by supernaturals coast to coast. Will has been avoiding the human paparazzi for months, and while he thinks he's ready for them now, *our* paparazzi are *different*. They make my aunt's naughty gargoyles look like friendly cherubs by comparison.

I cast him a worried look. "Are you sure you're ready for the extra media exposure?"

Will puts his arm around my waist, pulls me close, and smiles down at me. "Of course!" His velvety-brown eyes soften as he gazes at me, and I feel another of my walls crumbling. My breath catches in my throat.

He nods at Sophie. "Go ahead, take some photos."

I realize my mouth is gaping open so I hastily turn my silent *O* into a friendly smile. Sophie snaps a bunch of photos and thanks Will for the free publicity.

"Well now," says Will. "It's not entirely free."

Sophie raises an eyebrow. "Is that so? Name your price."

"A couple of cappuccinos and some cookies, if you please."

"For you, anything." Sophie winks at Will. "You can have all my cookies."

"I think you better stop promising all your cookies to every good-looking guy who comes through the door. You're going to make Teddy very jealous." Teddy Barker is Sophie's soon-to-be husband and about as un-jealous as anyone could get, but Sophie and I love to tease each other.

Sophie's eyes sparkle. "You've gone and done it now, cuz."

"What do you mean?"

"You've just told Will Rossi you think he's good look-ing. It'll go right to his head." Sophie folds her arms and grins at me. I'd like to pinch her right now; one good turn does not deserve another.

I'm feeling uncomfortably warm inside my puffer coat. "Will knows how he looks," I say, lamely. "He's had enough female fans over the years."

Will waggles his eyebrows innocently. "But I thought all those ladies liked me for my music. You're not saying they only liked me for my looks, are you?" He brings his hands up to his heart, pretending to be crushed by the revelation.

I flush up to my hair roots and unzip my coat to cool off. "Of course they liked your music. They also liked you, and um, your overall appearance." Will's grin deepens; he seems to be enjoying watching my face turn the color of winterberries.

Sophie decides to rescue me. "Two cappuccinos and a plate of warm cookies coming right up. Why don't you sit over by the window?"

Sophie indicates my favorite spot in the bakery, a sun-drenched corner by the front window where she squeezed in a couple of glass-topped tables and wrought iron chairs. I nod gratefully, drape my coat over one of the chairs, and take a seat. Will removes his parka and sits opposite me.

His eyes have a little twinkle in them as he asks, "What else have you planned for my Riddle Hill walking tour?"

We're sitting two feet apart, and I'm blushing again at the way he's looking at me, as if I'm the only woman in the world. I pull my tablet out of my purse, relieved to have something to do other than stare at his handsome face.

"Let's see. The bride's mother wants to expand her dessert selection for Saturday's wedding, so Sophie and I still need to go over the original order and decide what we're adding. Afterward, we're stopping at Malaki's Menswear because they're supplying the tuxes for the groomsmen, and I've just received the final measurements. And then we'll visit Bibbidy Bouquets and Baubles because we're adding one more table—the bride's cousins from Mexico are able to join us, so we'll need another centerpiece."

Will shakes his head. "My head's spinning just listening to you." He takes a sip of the cappuccino delivered by one of Sophie's helpers. "It seems to me your job would be simpler if you did more ordering online from the bigger stores and franchises. You'd save yourself a lot of time."

I can't tell Will that supernaturals comprise less than three percent of the world's population. There just aren't that many of us, and we tend to stick together. Plus no one, not even faeries, can make gold grow on trees, which means supernaturals work just as hard as everyone else. And while our magic might make some things easier, like my brother's werewolf strength, or taste better, like my uncle's daily specials, we need to pull our own weight.

I brush back my long bangs and try explaining it to Will. "I'm in the relationship business with the brides and grooms, with their assorted relatives and friends, and also with my suppliers. They're like my extended family, and some of them are my actual family, which makes it more fun. Besides, who'd want to use online ordering and miss out on this!" I point to the plate of decorated spritz cookies.

Will bites into one of Sophie's buttery cookies, still warm from the oven. "Hmm… delicious. I can see I'll have to start using Sam's treadmill *twice* a day while I'm in Riddle Hill."

Sophie wanders over and taps the plate of cookies. "Well, what do you think?"

Will wipes his mouth on a napkin. "The best spritz cookies I've ever tasted. Your family does know its way around good food."

Sophie grins. "Thanks. But truthfully, there are a lot of great places to eat in Door County. We're known for our food."

"And our craft beers, fruit wines, homemade chocolate, and fudge," I say. "And given the number of orchards, which are covered by snow at the moment, we're also known for our cherries."

"And the fact your residents consume more tart cherry juice per capita than anywhere else," quips Will.

Sophie glances at me. She rolls her lips together, probably to keep from chuckling out loud. We both know why so much cherry juice is served in Riddle Hill, but Will of course does not.

Now it's my turn to rescue Sophie from a giggling fit. Besides, it's time for us to get to work. I tell her about the extra guests coming to the wedding, and we start talking shop.

I can feel Will's eyes on me as Sophie and I are talking, and the part of me that's not scared senseless is totally thrilled. If I were more like my cousin, brave and confident, then I might be able to handle Will Rossi.

But despite my surging pulse and rosy cheeks whenever he glances my way, I'm still ready to bolt.

CHAPTER 10

HOUND DOG SERENADE

WILL

Tuesday Evening

After I take the dogs out for a walk and towel dry their snowy paws, I brew some coffee. Carrying my mug into the great room, I pause in front of Estee's creepy bat art on the left-hand wall. She has bat sketches, bat watercolors, bat oil paintings, and an oversized marble statue of a bat dangling upside down, wings fully extended. All the bats have large, round eyes that seem to follow me whenever I enter the room.

"Here's to your health, bat peeps!" I raise my coffee cup and toast them with a chuckle before settling down on Sam's *U*-shaped sofa. My buddy has a cord of wood in his shed out back, and I've built a nice, cheery blaze in the stone fireplace. Sleepy and Grumpy hop up on either side of me on the couch, and Dopey curls up in front of the hearth.

I pick up the remote and click through the channels

on Sam's flat-panel television, mounted on the wall above the fireplace. Every Christmas movie I flip through tonight has a supernatural element I never paid much attention to before: an angel, an elf, a ghost, a miracle, or a bit of unexplained magic.

My head goes immediately to Cassia, and I wish for some Christmas magic of my own. Sometimes I think I'm making progress with her, and other times I can almost feel her retreating back into her shell.

I'm flipping mad at her ex for putting her through so much grief she's afraid to believe in anyone else.

But I wonder whether my own tarnished reputation is partly to blame for her reluctance to trust me.

I'm not exactly filling ballparks these days... or even nightclubs. And while I've *started* composing some new material, I haven't actually *finished* anything in the past year. I've definitely hit a bump... or more like a slump.

If I want to make a lasting impression on Cassia, if I want an actual relationship with her, then I have to demonstrate I'm a solid, dependable guy. I need to start working again.

It's time to stop procrastinating and call my new manager—actually, my original manager back in Nashville—whom Roxie fired when she decided we needed to move to New York to bootstrap our careers.

She was right about the boost to our band's image and bottom line. And we did fill those stadiums everywhere we went, but it wasn't long before I became disenchanted with the whole scene. I started to miss the old days, when we performed in smaller towns and clubs, where our ticket prices were more in line with what an average guy or gal could afford.

I even begged Roxie to add a few of the old places back to our schedule, but she wouldn't hear of it. Told me I was being a sentimental fool. Perhaps. But we also started losing some of our most loyal fans, the folks who'd been with us from the start.

My biggest mistake, however, was allowing Roxie and Junior to manage our finances. It was a colossal error in judgment.

With Roxie's high-spending ways, Junior's large fees, and then the divorce and Mom's cancer treatments, I'm not as well off as most folks assume.

The tabloids, of course, have gotten it wrong. Creditors aren't hounding me; they're hounding my parents, who have huge medical bills that I'm now paying.

My new-old manager finally answers the phone. I try sounding nonchalant. "Hey, Mack, how's it going?"

Mack seems in a hurry. "Can't talk now, buddy, but I'm chasing down a few leads for you. I'll call soon, promise." Mack hangs up.

I frown at the phone.

I may have to take matters into my own hands and figure out how to manage my career by myself. But I'm terribly disorganized, hate negotiating, and dislike the internal workings of the music business.

I pace around the sofa, restless and ready for change. My eyes settle on my guitar case, stashed in the corner behind the taupe leather recliner.

I grab the case and pull out my fire-engine-red, twelve-string, custom guitar, purchased with my first paycheck as a professional musician. I've used many other guitars over the past decade, but this is my favorite, the one I always return to when I'm composing.

I sit back down on the sofa with my guitar and my music composition book, which I spread out on the square coffee table. I tune my guitar and turn the pages until I find the song I started composing during my flight from New York. Strumming the chords and humming, I pause periodically to jot down some lyrics.

I feel the need to write something grittier and somehow truer than what I've been composing for the past few years. I'm itching to revisit my country-rock musical roots.

Sleepy grunts, hops off, and saunters down the hall toward the master bedroom. "Guess you're not a fan, eh?" I call after the dog with a chuckle.

I return to my composition book, humming, strumming, and revising. Finally I lean back, satisfied with my draft. I decided to test it with my audience: Dopey, who's taken Sleepy's spot on the sofa next to me, and Grumpy, who's now sprawled out on the recliner in the corner.

I sing in my stage voice, projecting as if I'm playing to a sellout crowd. Grumpy jumps up and begins to whine, and Dopey rolls over to join him. Sleepy emerges from the bedroom, and then the strangest thing happens.

The dogs hum and howl in perfect harmony all the way through the song.

I'm so fired up about the music and the weirdness of performing with dogs that I go back to the beginning and do it all again.

And those three crazy hounds join me once more.

I'm flabbergasted. I don't know whether to laugh out loud, find a shrink, or go to a bar.

Instead, I send Sam a text. "Either I'm crazy, or your dogs just yowled in three-part harmony."

Then I add, "Speaking of crazy, I'm falling hard for Cassia Spellman. Any advice?"

CHAPTER II

ELVES, LOVE, AND GREEN BAY PACKERS

CASSIA

Wednesday, December 12

The gargoyles are sticking their fingers up their noses again. Ugh, how gross. Why can't I work in a normal restaurant? Well, maybe not entirely normal, but a supernatural version without disgusting little beasties like these? Phoebe needs to scold them because they won't listen to me.

I turn my back on them and read Mona's text. Then I slip the phone into my jeans pocket, adjust my Sit for a Spell apron, and sigh.

"What's up?" asks Phoebe.

"I asked Mona whether she could spare someone to help me pick up the supplies for Saturday's wedding, but she doesn't have anyone available."

I use the same company to supply most of the decorations, party favors, and other little necessities for my clients' weddings. My orders vary considerably depending on the theme, such as the dozen boxes of dark green and gold tulle—the team colors of the Green Bay Packers—which I'll be using to decorate the ballroom for Saturday's wedding. I also ordered Packers' tree ornaments for the party favors I'll be assembling.

Marie Ramos, the bride, is a willowy elf whose parents moved to Riddle Hill after selling their toy-making company. Her fiancé, Beau O'Mara, is a tall, ginger-haired elf whose extended family owns a string of shoe repair shops throughout Wisconsin.

These days, both the bride and groom are big Packers' fans, but when they were younger, they couldn't agree on anything.

Marie and Beau hated each other in high school, competing with a vengeance in every class and club. She'd been valedictorian, edging out Beau for first place. He'd been president of the student council, defeating Marie by three votes. She'd been debate-team captain, and the list went on and on.

Seven years later, Marie and Beau wound up as young associates in the same Wisconsin law firm. They decided to bury the hatchet over drinks after work, and they've been inseparable ever since.

I'm a sucker for a good romance, and Marie and Beau's story fills me with hope. I've grown very fond of these two elves and want to make sure their wedding is flawless.

My aunt glances out at the café's lunch crowd like she's looking for someone to help me shift boxes. I look too.

There *appears to be* four older men in ball caps at the

counter, two families sitting at tables, one couple in a booth, and a dark-haired, dashing human, who's seated in an adjacent booth, sipping coffee, and reading on his tablet.

What I *actually see* are a group of older gnomes in pointed hats at the counter, one vampire family, one faerie family, a werewolf couple, and Will Rossi.

My heart does a backward flip every time I'm near him, which is nerve-wracking; it's a good thing my eyebrows and ears are behaving. I'm doing my best to resist Will's charms, but he's not making it easy for me. And I can't very well ignore him the way I can the gargoyles.

"How about asking Will to tag along?" suggests Phoebe. "Didn't you say he asked for a tour of the county?"

I stiffen, like I've been caught red-handed thinking about Will. "I already gave him a walking tour of Riddle Hill. And I showed him around a bit when Dopey needed a ride to the clinic. It's not like I'm Will Rossi's personal tour guide or anything."

"What's gotten into you all of a sudden?"

"Nothing." I don't know why I'm being ornery with Phoebe. But I just don't want to ask Will for any favors. I don't know if it's my independent streak, or the way he's affecting me, or both, but I'll manage the boxes myself.

Phoebe pats my arm. "At least give the man some more coffee. He's been trying to make eye contact with you for the past five minutes."

"Fine," I grumble, picking up the juice carafe and coffee pot. I top up the gnomes at the counter, and then the three vampires, four faeries, and two werewolves, before pausing in front of Will. I notice he's drinking both coffee *and* tart cherry juice, just like my vampire customers. I suck on the insides of my cheeks to keep from chuckling.

"Thanks." Will nods as I top up his beverages. He looks at me expectantly. "Are you going to ask me or not?"

"Ask you what?"

"To give you a hand with some boxes." Will takes a long sip of coffee and places his cup on the table.

I wonder whether Will overheard my conversation with Phoebe, but he clarifies things. "Phoebe mentioned you needed to make a run. She thought I'd like to tag along, seeing how you could use a hand with some boxes, and I wanted to explore more of Door County."

I shake my head. *How on earth did Phoebe manage to know I'd need help and line up Will for me, even before I knew it?*

"So you don't need my help?" asks Will, sounding slightly deflated.

"Oh no, it's not that, it's..." I quickly backpedal. "It's that I'm not quite ready to go."

Will smiles. "No problem. Let me know when you want to leave."

Twenty minutes later we're on the highway heading south toward Sturgeon Bay. I point out places of interest, such as the best places to cross-country ski, sled down a hill, or rent a snowmobile.

As we pass a road sign announcing a lighthouse museum inside the state park, Will says, "I think that's the third lighthouse I've passed. Seems like a lot for such a small peninsula."

I enjoy sharing local lore. "Actually, there are eleven lighthouses up here—not so many when you know the history of the area. Door County has three hundred miles of rocky coastline, beautiful to look at but also treacherous, especially back when most goods were transported on ships. Not only do we have a lot of lighthouses, but the waters around here contain a lot of shipwrecks."

"I'll bet you get a great view from the top of those lighthouse towers."

"Olivia and I climb a different one every year during the Lighthouse Festival. But if you're thinking of climbing one, you'll need to wait until they're open for public tours."

We listen to the radio for a while, until a Roxie and Rossi song from their latest album comes on. I switch to another channel, and Will glances over. "I thought you were a fan."

"Guilty as charged," I say with a smile. I follow the traffic circle onto a side road leading to downtown Sturgeon Bay.

"Just not of the last album?"

I hesitate before answering. "I thought you might not want to listen to it."

Will rubs the stubble on his chin and shrugs. "It doesn't bother me, if that's what you're thinking. Though it's my least favorite album and that was my least favorite song."

That surprises me, because I feel the same way and

tell him so. "I'm no expert," I add. "But I like your older stuff—all of your older stuff—much better."

"So do I," says Will. "Roxie disagrees, of course, and that's okay. She's entitled to move in a new direction, with new songwriters and performers."

After we load the boxes of wedding paraphernalia into my Honda's trunk—I have to drop the rear seats to fit everything inside—we walk a few blocks to a local coffee roaster, where I order us two coffees to go. Handing a cup to Will, I give him a conspiratorial wink. "Best coffee anywhere."

"What about your coffee at the Sit for a Spell Café? Aren't you being disloyal to your own brand?"

I grin. "Taste it and tell me what you think."

Will takes a sip and chuckles. "You had me going there. This is the café's coffee supplier, right?"

"Yep." I nod. "They supply—"

"Hey Cassia!" a man's voice calls out behind us.

I turn around and wait for Rob Wolferman, my brother's best friend and my aunt's latest matchmaking attempt, to catch up with us.

Large and muscular, with short, sandy-colored hair and matching beard, Rob has a hearty laugh and booming voice that often make me wince. He's constantly glued to his phone doing business deals, even on a date. I find him exhausting, except during a full moon, when he wolfs out with Jake and the rest of the Riddle Hill pack. It's the one time of the month when he doesn't use his phone.

Rob extends a hand to Will and introduces himself.

Will shakes his hand. "I think I've seen your name somewhere before."

Rob puffs out his chest. "Probably on real estate signs and listings. I'm Riddle Hill's number one broker three years running."

"Congratulations, that can't be easy," says Will with a smile.

"Especially when dealing with supers!" exclaims Rob.

I can't believe Rob just said that; I roll my eyes at him.

Will draws his brows together. "Supers?"

Rob spots my eye roll and realizes his error. He fake-coughs and then turns to me. "What time are we meeting on Friday night?"

I completely forgot Rob, who's also a volunteer fire-fighter, is supposed to pick me up after Marie's wedding rehearsal. I'm his date for the Firemen's Ball. Now Will's eyebrows are arched in surprise. He probably can't imagine Rob and me going out together.

Here's the truth: When you grow up in a small, supernatural town and know everyone, and your brother's best friend can't find a date because he's so annoying, sometimes you just do the decent thing. Besides, I was already planning to go to the ball, just not with Rob.

Every year, I help decorate the high-school gymnasium for the fire department's December fundraiser, and Phoebe and Nash cater the event. I almost turned down Marie's request to plan her wedding because of the conflict with the Firemen's Ball, which is a longstanding family tradition given Jake's role as fire chief. But when Marie pleaded for my help, I couldn't say no.

However, this is the first year I have to work at the café in the morning, decorate the gymnasium in the afternoon, manage a wedding rehearsal in the early evening, and attend the Firemen's Ball later that night. I'm supposed to be providing moral support for Jake, but it might turn out to be the other way around. My brother might have to help keep me vertical.

Olivia will be staying at her best friend's house for her first-ever sleepover, and she's already packed her kid-sized, purple suitcase I bought for the occasion. I've always planned to spend my first evening home alone with a giant bowl of popcorn and a bottle of wine, watching rom-coms until two in the morning.

Phoebe likes to remind me too much planning is a waste of time, and I'm beginning to think she's right, as usual.

"Can you swing by Mooncrest Chapel at six-thirty?" I say to Rob. "I should be finished with the rehearsal by then."

Rob's cell phone rings, so he gives me a thumb's up, waves at Will, and ducks inside the coffee house to take the call.

As we walk back to my car, Will asks, "What's happening on Friday night?"

I explain about my busy Friday and the Firemen's Ball. When I'm finished, Will says, "I'd like to support the fire department by purchasing a ticket to the fundraiser. I might even decide to drop in and check it out on Friday night. Where can I make a donation?"

"You can buy tickets at the fire station and at the

café. But please don't feel obligated. It's a Riddle Hill thing. I doubt you'd enjoy yourself."

"Why is that?" Will asks as he opens the passenger door to my Honda, which is packed from our seat backs all the way to the trunk door with boxes.

I close my door and put my coffee cup down in one of the holders. "You've traveled and performed all over the country. You've even performed for the Prince of Wales one time, before he became King—"

"Twice, actually," Will interrupts.

"My point exactly. Look, I love Riddle Hill. I wouldn't stay here if I didn't, but it's not for everyone, and it's definitely not for someone like you." I start the car, pulling away from the curb.

"Someone like me?"

I blow out a puff of air, trying to figure out how to explain it without unveiling all the reasons why I live in Riddle Hill, including the fact I'm raising a precocious faerie child who'll need magical instruction as she grows older. Where better to find that support than in a town founded by faeries, where my family and friends are around to give me a helping hand?

The traffic light turns red, and I glance over at Will. "You're a celebrity who's lying low in a little Wisconsin town for a few weeks, and then returning to the hustle and bustle of New York City. Why would some fundraiser in our little town hold any appeal for you?"

Will pulls off his brown wool cap and runs a hand through his hair, making it stand up in wavy spikes. He looks younger, like I've caught him in an unguarded moment. My heart squeezes inside my chest. I really wish I were going to the Firemen's Ball with Will and not Rob.

"The way I see it, I'm just Will Rossi from Nashville, Tennessee—a guy who got really lucky and was able to live out his dream, except the dream didn't turn out to be what he expected—so he's stepped off the fast track for a bit. It's true I live in New York for now, but I have no set plans beyond dog sitting for Sam and Estee, working on some new material, and paying my rent." Will stops, as if he might have said too much.

I feel guilty, like I forced a confession out of him, when all I'd been trying to do was explain about the Firemen's Ball and why Will probably would think it was too homespun for his tastes. Besides, last year, some of the rowdier guys and gals let some fur fly—literally—and I definitely don't want Will to see *that*.

"I'm sorry," I say. "I didn't mean to imply you're not welcome. Please come to the Firemen's Ball if you'd like —no need to make a donation. Come as our guest."

Will clears his throat. "I appreciate the offer, but I'll be purchasing a ticket, same as anyone else."

Oh no, did I just insult him again? I don't want Will to think that I think he's a charity case. "Great, and thank you," I say cheerily, "the entire Riddle Hill Fire Department will be honored to have you attend."

Will nods, looking a bit defeated.

I realize too late I didn't say I'd be happy to see him there too.

CHAPTER 12
THREE-ALARM FIRE

CASSIA

THURSDAY, DECEMBER 13

The gargoyles blink up at me so sweetly this morning I'm almost ready to forgive all their past rudeness. But then they start tittering and hooting very loudly when I walk past them. Cousin Heliotrope *tsks* at them from her picture frame, but they ignore her scolding.

They're icky little fiends.

"3A fire. Can u walk Sam's dogs? Will's out, back late." I scroll through the text from Jake several times to decipher it. Jake's dealing with a "3A" or three-alarm fire.

Will must have asked Jake to walk the dogs while he went somewhere for the day. I'm disappointed in Will because it's the sort of thing Derek would have done. Where is Will going... and why?

"I'll walk the dogs, be safe," I text Jake.

My brother sends me the garage code and a thumbs-up.

I put my phone away and return to my customers, dropping off checks at several tables. I spend some time chatting with a lively group of elderly vampires, faeries, werewolves, and witches from the Riddle Hill Senior Center, out for an afternoon of Christmas shopping.

My shift runs over, and I slip away later than expected. I hear Grumpy's shrill barking as soon as I punch in the garage code. Dopey and Grumpy greet me with wagging tails and happy yaps when I step into the white kitchen. Sleepy rouses himself enough to lick my hand when I snap on his leash.

I take the trio for a lengthy walk; I figure they deserve it. The day is warm for December, the temperature hovering around thirty degrees before plunging again later tonight. Returning to Estee's kitchen, I hang up leashes, dry off paws, refill food and water bowls, and hand out dog biscuits. I search on top of the counters and inside each of the white cabinets, trying to find Dopey's medicine.

I wander into the great room, thinking I might find the dog's stomach enzymes out here, but no such luck. Turning to leave, I can't help but notice Will's music composition notebook lying on the coffee table. I debate with myself for maybe five seconds, but my curiosity wins.

Gingerly spreading open the first page, I hum all the way to the last bar. Turning the page, I keep humming. Ten years of piano and voice lessons with Granny Catbeam are finally paying off. I have a sneak peek at Will's new material, and his music is better than ever.

Some of the pages contain fragments of lyrics; others

have complete verses. The lyrics are more mature than the old Roxie and Rossi standards and just as witty. One melody, untitled and toward the back of the notebook, lifts my spirits unexpectedly. I ponder the power of music to move me.

Closing the notebook and placing it back on the table, I have a new appreciation for Will's talent. I also realize Will was the true genius behind the band's music, despite the fact Roxie was listed as co-author on everything the band produced.

I close the garage door and climb into my Honda. Shaking my head, I wonder why Will allowed his ex-wife to take credit for co-writing all his songs. Then I recall the early years of my marriage to Derek. I encouraged him, supported him financially, and traveled around the country with him, until he finally took too much.

Did something similar happen to Will?

I shrug and remind myself he's not so very different from Derek. Will is off doing his own thing at the moment, while I'm here feeding and walking the dogs entrusted to his care.

And yet, how could a man write that music, those lyrics, and not feel a deep connection to others? It makes no sense.

As I'm driving home, I catch myself humming Will's unnamed melody. I reach over and turn on the radio to drown out his song.

～

I TURN down the heat under the pot of chili on my stove and head into my dining-and-living-combo room. It's decorated in shades of gray, white, and my favorite color, bright pink. My vintage maple dining table—which I picked up for almost nothing last summer, along with four matching chairs and a small buffet—is set for three.

Jake sent me a text to let me know he's coming over, which he often does after dealing with a difficult fire. I'm apprehensive because Jake's given no indication of how things went today. That's never a good sign with my brother.

The doorbell rings, and Olivia dashes over to answer it. When she throws open the door to greet her uncle, I take one look at Jake's stooped shoulders and dark circles under his eyes and say, "Have a seat. I'll get you a beer."

Jake nods his thanks, tosses his jacket onto a fuchsia armchair, and drops onto my sofa. Olivia climbs up next to her uncle and drapes a fluffy, pink-and-white throw across their knees. Then she proceeds to tell Jake about her day at school, which I know from personal experience is often great therapy for world-weary adults.

After I hand Jake a beer and ask Olivia to finish her homework in the kitchen, I ask, "Rough day?"

Jake nods. "Apartment fire today. Four families lost everything, but thankfully, no one was seriously hurt. We even saved a pregnant, nine-tailed fox named Hoshi."

My eyes cloud over. "But it was a close call, wasn't it?"

Jake takes a long swallow. "Almost lost two fire-fighters when the roof caved in." He looks at me and adds, "I never want to go to a crew member's family and tell them their mom or dad isn't coming home."

I know he's remembering the night the police arrived with the news of our parents' car accident. Phoebe had been watching us and opened the front door, with Jake and me trailing in her wake. I remember my aunt's tears, along with mine and Jake's. The memories of that night still haunt us.

"I understand… and I also know how careful you are with your crew."

Jake puts his beer down on a side table and scratches his neatly trimmed brown beard. "I realized tonight that if something happened to me, there'd be no one at home to mourn me."

I start to object, but he puts up a hand to continue. "Of course you, Olivia, and our family would miss me. I'm not saying that. What I'm trying to say is that I wouldn't be leaving much behind, no wife or child or anything."

I often tease Jake about his lack of commitment to a long-lasting relationship. He's never had a serious girl-friend. Maybe something's shifting inside him; whatever it is, I want to encourage him. "It sounds like what you're saying is you want to leave a legacy of some sort. Is that what you mean?"

Jake snaps his fingers. "Yes! That's what's been rattling around inside my head all day." He pauses and adds, "How'd you get to be so smart?"

I grin. "It goes with being a mom. We get pretty good at discerning what's going on inside here." I tap the side of my head with a finger.

Jake picks up his beer and examines the amber liquid. Taking another long swallow, he says, "Just don't tell Aunt Phoebe about this. The last thing I need is match-making advice from her, or Nash, or Sophie, or you, much as I love you all. And I definitely don't want suggestions from any of the old vampires and were-wolves who sit at the café's counter nursing their cherry juice and coffee every morning."

I run my thumb and forefinger across my mouth as if zipping it closed. "My lips are sealed."

Olivia calls out from the kitchen, "My homework's done! Can we eat now?"

I smile and ask Jake, "Do you think you can handle a bowl of chili with a side of cheesy nachos?"

"Definitely!" He stands up. "I'm starving. Let's eat."

As Jake scrubs the chili pot after dinner, he says, "Oh, I almost forgot. Thanks for walking the dogs today. Sorry to dump that on you."

"No need to apologize to me. Those dogs are Will's responsibility, not yours. It seems like he dumped them on you."

"Not at all. Will asked me if he could pay someone to walk the dogs in the afternoon, since he'd be gone all day. I offered to walk the dogs myself."

"Now why would you do that?"

"Can't I just be a nice guy without you getting suspicious?"

I laugh. "Sure, but I'm detecting an ulterior motive."

Jake chuckles. "I like to keep my donors happy, and Will Rossi made a significant donation to our fundraiser."

"So he bought a ticket to the Firemen's Ball?"

"He bought a hundred tickets." Jake hands me the clean pot to dry off. "Can you think of any reason for his sudden burst of generosity?"

Will Rossi purchased a hundred tickets to the Firemen's Ball!

I'm speechless. Ten tickets would have been generous. But a hundred tickets?

That's a statement.

Will is trying to say something. Whatever it is, *I think he's saying it to me.*

I'm nervous, excited, unsure what to think, and terrified he's actually attending the dance tomorrow night.

Jake is waiting for me to respond, so I mumble, "I have no idea why Will Rossi did that."

My brother shoots me a sidelong glance. "No idea, huh?"

I lift my shoulders. "I guess Will Rossi has a soft spot for small towns and good causes."

"Speaking of good causes, we've decided to donate the proceeds from the Firemen's Ball this year to the four families who are now homeless due to the fire. We want to help them get back on their feet, maybe even purchase new Christmas gifts for the kids."

I give him a bear hug. "Jake, that's a wonderful idea. I want to help too."

Olivia must have been listening to us because she says, "Me too."

Jake ruffles her hair. "Thank you, sweetie. You and your mom can help organize the food and clothing purchases for the families. We want to give them a good Christmas, despite everything that's happened to them."

Jake and I decide December twenty-third is the best date for delivering the food, clothing, and gifts to the families, all of whom are staying in temporary housing. I'm going to pull together a few volunteers from the community to help organize the special drive.

Jake reads Olivia a story before she goes off to bed. As he slips on his jacket and boots, I ask him, "Are you heading over to the pub?"

Firefighters and their families often gather at Howling Shores Pub after a particularly difficult fire; they need that extra connection to each other and their community.

Jake nods, and I wish I could go with him tonight. I reach up to give Jake a peck on the cheek as he leaves, incredibly thankful he wasn't on that roof when it collapsed. I can't bear the thought of anything bad happening to my brother—or to anyone else I love.

Then Will Rossi's dreamy brown eyes and stubbled jaw pop into my head. I roll my eyes, not sure what Will thinks he's doing, invading my thoughts like this.

Go away, I mutter half-heartedly.

But I don't sound particularly convincing.

CHAPTER 13
HOWLING SHORES PUB

Thursday Evening

It's well after sunset when I enter Sam and Estee's tidy blue ranch. I'm greeted by Grumpy's high-pitched bark and the two labs' deeper woofs. I wrestle a red sweater on the schnauzer, take the dogs out for a walk, and refill their bowls.

After grabbing a beer from the fridge, I head into the great room and salute Estee's bat paintings with my raised can before sprawling on the sofa with my canine companions. I'm out of firewood and don't feel like traipsing out to Sam's shed to bring in more. I'm bushed from the nine-hour, round-trip drive to O'Hare Airport, but I'm also relieved.

My mom is looking much better; her hair's grown back, and she's now sporting a cute, gray pixie cut. Dad looks the same, perhaps with more silver than black in his thinning hair.

I'm happy they're finally taking their long-awaited, often-postponed Caribbean cruise—which is my Christmas gift to them. They're now on their way to Miami and will be onboard their ship by noon tomorrow.

Mom tried convincing me to spend Christmas with my sister, Maggie, and her family. I know Mom's worried about me being alone over the holidays. But her face lit up when I told her I've met someone special and want to leave my options open for where I spend Christmas.

I finish my beer and head back into the kitchen, flip on the overhead lights, and wait for my eyes to adjust to the bright, white walls. I peek inside the freezer, hoping to find something I can pop into the microwave. I never made it to the grocery store yesterday, so I'm not surprised to discover only ice cubes.

Argh.

Next, I check the pantry... which has twenty gallons of tart cherry juice, several cases of dog food, and not much else.

Looks like I'm heading into town to find someplace that's still serving dinner. I really wish the Sit for a Spell Café was open right now. I'm starving, and not just for supper; I miss Cassia something fierce.

Tomorrow, I promise myself. I'll see her at the café *and* at the Firemen's Ball. I'll be wearing my new blazer from Malaki's, which is pretty dapper, if I do say so myself. I'm going to ask Cassia to dance.

I aim to sweep that woman off her feet and into my arms.

Yeah, I know she has a date, but I doubt Rob

Wolferman is going to care. He seems too interested in his business deals to notice anything or anyone else.

At least I hope so.

I PARK DOWN the road from Howling Shores Pub, the only building on Main Street with any activity this late in the evening. I walk up to the thick, wooden door with a porthole window, give it a hard tug, and step inside. Squinting into the gloom, I attempt to get my bearings.

A scarred oak bar with brass footrails runs along the mirrored wall in the back. Nautical-themed artwork, prints of old ships tossing at sea, and a fair number of mermaids, merman, and other sea creatures I can't identify covers the three other walls. Fishnets overflowing with starfish and shells hang from the corners of the room.

The buzz of conversation gradually dwindles until all I hear are mugs hitting tables and chairs scraping floors. An awkward silence descends.

Something—make that many somethings—is definitely off here.

It takes my brain a few moments to realize I'm standing in a bar with a bunch of giant wolves. I can't tell you whether there's a difference between the guys and the gals because all I see is fur, claws, fangs, and tails everywhere I look.

This is Little Red Riding Hood's worst nightmare.

I shriek and bolt, smacking my head as I wrestle open

the heavy door. I run for my SUV like it's a lifeboat in a monster-filled sea.

"Will! Will! Wait up! Are you okay?"

That sounds like Jake Spellman. Does he realize he's living in Freaksville, USA? More importantly, does Cassia?

I keep running, my adrenaline pumping so hard I couldn't stop myself even if I wanted to, which I don't.

Jake catches up to me. (The man is massive, and a firefighter, and he apparently can outrun me despite the fact I'm sprinting for dear life.) He claps a big hand on my shoulder, stopping my mad dash across the frosty sidewalk.

"What's wrong? You're acting like you saw a ghost or something just now."

If Jake was inside that pub, does that make him a wolfman... er, werewolf? I'm not up on my paranormal monster types. That's my sister's favorite genre, not mine. Give me a mystery-thriller any day.

My chest is heaving for air as I slowly turn around to face Jake. I'm overwhelmed with relief to see he's the same large, bearded man I met at the fire station. He's not wearing a jacket, probably because he ran outside after me.

Just because Jake is normal doesn't mean everyone else in that joint is. I glance at the lit sign above the pub's entrance and flinch. *Howling Shores*. Even the name gives it away.

I point at the sign. "Howling Shores is a werewolf hangout, isn't it?"

Jake gapes at me, his mouth hanging open as if in

shock. "What are you talking about? I saw you hit your head as you were leaving... I think maybe you need to come back inside with me and sit down. I'm worried it's not safe for you to drive home right now."

Jake's brow is furrowed, and he seems genuinely concerned about me. I decide to trust him. After all, he *is* Cassia's brother, and the fire chief, and the mayor of this wackadoodle town.

I rub my head, which has a bump near the hairline. "Look, I know what I saw just now. A lot of big, furry wolves were milling around that bar."

Jake takes my arm and leads me back toward the door with the porthole window. "A couple of the guys are dog sledders, and they brought their dogs—which probably looked like wolves—into the bar. I'm really sorry they startled you, Will. I'm going to make sure the owner doesn't permit that again."

He pulls open the door and propels me inside the pub... which looks standard issue. Guys and gals are standing by the bar and sitting at tables. In the back, I notice the bartender hustling the last of the very large dogs out a side entrance.

I'm mortified at the way I overreacted, and I apologize to Jake. But he just smiles and guides me over to a long table, which is actually several smaller tables shoved together. Jake points to an empty spot across from Rob Wolferman, Cassia's possible suitor, who gives me a friendly smile.

About ten other men and women sit hunched over their beers around the table. I get the sense I've interrupted something important, and now I feel kind of guilty.

Jake introduces me, but I'm terrible with names, forgetting most of them almost as soon as I'm introduced. Nearly everyone has a connection with the fire station, except for Nash Brownlee, whom I met earlier this week, when the large man briefly emerged from the café's kitchen.

The guy sitting next to Nash nods at me. He's a big, blue-eyed, blond man who looks as if he walked off the cover of some book on Norse mythology. I think his name is Teddy. "Sophie tells me you stopped by her shop this week."

I scratch the stubble on my chin. Is Sophie the bakery owner, the florist, or the wedding decorations supplier in Sturgeon Bay? "Sorry, but I've met a lot of new people this week..."

Teddy grins. "Sophie Brownlee, owns the bakery in town? She is Nash's daughter. And my fiancée. We're getting married right before Christmas."

I reach across the table to shake his hand and congratulate him. Jake pours a mug of beer for me from one of the pitchers scattered haphazardly around the table. Pushing the mug toward me, Jake says, "I guess you must have heard about the fire."

I shake my head. "I just got back to town. What fire?" My head goes immediately to Cassia, but I don't think her brother and uncle would be out drinking beer if she and Olivia were injured. "Is everyone okay?"

Jake nods. "We were very lucky today. We got

everyone out of the apartment building before it collapsed.”

Nash stands up, clinking his mug with a spoon until the entire pub quiets down. Raising his glass, he shouts, “Here’s to the brave men and women who fight fires every day, in every city, town, and borough. May they all return safely home again!”

Every patron in the place raises their glass, downs the contents, and then claps and cheers. Nash puts his empty mug on the table and zips up his parka. “I’m off to bed, lads and ladies, unless I have a volunteer to get my dough started around three in the morning?” He looks around the table with a broad smile and laughs. “Didn’t think so, but it never hurts to ask.”

Everyone else pulls on parkas and coats, scraping their chairs against the scratched-up floor as they shout goodnight.

Jake insists on walking me back to my SUV. I glance at him as I’m opening the door. “Thanks for rescuing me from a full-blown panic attack. I don’t know what you must think of me.”

Jake shakes his head. “You don’t need to thank me. It was an honest mistake. I’m just glad we were able to clear up any misunderstanding.”

“Definitely... and er, I’d appreciate it if you don’t mention my foolishness to Cassia.”

Jake arches an eyebrow, looking slightly confused. Maybe it’s just dawned on him I’m crazy about his sister. Then he slowly nods. “Sure, no problem.”

I say goodnight and climb into my SUV. As I pull

away, I spot a couple of those big dogs chasing each other down the street.

Ramos–O'Mara Wedding

The honor of your presence
is requested at the marriage of

Marie Eliza Ramos
to
Beau Riley O'Mara

Saturday, the fifteenth of December
at five o'clock in the afternoon

Mooncrest Inn
Door County, Wisconsin

Reception to follow

CHAPTER 14

FIREMEN'S BALL

CASSIA

FRIDAY, DECEMBER 14

A small army of volunteers is helping me turn the school's large, boxy gymnasium into a sparkly winter wonderland. "We need to add some extra mistletoe over there," I tell a burly firefighter, who grabs the mistletoe from my hand and gives me a jaunty salute.

Grinning, I take a spin around the gym, pointing out where the lights need to be strung higher, the dangling snowflakes distributed more evenly, or a few more gold and silver ornaments hung on the white-frosted Christmas trees dotting the edges of the room.

"I believe we're done. Thanks, everyone!" I call out from the center of the wooden floor. I'm greeted by cheers and a smattering of applause. My helpers don their coats and scarves, heading back out into the bitter cold.

But I'm not ready to leave yet.

I feel fluttery just thinking about the Firemen's Ball tonight—and seeing Will again. We missed each other this morning at the café; I started my shift late so I could take Olivia to the pediatrician's office for her wellness checkup.

I remind myself I can't afford to fall for another performer who puts his aspirations ahead of everything else. Especially one who's leaving soon anyway. And who has no idea supernaturals even exist. And who disappeared yesterday without any explanation.

I see nothing but roadblocks ahead for me and Will Rossi.

Then why do I feel warm and tingly whenever he's around? I shake my head and chalk it up to wishful thinking... and loneliness.

I want to fall in love again, but with the *right man* this time. And regardless of how hot he is, that man is *not* Will Rossi.

I HEAD HOME to shower and change out of my jeans. After discarding nearly everything in my closet, I select my tall, black leather boots with spiky heels, fishnet tights, and the only piece of designer clothing I own, a little black dress. I pin my hair up in a French twist, leaving some loose tendrils around my face.

Before I head out, I place a quick call to Olivia in case she's homesick and wants to skip her first sleepover. My neighbor, a grandmother who raised four boys, offered to be my backup sitter for the evening.

Olivia chats about a game she's been playing and then blows air kisses over the phone. I hang up, surprised and more than a little proud of how well she's handling the separation. Definitely better than me; I want to dash over to my friend's house and shower Olivia with real kisses.

Marie and Beau's rehearsal goes well, making me almost nervous at how smoothly things are running the day before the wedding. Rob walks into the chapel promptly at six-thirty and helps me into my cranberry-colored, dressy wool coat. I withdraw a pair of dangly crystal earrings from my purse and slip them on as Rob drives us to the school.

We park, follow the crowd, and pause outside the gym entrance to hang up our coats on the freestanding racks. When we walk through the doors I'm smiling, delighted with how lovely everything looks. I decide this is my best winter wonderland yet.

Rob quickly scans the room. "I see one of my clients over there. Meet you at the bar in a bit?"

"Sure," I say, but he's already walking away.

Someone comes up behind me and gives a low whistle.

"You did all this?" Will asks, glancing around the gym with its white faerie lights crisscrossing overhead and giant snowflakes dangling at varying lengths like upside-down lollipops. Decorator snow dusts the Christmas tree branches and the floor underneath the trees, creating an enchanted forest feeling.

"With a lot of help." I smile and turn to greet him, but I wind up taking a step back in surprise.

Dressed like he's stepped off the cover of *GQ*, in a brown-and-beige tweed blazer, beige turtleneck, and brown flannel pants, his dark hair combed back over his collar, Will flashes his often-photographed celebrity grin. "I clean up pretty well, don't I?"

"Uh huh." I say lamely. The man is drop-dead gorgeous, and he's focusing his dreamy brown eyes on me. Butterflies spin and dance in my stomach, and I take a deep breath to calm my skittering pulse.

He looks me over—not in a creepy way, but like he appreciates what he's seeing—and says, "I like your dress."

"Thanks." I reach up to tuck a loose curl behind my ear, but Will takes my hand in his.

"Your hair's perfect just like that." He scans the room, adding, "I thought you had a date for tonight."

"Oh, Rob's around here somewhere. He's speaking with a client."

"Then he won't mind if I keep you company," Will says, not so much asking permission but making a declarative statement.

"I'm sure he won't mind." I want to add, "*Rob and I are just friends,*" but that might sound like I'm expecting something from Will.

Curious about his absence the day before, I decide to probe a bit. "So what have you been up to lately, besides dog sitting?"

Will points a thumb at his blazer. "I spent quite a bit of time earlier this week at the menswear shop, where I became Malaki's new best friend. I bought this jacket, a new suit, plus a couple of slacks and sweaters. Oh, and a new parka and pair of snow boots."

"Ah," I say teasingly. "Planning on posing for paparazzi?"

Will winks. "Afraid not; they stick to the big cities. However, I believe I've mentioned my only flaw?"

I purse my lips, pretending to concentrate. "You forget important items, like ties and vests?"

Will laughs. "You're one hundred percent correct. I'm not very well organized and didn't pack the right clothes for winter in Wisconsin. I've been borrowing heavily from Sam's closet but decided I need an upgrade."

"Why the upgrade? Have the dogs been complaining?"

"There's a special woman I want to impress." Will flashes me his knee-buckling grin again, and a drum roll awakens inside my chest. I try to tuck another lock of hair behind my ear, but my hand is still firmly in Will's grasp.

Somewhere in the back of my frazzled brain a memory surfaces. Ah, yes, Will's unexplained absence yesterday. Plus he's human. And a singer accustomed to traveling and performing across the country.

I hold fast to all the reasons why he's wrong for me, but it's like clinging to a tiny floatie in the middle of Green Bay. Any minute now I'm liable to go under.

We wander over to the section of the gym set up with tables, chairs, and a bar staffed by volunteers. Spotting Teddy and Sophie serving beverages, we stand in line to say hello and secure a couple glasses of wine.

We walk away from the crowd standing near the bar

and watch everyone milling around the room, Rob's voice occasionally rising above the rest.

Will takes a sip of wine and says, "Reminds me of fundraisers back home in Tennessee. Folks turn out to contribute to a good cause, visit with each other, and have a good time." He pauses and adds, "I'm beginning to understand why people are so loyal to this town. There's a strong sense of community here."

Even stronger—and stranger—than you can imagine!

"But not in New York?" I ask, curious whether he enjoys city living.

Will hesitates a moment before answering. "It's difficult to compare them. New York is a remarkable city to be sure, but it can be a pretty isolating place if you're alone."

I hear such wistfulness in his tone. "So why do you stay?"

Will shrugs. "Because it's home for now, at least until I figure out my game plan. No point in moving until I can jump-start my solo career and start earning a living again."

I don't know much about the music industry, but I learned quite a bit about the entertainment business during my marriage to Derek. "But you must be earning some residuals from all of your previous albums, right?"

Will nods. "Sure, but not as much as you might think. Junior's commission is thirty-five percent in perpetuity, and Roxie and I split the remainder. After taxes, insurance, divorce lawyers, and my mom's treatments... let's just say my cut covers the basics and a little extra."

"I didn't know your mom's been ill," I say quietly.

Will squints into his glass and tells me, haltingly at times, about the shock of his mother's cancer diagnosis, how difficult it's been for the entire family, and how his parents lost almost everything, trying to cover the medical bills. "But Mom's in remission now, and they just left for their first cruise. In fact, I drove to O'Hare and back yesterday to see them off."

I'm now completely ashamed of myself for assuming Will was goofing off yesterday, dumping his dog-walking duties first on Jake, and then by default on me. He's obviously crazy about his family... He's even helping his parents financially.

I've really misjudged Will Rossi.

"There you are! I've been looking for you." Jake reaches out his hand to Will, and they shake. "Thanks again for your generous donation to our fundraiser."

"It's a good cause, and I'm enjoying the company. By the way, thanks again for walking the dogs yesterday."

Jake waves in my direction. "Thank my sister. I had the three-alarm fire to contend with, so she stepped in for both of us."

Will's brown eyes lock onto mine. "Every time I need help with something, you step up. I'm going to have to find a way to thank you properly."

Those eyes, this man, his smile. Even though the gym is drafty, I'm growing uncomfortably warm under Will's gaze. My pulse is racing, and I'm beginning to perspire inside my dress.

"You don't need to thank me." I glance away and take a few sips from my plastic wine glass before depositing it on a nearby tray. "I'm glad you could see your parents yesterday." What I really need is a fan on my face or a cold washcloth. Maybe I should just go stand outside in the freezing temps for a while to cool down.

"Sorry I was gone so long," says Rob as he joins us. He launches into a boring explanation about a sales contract that fell through and how the deal is back on again. Glancing at Jake, he says, "How are you feeling after your close call on the roof yesterday?"

I whip my head around, narrowing my eyes at my brother. "*Your* close call? Were you on that apartment roof yesterday when it caved in?"

Grimacing, Jake says, "I had one foot on the ladder, so technically I was only partly on the roof when it gave way."

I gasp, and my eyes well unexpectedly. A fat tear rolls down my cheek, which I swipe with the back of my hand. "I can't believe you almost—" But I can't say it out loud. I can't say that my overprotective, big brother almost *died*! It hurts too much to even think about it, let alone verbalize it.

Now I'm really crying, and Jake pulls me into a bear hug. "Hush now. I'm fine, really."

I hit his shoulder with my fist. "Don't ever, ever lie to me again! We need to be able to trust each other, no matter what."

Jake nods. "You're right, and I'm sorry. I just didn't want you to worry."

"That goes with the territory. When you care about someone, you're going to worry about them." I notice Will nodding at me sympathetically. He must feel the same way about his mom and her illness.

"I promise I'll tell you the truth—the whole truth—from now on." Jake drapes his arm around me and adds, "Deal?"

"Deal." I sniffle.

"Sorry," says Rob. "I didn't mean to spill the beans. I guess all's well that ends well, right?" His phone rings, and he steps away to take the call.

I want to take Rob's phone and toss it behind one of the Christmas trees. Will smiles at me, as if reading my thoughts. I give Will a sheepish grin and then ask my brother, "Don't you have to give a speech soon?"

Jake nods, puts his drink down, and heads over to the dais where the DJ has set up his equipment. After Jake welcomes everyone and thanks them for supporting their local fire department, he announces that all proceeds from the fundraiser will go to the aid families who'd lost their homes. Then he switches into mayor-mode and makes a series of announcements about the upcoming Riddle Hill holiday celebrations.

After Jake finishes speaking, Will turns to me. "Let me get this straight. Your town hosts an outdoor Christmas festival in the middle of winter?"

I chuckle. "Of course. The Holly Festival lasts all week; Olivia loves it."

"What about the ice and snow and sub-freezing temperatures?"

"Aren't they a part of Christmas?" I ask, adding in a stage whisper, "We do have a well-kept secret." Will leans in closer, and I inhale the spicy scent of his cologne. "All the shops serve hot cocoa and cookies to any passersby. When it's super cold outside, most of the action is at the bakery and the café, which stay open later than usual."

"Ah," says Will with a conspiratorial wink. "You're still human after all! I was beginning to wonder."

My eyes widen, wondering whether Will has figured out the truth about us. But then he chuckles, and I realize he's joking.

After a spaghetti and meatball dinner catered by Phoebe and Nash, and served by Riddle Hill firefighters, the DJ cranks up the music. As chairs scrape against the gymnasium's waxed floor, Will asks, "Do you think Rob would mind if we took a turn around the dance floor?" Without waiting for an answer, he reaches out his hand and leads me over to the section reserved for dancing.

The first few dances are fast numbers, with even one disco tune from the eighties, and I manage to keep pace with Will, who is accustomed to dancing on stage. Then the DJ switches the tempo, and one of Roxie and Rossi's slow numbers blares from the speakers. It's one of their early love songs, and I ask, "Do you want to sit this one out?"

Will shakes his head and pulls me closer. "I've been sitting out, more like hiding out, for months. Not any longer."

I smile and allow myself to be drawn into the music and into Will's arms, surprised at how well I seem to fit there.

"This is a beautiful song. I remember the summer it came out; I used to sing it to Olivia all the time. You should be proud of all the joy your music has brought your fans through the years."

Will has a far-off look in his eyes. "I haven't thought about it in a long time, so thank you for reminding me."

My chest feels suddenly tight, and I take a step back.

What am I doing here with Will? I know this isn't going to end well for me. I need to create some distance... like right now. I excuse myself to find the ladies room, forcing myself not to run across the gym's wooden floors.

Rob spots me in the hallway and jogs over. "I'm really sorry about this, but I need to drop off a revised sales contract tonight. Do you think you could get a ride home with Jake? Or with that Rossi fella who's been hanging around us?"

"No problem," I say, with more gusto than I intend, but Rob doesn't seem to notice.

I take my time freshening up, reminding myself of all the reasons why Will and I could never work. I'm finally ready to return to the dance floor, when I run into Sophie just outside the door. She starts to say something, but I can feel my phone vibrating and pull it out of my purse.

"This could be about the wedding tomorrow," I tell her. "I better take it."

Sophie nods. "Go ahead, I'll wait for you."

Cupping my ear to hear better, it sounds like the call is from the manager of the band for tomorrow's reception. Marie wants a nine-piece band that can play Irish folk music and Mexican love songs. I spent hours searching until I found the perfect band in Illinois.

"I'm sorry, could you please repeat that? I'm having trouble hearing you." I hear something about a broken axle, waiting for a spare part, and stuck in Indiana. There are a lot of apologies as well, but I'm already starting to panic as I drop the phone in my purse.

Sweet moonglow. I've lost the band for Marie and Beau's wedding tomorrow!

"Looks like bad news." Sophie's brow creases in sympathy. "Something about a van?"

"We justh losth th' ban' fer tomowhoa," I reply. My tongue's suddenly sticking to the roof of my mouth.

"Huh?"

My ears and eyebrows are tingling. "Ah noo!" I whimper, scurrying back into the restroom.

Sophie runs in after me. "Are you okay? Is there anything I can do?"

"Nah fanks." I shake my head, lean over the sink, and lap up some water from the faucet to unstick my tongue.

I lift my head and stare at my reflection in the mirror above the sink. My eyebrows tip upward and my ears are pointy. I turn sideways; at least my faerie wings are nothing more than tiny bumps beneath my shoulder blades. Even so, I can't let Will see me like this.

I sigh. "I guess I'm stuck in the ladies room until my symptoms clear up."

"Oh no you don't!" says my bossy cousin. "I saw you and Will dancing just now. You were laughing and having *fun*! You're going right back out there, no excuses!"

"Are you crazy? Look at me!"

"So? We all know you're half faerie. Well, not Will Rossi, but everyone else does." Sophie glances at my reflection. "Look, let's pull out your hair pins. With your hair down, your ears are covered. And if you brush out your long bangs, you'll be able to hide the tips of your brows. It'll be fine. All Will is going to see is your long, blonde hair and nothing else."

Sophie helps me with my hair, and she's right; I don't think Will is going to notice anything about my appearance. "Thanks, Soph. Now comes the really hard part."

"But we've covered your faerie features," she says.

I open the door and exit the ladies room. "I mean about finding another band on such short notice."

"You'll think of something. You always do." Sophie gives me a little push toward Will, who's chatting with Jake, and then she heads back to the bar to give Teddy a hand with the thirsty crowd.

Will frowns; he must see that I'm worried about something. "What's wrong? Is it Olivia?"

"Olivia's at her first sleepover and in seventh heaven," I say, touched by Will's concern for my daughter. I remind myself things could be much worse. "It's the band for the wedding tomorrow night."

"What about them?" asks Jake.

"There isn't one. Their van broke down somewhere in Indiana, and they're not going to make it."

Will shakes his head, "Can't they rent another van?"

I sigh. "Apparently not."

"This is an easy save," says Jake, who glances at Will. "I have a proposition for you."

Will squints at Jake, a confused expression on his handsome face. "I'm not sure I'm following what you're thinking."

Jake says, "It's only for a few hours, and think how much it would help my sister."

"What would help me?" I've lost the thread of their conversation. I'm trying to figure out whom to call and so far, I've only come up with one of Nash's cousins who plays the ukulele.

Jake replies, "If I could rustle up a few of the guys to play tomorrow night—" pointing at Will he adds "—and if our local celebrity here joins us, wouldn't that help you out?"

"Are you offering to pull together your band for the reception tomorrow?" I feel a faint glimmer of hope return. Finding even a keyboardist and a singer would be nearly impossible on such short notice, especially this close to Christmas. Jake's band is actually pretty good. They might even pull off an Irish jig and a Mexican love song or two.

I turn to Will. "Please don't feel like you need to do this. I don't want you to feel pressured in any way."

"Would this really help you?" he asks.

I look down at my beaded evening purse, which I'm twisting in my hands. "Lots, but I—"

"Then it's settled. I'll do it." He turns back to Jake. "We better schedule a rehearsal tomorrow after lunch."

Jake snorts. "We better schedule a rehearsal tomorrow after breakfast, and again after lunch."

"That rusty, huh?" Will whistles.

"We're an all-volunteer band who hasn't played together since Halloween."

"Meet you at the fire station after breakfast, then." Will takes my hand. "Now if you'll excuse us, I think they're playing our song."

"Our song is *Jingle Bell Rock*?" I smile up at Will. I can

feel my stress symptoms already starting to fade; I'm not even worried if I forget and tuck my hair behind my almost-normal ears.

"It's a personal favorite." Will grins. "A Christmas song that's especially good for dancing."

I chuckle and play along with Will, pretending we have a song... pretending we're in a relationship... pretending I'm not falling for him.

CHAPTER 15

DANCING WITH CASSIA

WILL

Friday Night

What a night—I'm ecstatic!

A little while ago, Cassia returned from the ladies' room with her blonde hair tumbling down her shoulders and a look of vulnerability in her jade-green eyes. Her beauty knocked the air out of my lungs. I don't know what happened while she was gone, but when she returned to the gym... wow!

I wanted to rush right over, draw her into my arms, and kiss away every anxious thought.

The solution to her immediate problem is an easy one; I'm glad I'll be able to help her out by singing with Jake's band tomorrow night. Besides, I get to spend more time with Cassia. And I can tell she's more relaxed now, no longer so worried.

It's getting late, and the gym is starting to clear out. Yet we're still dancing, this time to a nice, slow number. I can feel the warmth of her body inside her wool dress, which shows off her curves far better than those aprons she wears at work.

Rob, her date for the evening, left her high and dry—how lucky is that?

Cassia needs a ride home, and I'm only too happy to oblige. I'm going to walk her to the door and give her a goodnight kiss that'll leave her breathless... and will leave me panting for more. Maybe she'll invite me in for a nightcap, but I doubt it, not with her crazy work schedule.

I hear sudden scuffling behind me on the dance floor, which I try to ignore. I don't want any interruptions as I hold Cassia in my arms.

But the commotion draws Cassia's attention away from me, and she gasps. "Oh no!" She stops dancing, a look of horror on her face. "What's *Rafe* doing here? Poor Sophie!"

"Who's Rafe?" I ask, turning around as someone—big, blond, Norseman Teddy—hits the floor.

Teddy scrambles back to his feet and tackles another huge fellow with pale skin, jet-black hair, and body-builder muscles straining his olive jacket. There's something almost feral about this man, and the way he's pounding on Teddy tells me he's out of control.

Sophie shrieks for them to stop as Cassia runs over to comfort her cousin. Since I'm the closest guy, I rush into the fray.

I manage to come between the two heavyweights and hold up my hands, arms outstretched. "Let's stop right now, fellas. You're ruining the holiday feeling and making Sophie cry."

I can see Jake and a few of the other firefighters jogging over to us from the other side of the room.

But they're not fast enough.

This Rafe character draws back his fist, *which is now covered in fur*. He punches me in the face, and now it's my turn to take a tumble. I'm waiting for the impact, for my skull to smash into the hard, wooden floor.

But something weirdly amazing happens.

Cassia screams my name, and an invisible cocoon seems to form around me. I fall in slow motion until I'm lying flat out on the floor. My right eye where Rafe socked me hurts like heck, but the back of my head is only a little sore.

"Oh, Will! Say something, please!" Cassia is crying, and I want to reassure her.

But as I look up, I can't find her lovely face. All I see are furry visages with long snouts and sharpened teeth hanging over me.

"Monsters!" I yelp before passing out.

I'M LYING on Sam's gray sofa with an ice pack covering the top half of my face. I feel like someone used my head for target practice. My memory is fuzzy; I can remember dancing with Cassia and how gorgeous she looked but nothing else.

My pillow starts shifting beneath me, and I cry out, "What the—"

"Shh, Will. It's just me. You're safe now," says Cassia, who is cradling my head in her lap.

I would prefer a kiss, but I'll take what I can get.

I hear Jake in the kitchen, talking quietly on his phone. It sounds like he's speaking with someone at the police department. "Definitely a 360 restraining order. Not only did Rafaellus MacTire attack a super unprovoked, but even worse, he hit a defenseless human." Jake listens a bit and then says, "Uh huh, will do."

I start to pucker my forehead in confusion, but that hurts. Instead, I murmur, "What's a 360 restraining order?"

Jake must have superpower hearing because he returns from the kitchen to answer me. "It carries more weight than a typical restraining order."

"Oh," I say. Then I recall what else Jake said. "Why did you say that dude—Rafaellus?—hit a human? We're all humans, aren't we?"

I leave out the part about me being defenseless; I'm still a guy with an ego that's pretty bruised at the moment. Not only can't I take Cassia into my arms for a proper kiss, I can't even stand up. Some date I turned out to be.

Neither Jake nor Cassia responds immediately. I can't see anything with the ice pack covering my eyes, but I can sense Cassia tensing.

Jake says, "We have some very specific statutes in Riddle Hill that require me to state the obvious."

"Huh," I reply. Jake has to specify to the police that Rafaellus hit a human? That's just plain ridiculous. Talk about unnecessary bureaucracy!

I decide to drop it for now and bask in Cassia's attention... and the feel of her soft thighs beneath my aching head. I won't relish the shiner I'll have in the morning, but it's worth it for this moment right—

"Cassia, now that Will's awake, I think it's okay to leave. I'll drop you off before I head to the police station. I want to make sure Rafe remains in lockup until he's sober and understands he can't go near Sophie or Teddy again."

"Alright," says Cassia, who gently shifts out from beneath me, placing a pillow under my head. Then she leans down to pull the ice pack away from my face.

"Ooh..." Her full, pink lips are puckered in sympathy. "Your poor eye. I'm so sorry, Will."

If I didn't feel so lousy, I'd pull Cassia down for a kiss her right in front of her big brother. But my head is killing me.

"Me too," says Jake. "I'm terribly sorry you were assaulted at a fundraiser sponsored by the fire department. I take full responsibility for what happened."

"No one's to blame but the guy who hit me. Who is he, by the way?"

"Rafe and Sophie dated briefly," says Cassia. "He blames Teddy for coming between them."

She refills the ice pack in the kitchen and then returns, handing it to me. "Wait twenty minutes, and then put this back on your eye for no longer than fifteen minutes. If you get sleepy, leave it off. And if you need anything, call me."

Jake glances at her with a frown. "You're working the early shift tomorrow and then managing a wedding. You need your sleep." He nods at me. "Call me if you need any help."

"I'll be fine. Thanks for the lift home and the ice pack."

No way am I calling overprotective Jake Spellman.

Cassia pats my shoulder and murmurs, "I'm just so thankful you weren't seriously injured."

After she leaves, I can still feel the imprint of her hand on my arm.

I groan, missing her already.

CHAPTER 16
FAERIE DUST

CASSIA

Early Saturday, December 15

I'm exhausted and in no mood for my aunt's uncouth gargoyles this morning. But as soon as they spot me slipping on my black apron, they turn around, bend over, and moon me.

Captain Killian leans out from the wall and waggles his handlebar mustache. "I say, old chaps, showing one's bum in public is not the done thing!"

Cousin Heliotrope is so offended she tosses her purple scarf over her face. Hisses, boos, and a few giggles emerge from the rest of the ancestors in their frames, which is rare. Very little gets a rise out of them.

Aunt Phoebe hears the racket from the kitchen, pushes open the swinging doors, and catches her tiny demons in the act. She snaps her fingers and a flurry of gold faerie dust swirls around the gargoyles. I hear a loud thwack, and each of the stone monsters cries out.

My aunt's magic just spanked their butts!

I burst out laughing as the gargoyles whip around and stand like perfect little sentries. Phoebe glances over at me, her eyes clouded. "How's Will doing?"

I'd texted her the details of what happened last night, and I'm sure Sophie and Jake did the same. My aunt was furious at Rafe, concerned for Sophie, and worried about Will.

It's illegal for a werewolf to take a swing at a human, and it almost never happens. A 360 restraining order means Rafe will have to deal with both the human and supernatural legal systems.

"Other than a headache, a cut over his eye, and some bruising and swelling, Will seems fine." My lower lip trembles as I whisper, "He could have lost an eye or worse!"

"But he didn't because you were there to look out for him," says my aunt.

I shake my head. "I didn't do anything, except scream!"

When Rafe punched Will, I was terrified he'd crack his skull open on the hard floor. All I wanted was to throw my arms around Will, cushion his fall, and make sure no one hurt him again. That's why later, after Jake laid him on the sofa, I cradled his head in my lap.

I held Will close so he'd know he wasn't alone.

I realized last night I've completely misjudged him. I was sure he'd ditched his dog duties on Thursday for something frivolous. Instead Will drove to O'Hare and back to visit his mom and dad.

I've been comparing Will to Derek, which isn't fair.

My ex has always been more focused on his career than me and Olivia. But I can see now that Will is wired completely differently... He's a man who adores his family.

My aunt says, "According to Sophie and Jake, you did a whole lot more than just scream. They both felt a massive surge of energy leave you and surround Will, breaking his fall. Your magic saved Will from serious injury."

"*My magic saved Will?*" I drop onto a stool and lean my elbows on the counter. It's still early; the café doesn't open for another half hour. "But how? I didn't conjure or incant or anything."

"It was pure instinct on your part. Without even realizing it, you reached for the faerie magic deep within and poured all your intention and energy into protecting Will from harm. Did you feel your magic leaving you?"

I shake my head. "I felt completely drained after his fall—and I still do."

"Of course." Phoebe drapes an arm around my shoulder. "It's only natural, since you're unaccustomed to using magic. But you do realize what this means, don't you?"

"Not really."

"It means you can't just *see* the magic of others—you *have* magic too! You're a faerie!"

I roll my eyes. "I'm half a faerie at best. And if this is how I'll feel whenever I wield magic—if I can even do it again, which is doubtful—no thank you. I think I could sleep for a week."

Phoebe pours me a cup of coffee. "You need to rebuild

your energy. I'll have Nash whip you up the daily special. Just sit until the doors open. I'll finish setting up."

I stifle a yawn and give in to my aunt. She's right; suddenly I'm ravenous.

As I savor Nash's goat cheese, caramelized onion, and spicy chorizo omelet, I remember last night and dancing with Will. His arms around me, holding me close, gazing at me with his dreamy brown eyes. For the first time in... well, longer than I can remember... I felt safe.

And then Rafe ruined it all by throwing a punch at Will. I keep seeing Will tumbling backward, about to hit his head, and I'm scared all over again.

I'm frightened for Will, and how much worse he could have been hurt.

And for me, because now I'm the one falling.

I'm falling for an unemployed singer who's leaving town in another week, for a man who's one hundred percent human and has no idea I used magic to save him.

I'm falling hard for Will Rossi.

And I know I won't be able to save myself from another broken heart.

CHAPTER 17

FIRE STATION BAND

WILL

Saturday Morning

After a long, hot shower in Sam's steely gray bathroom, I wipe the steam from the mirror and stare at my reflection. *Gah, that Rafe really packs a punch!* The right side of my face is black and blue; my right eye is swollen half-shut, and there's a cut on my brow where Rafe's ring made contact. I'll need to wear shades to hide the damage.

I turn up at the fire station at nine-thirty bearing a tray of Sophie's pastries (she refused to let me pay for them) and my guitar case. As I wait in the blue lobby for Jake, I skim the usual community events calendar and real estate listings along with the fire safety posters tacked up on the walls. This time I notice Rob Wolferman's name as the sales agent for half the properties, including the lot with the old barn and sound stage.

I chuckle to myself; Wolferman is so busy chasing

leads he's blind to the most beautiful woman in Riddle Hill. I ought to thank the guy.

Jake emerges from his office, takes one look at my battered face, and grimaces. "How are you feeling today?"

"A bit rough, but I'll be fine."

"I feel terrible about this, Will." Jake shakes his head.

"It wasn't your fault. Let's forget it and get down to work. I want to hear this band of yours."

Jake nods, and I follow him down the hallway to the boxy band room at the end, with the gray carpeting, navy walls, and raised platform along the back wall. There's a portable card table and some metal chairs off to the side. He introduces me to the band members, most of whom I met last night. They're unpacking and setting up their equipment: drums, keyboard, alto saxophone, trumpet, and lead guitar. Jake's bass guitar sits near one of the amplifiers.

After we tune our instruments, I ask the band to pick a song they know by heart and play it for me. I close my eyes to help me focus, listening to the blend of their vocals and instruments. *Not half bad.*

When they're finished, I say, "With some solid practice, I think we can pull this off. Except for one thing."

"What's that?" asks Jake.

"This is a wedding. We need to practice songs the bride wants to hear. And based on what Cassia has told me about the bride, she's not going to want heavy metal at her reception."

"What about the groom? Doesn't he get to pick anything?" grumbles the drummer, a brawny fellow with a ginger topknot. Actually, all the band members—four guys and two gals—are packing some serious muscle.

Jake points at me. "Will's the expert here. Let's listen up."

We practice throughout the morning, losing track of time until Cassia surprises us with take-out lunch from the café.

She's wearing black jeans, a bright pink turtleneck, and lipstick the same shade as her sweater. Her hair is pulled back in her usual ponytail.

Forget about band practice.

Cassia looks so hot I don't think I'll be able to concentrate on my music. All I want to do is take her in my arms, run my hands through her honey-blonde tresses, and kiss her full, pink lips until dinnertime.

Instead, she gazes up at me and winces.

I guess I won't be sweeping Cassia off my feet with this face. My only consolation is the way her eyes soften when she reaches up, removes my shades, and gasps. She purses her lovely bow-shaped mouth. "Oh, Will! It's not too late to take you to the clinic. I can drive you right now. I'll just text Phoebe."

As much as I'd like to get in the car with Cassia and bask in her sympathy, I can feel Jake's eyes boring into the back of my head. I don't think he objects to me personally, so much as he's worried about his sister getting hurt again. But if I'm ever lucky enough to win Cassia's heart, I'll never let her go.

I shake my head. I'm not a quitter, despite what the tabloids claim. I committed to playing this wedding gig tonight, and we have three more hours to rehearse. "No, thanks. I'll be fine. Besides, we still need to practice. I wouldn't want to disappoint the bride—or you." I replace my shades and take a bite of my turkey avocado panini.

Cassia gives me a shy smile. "How's it going?" she asks, pulling out one of the folding metal chairs and taking a seat beside me. "Do you think the band can be ready in time? Is there anything I can do to help?"

I wipe my mouth on a napkin. Counting down on my fingers, I reply, "One, pretty well. Two, more or less. Three, we need an audience."

Cassia sits up straight. "Great, I'm ready when you are."

I glance at Jake, who's obviously listening to every word. He tells the band, "Ten more minutes for lunch, and then we're playing a set for Cassia."

We play mostly oldies from the eighties and nineties, plus a fair number of Roxie and Rossi standards from the past decade. Cassia claps enthusiastically, praising our performance and asking for an encore.

After we play a poignant version of *Danny Boy*—a nod to Beau O'Mara's Irish heritage—she asks, "What are you going to play for the traditional father-daughter dance?"

"Huh?" says the drummer.

"You know, that special song where the bride dances with her father, and then the groom dances with his mother? Everyone gets slightly teary eyed?"

"Can't we skip the father-daughter dance?" asks Jake.

"Marie specifically requested it."

"Okay," I reply. "Then we need some suggestions."

Cassia ticks off a number of song titles. At each suggestion, the band shakes their heads, either because they don't know the song or don't want to perform it.

"Wait a minute," Cassia snaps her fingers and turns to me. "If you skipped the second verse, you could play *Into His Arms*. It's perfect... who knows, you might even start a new father-daughter dance trend!"

I rub the stubble on my chin, considering. *Into His Arms* was my old band's first big hit. It's a bittersweet song about a woman finding true love after a failed relationship. I can see Cassia's point; if we skip the verse about the painful breakup, the song celebrates new love.

I grin at her. "You know what? I think it could work." Looking at the others, I say, "Come on, mates, we have another song to spin up and learn." The band gives me a good-natured groan.

"I'll leave you to it," says Cassia. "Mona is expecting you at the inn at three-thirty sharp to set up."

As her hand touches the doorknob, she turns back to ask, "Wait a minute, what's your band's name? Somehow, I don't think 'Red Hot Howlers' is what we're going for." Apparently Red Hot Howlers is the name of Jake's band, something he and his friends cooked up one night after too many beers at Howling Shores Pub.

Jake waves her out the door. "Details, details, sis. Don't sweat the small stuff. We'll think of something."

The band's name triggers a half-buried memory. Something to do with fur, claws, and fangs.

But it's gone, retreating once more into my foggy brain.

I shrug. A hard knock to the head can do that sometimes.

WE'RE in the ballroom at the inn, setting up our instruments on a large, raised dais next to the parquet dance floor. The room looks completely different for this wedding. It's decorated in shades of green and gold, and Green Bay Packers memorabilia is scattered across the green tablecloths. There are huge vases on each table filled with bright yellow, orange, and white flowers and lots of green foliage.

I'm impressed all over again at Cassia's design skills, along with her amazing organizational abilities.

Sophie arrives with a four-tiered wedding cake that she wheels to the other side of the room. Mona, the inn's special events manager, helps her wrestle it onto a linen-draped dessert table.

As Sophie straightens, I overhear her ask, "What are *they* doing here?"

By "they" I assume she means Jake, the band, and me.

"Last minute substitution," says Mona. "Since the original band is stuck in Indiana."

Sophie huffs. "So they get Will Rossi instead? Meanwhile I'm having a high-school football coach who moonlights as a DJ for my wedding next week?" She smooths down her hair and says, "We'll see about that."

"But you haven't heard them play yet. What if they're not very good?" says Mona.

"Who cares? That's Will Rossi over there. I want him to sing at *my* wedding."

I'm starting to feel uncomfortable and focus on adjusting the sound system.

Jake spots his cousin staring at us and calls out to her, "Hey, Soph, your cake looks good enough to eat!"

"Ha-ha," replies Sophie. "Very funny." Then she walks over and watches as I test the speakers.

When I'm finished, I give her a friendly smile and thank her for the pastries this morning. Then I say, "I guess you're next down the aisle, aren't you?"

Nodding, Sophie takes a deep breath. "Yes, and my special day would sure be even more special if you—" she flutters her hand to indicate me, Jake, and the rest of the band "—would play at my reception. It'd be a dream come true for me."

I get the feeling Cassia might not agree, but I'm stuck between a rock and a hard place. I glance over at Jake, who says, "It's your wedding, and if that's what you want, I'm in."

Jake looks at me, and I say, "Sure, I'd be honored." The other band members nod their heads in agreement.

I smile at Sophie. "It's all settled then. I suppose you'll let Cassia know there's been a change in plans?"

Sophie hesitates briefly before answering. "Sure, no problem. I'll tell Cassia. And thanks, guys! Teddy will literally howl with excitement!"

CHAPTER 18
MARIE AND BEAU'S WEDDING

CASSIA

Saturday Evening

I pop into the ballroom for a final check on the reception setup before heading to the chapel. Mona gives me a thumbs-up as I pass, which tells me the food and beverage details are set. Scanning the ballroom, I nod my approval. Marie's grandparents shipped sixteen colorful Talavera vases from Mexico, which Auntie Bibbidy has filled with yellow and white roses, orange lilies, white hydrangeas, and sprigs of dark green myrtle. The Green Bay Packers party favors I scattered around each of the elegant centerpieces add a fun, kitschy flair.

I head over to the band to see whether they need anything and overhear Jake, Will, and Sophie talking about a change of plans. "What change of plans?" I ask. "You know I'm not a fan of last-minute changes."

"We know!" they reply in unison, like I'm some old fuddy-duddy fearful of all change. My eyes sting at the implied insult. Change is fine; what I don't like are impromptu deviations from a good plan, which inevitably lead to unforeseen consequences and extra work.

Sophie grabs my hand and pulls me away from the band. I wait until we're out of earshot and then hiss, "What last-minute change?"

Sophie waves her hand in the band's direction. "I booked them for my reception next Saturday."

"You did what?" My jaw drops. I'm not sure I heard her correctly. Sophie knows I've already hired a local DJ, because that's what she told me she wanted for her reception.

"I booked the band," Sophie repeats. "I want Will Rossi to sing at my wedding. Isn't that exciting?"

"Why didn't you come to me first so we could talk about it?"

Sophie shrugs. "The moment seemed right for me to ask, so I did, and everyone said yes. I don't see what the big deal is."

I shake my head, frustrated at the way Sophie plunges ahead without considering the consequences. "Don't you think that's a real imposition on Will? And what about the DJ we hired? Who's going to tell him? At this point there'll be a cancellation fee."

Sophie says in a small voice, "That's exactly why I didn't want to discuss it with you first. You always have a hundred reasons for saying no!" Sophie turns around and adds, "I have dessert trays to unload, which I'm going to do right now, before I say anything I'll regret later." She stomps back to the service entrance.

I know she's pretty upset, but I think something else is bothering her. Maybe it's Rafe showing up last night, or maybe it's pre-wedding jitters. I sigh; there's nothing I can do about it now.

Heading back toward the chapel, I pass Mona, who offers her own opinion. "Don't be too hard on Sophie. She's still young."

"She's the same age as me," I snap, feeling defensive.

"Maybe in years, but not in life experiences. She looks up to you. Always has."

Sometimes I wish I lived in a big city like New York, where I could have a family quarrel without outside participation. Feeling a lump forming in my throat, I swallow hard and keep walking. I absolutely can't afford to get emotional in the middle of a wedding. Everyone else can fall apart, but I have to keep it together. That's why the brides hire me.

After the vows are exchanged, the main course consumed, and the wedding speeches given, Jake steps up to the microphone. He invites Marie and her father to the dance floor and promises them a special treat. As the band strikes up the opening chords of *Into His Arms*, I'm relieved at how good they sound and how polished they look. The guys changed into dark suits, and the gals are in snappy, black dresses.

I practically swoon as Will serenades the bride and her father. He's wearing a black jacket and slacks, a white shirt open at the neck, and a pair of shades to hide his bruising. He looks so handsome my knees go wobbly, and I grip the nearest seat back for support.

Then all of a sudden, every single elf in the place—

that's everyone, except for me, the werewolf band, and Will—drops their glamour. All the guests' shoes curl up at the toes, their ears grow long and pointy, cute top hats appear on their heads, and the men sprout very long, curly beards. They look absolutely adorable—as if they've just stepped away from Santa's toy shop for a dance break.

Will's voice falters, but he's a pro; he keeps right on singing.

Marie's mother must recall there's a human in our midst because she opens her hands and murmurs something. I see silvery sparkles ripple around the perimeter of the ballroom as Mrs. Ramos uses her magic to mask everyone's elvish features, creating the equivalent of a room-sized glamour.

I breathe a sigh of relief and take a peek at Will. He's frowning slightly, but he manages to finish the song and bow as the room erupts into cheering and applause.

I really wish I could tell Will the truth about Riddle Hill... and about me. But it's absolutely forbidden, unless the elder council decides to share our secret, as they did with my human mother. As mayor, Jake is authorized to tell a non-super the truth about us, but he's never done it.

Later, when the band takes a break, Will comes to find me. "That was so bizarre!"

"What was bizarre?" I ask, my pulse rate soaring because of his nearness, and because I'm afraid of what he's going to say next.

Will removes his shades and draws his brows together. "Don't tell me you didn't see it either. Jake has no idea what I'm talking about, and now I'm beginning to worry that punch shook something loose inside my skull."

"What do you mean?"

Will puts his sunglasses back on. "Never mind," he says. "It's not important."

I'm lying to Will and feel terrible about it. He obviously believes he's seeing things that aren't there. Changing the subject, I say, "*Into His Arms* worked out really well tonight. It's such a beautiful song, and the way you sang it was amazing. Thank you for making this a special night for Marie and Beau."

"I didn't do this for the bride and groom, although I was happy to help." Will picks up my hand, and my insides melt at his touch. And the way he's gazing at me... it's like I'm the only woman in the room. "I did this for you."

"I... I don't know how I can thank you enough," I stammer, my heart spinning like an out-of-control top.

"Oh, don't worry." Will offers me his most brilliant smile. "I'll think of something."

I believe he's gotten past the weirdness just now, when every elf in the room showed their true nature, but I still feel bad for pretending I didn't see it.

As Will leaves to get ready for the band's next set, I go searching for my brother. I spot Jake coming out of the restroom and pull him aside. "We have to tell Will about us," I hiss. "The poor man thinks he's seeing things!"

"Absolutely not!" exclaims Jake. "It's too risky. Besides, he's only here for another week, and then he'll be heading back to New York."

I feel a stab of pain in my chest at Jake's words. The truth really does hurt sometimes. I roll my lips together to keep them from trembling, but my brother knows me too well. He puts a hand on my shoulder and says more gently, "I know you like him, but this is not going to end well."

I whisper, "But Will is nothing like Derek."

"I'm sorry Cassia, but you have to be realistic. Will's a celebrity, and he's human, and he doesn't belong here. Period."

I wipe a stray tear. "But maybe—"

"There are no 'buts' about it." Jake shakes his head. "Stop now before you get hurt."

Now I have this dull aching inside me, thanks to Jake and his harsh honesty. I manage to get through the rest of the night by going into "wedding planner mode" as Sophie calls it. I smile, answer questions, solve problems, and ensure everyone's having a good time.

I thank the band as they're packing up their instruments and remember to ask, "Did you ever decide on a name? I need to cut you a check—you're all paid professionals now!"

That gets a chuckle from them. Will turns and gives me the sweetest smile—it's not his usual hundred-watt-wonder—and replies, "We're calling ourselves The Second Chance Band."

"That's Will Rossi and the Second Chance Band," corrects Jake, who's scowling at his guitar.

I have a feeling Jake was overruled by the rest of the band when they picked the name, which my brother knows speaks volumes to me. A lump forms in my throat as I whisper, "I like it. A lot." I can feel Will's eyes on me as I walk away.

Finally, I'm in my car, and the tears I've been holding back stream down my cheeks. I make sure to dry my face before I enter my condo, pay the sitter, and peek in on Olivia. My daughter wakes up long enough to ask for a hug, and I wrap my arms around her as she drifts back to sleep.

Later, as I'm lying in bed staring at the thin strips of moonlight seeping in through my blinds, I think about Will. I'm not the only one who'll be sad when he leaves. I also have Olivia to consider.

On school mornings and weekends when I'm working and don't have a sitter, Olivia usually sits at a small table in the back of the café. She'll color, play games, and possibly do homework, in that order. But all that changed with Will's arrival in Riddle Hill.

For the past week, Olivia has been sliding into Will's booth as soon as he walks into the restaurant. The two of them have become quite chummy. Will shares his toast with Olivia and tells her stories. I often hear her giggles from across the room, and I chuckle just hearing her laughter.

I sigh heavily. I don't know what to do about Will.

My phone pings, and I grab it from my nightstand, relieved for the interruption.

"I'm sorry." Sophie is texting me at one in the morning. I guess she can't sleep either. She adds a bunch of sad emoji faces and different colored hearts. My cousin's effusive personality comes through even in her messages. "Please don't be mad at me."

"I'm not mad," I write back, and it's true. "I'm sorry too, Soph. Love you." I send her a heart, which she hearts back, and then I try to get some sleep.

But I lay awake a long time, thinking about Will.

I like him too much to pretend otherwise, but I have more than myself to worry about.

I have to make sure Olivia doesn't get hurt either.

CHAPTER 19
SNOW SQUALLS AND SNOWBALLS

WILL

Sunday, December 16

It's a little after eight on Sunday morning, and I'm back in my regular booth at the café. The stone gargoyles are paused for the moment, perhaps for maintenance. I'm still wearing shades, even indoors, to hide the swelling around my eye. Cassia greets me with a tentative smile, like she's still not sure she can trust me. I suppose that's only fair, since we've known each other barely a week.

But I'm here to stay. Well, okay... I do need to find a new gig soon, which Mack in Nashville is working on. And I should get back to New York eventually. I have my goldfish, and my apartment, and my stack of mail (which I forgot to forward)... but I'm not in any hurry to return.

Cassia's daughter slips into the seat opposite me. She's the spitting image of her mother and just as smart.

I cut up my maple-butter toast into four smaller squares, place it on a napkin, and slide it across the table to her.

Olivia thanks me and points out the café's picture window. "It's snowing."

I glance outside and nod. "Sure is. Those are the little white flakes my grandaddy says means a snowstorm is coming. There's no doubt this'll be a white Christmas, with all the snow already on the ground and now this storm."

Olivia chews on a square of maple-butter toast. "I like snow."

"Me too," I tell her. "I love building snowmen and going sledding and throwing snowballs at my friends."

Olivia giggles. "Me too!"

Cassia swings by to pour my coffee and juice. "What's so funny?"

Olivia says, "Will likes throwing snowballs."

Cassia tilts her head at me, her ponytail tumbling over her shoulder. My mind wanders, as I think about freeing her blonde locks from that hair clip and the feel of their silky softness between my fingers. But alas, this is a restaurant, and there's a child present.

"Is this true, Mr. Rossi?" says Cassia. "You enjoy flinging snow around?"

I chuckle. "Guilty as charged. I find the white, fluffy stuff irresistible."

"Hmm…" Cassia purses her lovely lips and seems to be making up her mind about something. "In that case, you might want to swing by Riddle Hill Park around three this afternoon."

I tear my attention away from her bow-shaped mouth long enough to ask, "Why is that?"

"To join our annual snowball fight," says Cassia. "It's the unofficial kick off for the Riddle Hill Holly Festival."

Olivia claps her hands together. "You can be on our team!"

I glance at Cassia. "You have a team?"

She chuckles. "Since we have so many relatives in the area, all the Spellmans, Brownlees, and our friends—who've been dubbed the 'Friends of Spellman-Brownlee'—line up on one side of the park, and everyone else lines up on the other. We pelt each other until one side surrenders. It's always the other side because the winning side has to buy drinks for everyone."

I whistle. "Drinks for everyone? That sounds like a hefty bar bill."

"We're talking about hot cocoa with marshmallows." Cassia grins.

"And cookies," adds Olivia.

"An epic snowball fight culminating in hot cocoa and lots of cookies?" I rub my hands together. "Count me in!"

"Make sure you wear water-proof gloves," says Cassia. "You'd be surprised what a difference they make."

"You really take this seriously, don't you?"

Cassia picks up the coffee pot and cherry juice carafe. As she leaves, she calls over her shoulder, "We have to protect the Spellman-Brownlee reputation. And since you're now a Friend of Spellman-Brownlee, you'll have to do your part."

I glance at Olivia, who takes another bite of toast and shrugs.

~

"Incoming!" shouts Cassia as the first snowball hits Nash squarely in the chest.

The Spellman-Brownlee contingent has staked out the territory surrounding the quaint, gabled, gray stone village hall, hiding behind trees and a low wood-rail fence that runs along the empty parking lot.

Everyone else, whom Olivia calls "the enemy," is scattered in uneven clumps of adults and kids across the park grounds. A foot of good packing snow has already fallen, and forecasters predict another foot at least will fall by morning.

I stand between Olivia, clad in a purple snowsuit, and Cassia, who looks like an ice princess in her silver-and-white ski jacket, white wool hat, silver waterproof gloves, and a fluffy, pink-and-white scarf wrapped around her throat. Cassia's cheeks are glowing from the cold, and her rosy lips are so irresistible I nearly sink to my knees in the snow to cool down.

Olivia drops her first snowball, crunching it under her boots. Undeterred, she rolls another snowball and hands it to Nash, telling him to "make 'em pay!"

Shaking her head, Cassia says, "Olivia, remember these are our neighbors and friends."

"And our customers," adds Nash.

"It's just snow," replies Olivia, stacking a small mound of snowballs in front of her.

I say to Cassia, "You can't argue with her logic." I aim several snowballs at a couple of boys venturing too close to our section of fence. "Pragmatism seems to run in the family."

Cassia grabs a few of Olivia's balls and hurls them at the boys, who decide to pull back. "Are you suggesting something like the apple not falling far from the tree?"

"The Spellman ladies are charmingly pragmatic," I reply, firing off a volley of snowballs at the boys, who've brought in reinforcements. "I'm a big fan of common sense, a rare commodity in the music business."

"I'd say it's a rare commodity anywhere." Nash pauses as he leans his large bulk over the ground to snag some snowballs from Olivia's stockpile and tosses them at the advancing cluster of boys. "It was one of the qualities that attracted me to Phoebe. That, and her double-fudge chocolate cake." Nash pats his stomach and is rewarded with a flurry of snowballs hitting him just above the beltline.

"Here, allow me." I send half a dozen snowballs whizzing after the boys' retreating backs.

"Well done!" Nash chuckles. "They'll be ready for hot cocoa soon enough."

Cassia scoops up some snowballs and dashes after a couple of lads attempting an end-run around us. I chase after her, ostensibly to lend a hand with the snow fight, but mostly to stay near her. She tosses her snowballs at the two boys, hitting both in the back. Laughing, they quickly disperse.

Cassia pulls her arm back again, spins around, and lets loose another snowball that lands squarely in my face. She's hit me on purpose! I'm momentarily stunned as icy water blurs my shades and drips into my eyes. I decide to milk this opportunity for all it's worth.

"Foul ball!" I cry, clutching my face.

Cassia runs up to me. "Oh, Will, I'm so sorry! I was aiming for your chest. Are you okay?"

Shielding my face with one hand, I turn away, moaning. As Cassia tries to pull my hand away to inspect the damage, I bring my other hand up and shove a fistful of snow inside the back of her jacket.

Cassia yelps, "Cheater!" and gives me a push.

I topple backward into a snowbank. Cassia loses her footing and falls down on top of me. She's so stunning in this moment, with snowflakes on her eyelashes and her cheeks flushed with cold, I'm rendered speechless.

I wrap my arms around her waist and hug her to myself. My pulse is pounding so hard I'm sure she must feel it through the layers of winter clothing. Our noses are nearly touching, and my breath becomes ragged. Her lips part, probably in surprise, as I tilt my head and gently kiss her.

The warmth of her mouth against mine ripples through me like a heat wave. As I lean in to deepen the kiss, a pile of wet snow lands on our heads.

Cassia breaks free of my arms and jumps up, shaking the snow out of her long, honey-colored hair. She points at someone behind my head, scoops up some snow, and shouts, "Jake! You're gonna pay for that!"

Jake laughs. "Not if you can't catch me."

A low moan escapes from me as Cassia runs off,

chasing after her brother, who clearly doesn't want me chasing after his sister.

If Cassia doesn't have a word with Jake soon and tell him to butt out, I will.

A short while later the Spellman-Brownlees are declared the victors, and everyone troops back to the Sit for a Spell Café, stomping boots on the mats near the entrance and pulling off sodden mittens and caps.

I pause to take a sniff. Mingled with the delicious aroma of chocolate, cinnamon, and butter, I detect the not-so-pleasant odor of damp dog fur. I quickly scan the café but find no huge sled dogs on the premises. I see the gargoyles have changed positions though; now they're leaning forward, their noses wrinkled, as if they, too, detect wet canines close at hand.

I notice Jake, who scratches his neck as he nods in my direction. I set my jaw and give him a curt nod in return. Jake may be the mayor of Riddle Hill, but there's nothing he can say or do that'll dissuade me from pursuing Cassia Spellman.

CHAPTER 20
SNOWBOUND!

CASSIA

Monday, December 17

It's a little after four in the morning, and I can't sleep. I'm sitting at my kitchen table in the dark, nursing a cup of now-tepid tea and daydreaming about *the kiss*.

Just... wow!

When Will drew me into his arms, I was glad I was already lying down. Otherwise, I would have gone all trembly and swooned like some heroine in a BBC historical drama.

Then he brushed his lips against mine, and the last of my walls crumbled. I felt utterly defenseless and also completely safe. I wanted more, and so did Will. He pressed against me, and I leaned closer... and then my brother dumped snow on our heads.

I had a moment of pure frustration mingled with hot fury, until I realized I was lying in the snow in the park, necking with Will Rossi in front of my family, my seven-year-old daughter, and the entire village.

It's official. I've lost my mind. And my heart. And I'm still terrified, but I no longer want to bolt.

I did, however, chase down Jake, who allowed me to catch him and stuff some snow down his parka. Once I was finished making him pay, snowball-for-snowball, I said, "Don't ever do that again. If I want to kiss a man in Riddle Hill Park, I'm doing it."

Jake was brushing the snow out of his coat, but he paused to gaze at me. Then he dropped his eyes and shrugged. "You're right, and I'm sorry. I just don't want to see you go through another heartbreak when Will Rossi leaves. Because he's going to leave. He simply doesn't belong here."

"I understand your motives." I folded my arms across my chest. "But I need to make my own choices. I don't want to get hurt either... and I promise to be careful."

"Well alright then," said Jake. Then he gave me a mischievous grin and ran off, but not before he pommeled me with two snowballs to the chest. He's such a goof, but I adore him.

"Mommy," says Olivia, yawning as she pads into the kitchen wearing her fleecy slippers with rabbit's ears on top. She's in her favorite Disney flannel pajamas. I open my arms and make room so she can climb onto my lap.

"Is it still snowing?" she asks, leaning her head against my chest.

I run my fingers through her tousled hair. "Yes, it's still coming down. I don't think you'll have school today."

"No school! Yay!" says Olivia, jumping down from my lap. She runs to the frosted kitchen window overlooking our yard, which is buried under two feet of fresh snow. "Can we go sledding? Please?"

"Yes, later this afternoon. But we need to get dressed and head to the café first. The regulars will be showing up for breakfast, snow or no snow."

Even as I mention "the regulars" my mind goes immediately to Will, sitting in a booth up front, sampling one of Nash's walnut-and-cherry crepes or goat-cheese-and-pumpkin frittatas. Will arches an eyebrow when he encounters a new taste, and then he leans back and chews slowly, savoring the blend of flavors.

Somehow in the past week, Will has become a regular, and in another week, he'll be back home in New York. I can't quite reconcile the two opposing realities: Will's very real presence in Riddle Hill now, and his very real plans to depart before Christmas.

My mind is miles away, so I ask Olivia to repeat her question. "Can we invite Will to go sledding with us?"

I sigh. I'm well aware Will has to return home, and I'll prepare myself for his departure as best I can. But Olivia is a child; I'm concerned about her growing attachment to Will. "Olivia, we need to talk about Will."

"What about?"

"You remember Will's only *visiting* Riddle Hill, right? In fact, Will's going back to his own home in New York before Christmas."

Olivia draws her delicate blonde eyebrows together. I wait for her to explain what's on her mind. "I know, and that's why... that's why I want him to go sledding with us, and do other stuff. I want him to have a lot of fun, so maybe—"

"So maybe he'll stay after all?" I finish with a ghost of a smile. When Olivia nods, my heart cracks inside my chest, recalling all the times Olivia has tried to get Derek to "stay after all."

But her father never stayed, despite her sweet pleas and little ploys. Neither one of us rank high enough on Derek's list of priorities. And now I'm risking Olivia going through that pain and rejection again with Will.

I brush back her hair, my hand trembling slightly. "That's really thoughtful, but we need to remember that Will has to find work again, which means he could wind up anywhere in the country."

"Well maybe he'll find work here!"

"Maybe, but more likely in New York, or LA where your daddy lives, or Nashville, where he grew up. Besides, Will is one hundred percent human, which makes it even less likely he could ever settle here."

"Okay." Olivia shrugs. "Can we invite Will to go sledding?"

I decide I've taken the conversation, and the reality of Will's departure, as far as possible with Olivia. "Sure, let's ask him when we see him at the café."

When there's no sign of Will by mid-morning, Olivia starts walking past the picture window every five minutes or so, peering up and down the street for him. By lunchtime, Phoebe is nearly as anxious as Olivia, and I'm not far behind either of them.

Phoebe says, "Do you think there might be something wrong? This isn't like him."

I don't want to jump to conclusions, but I agree something feels off. I text Will: *Are you snowed in?* An hour later, when I still haven't received a reply, I send him a second text, "Swinging by on my way home to make sure everything's alright."

I see a pair of dogs' noses peering out of Estee and Sam's front window as I pull into the driveway, but I don't hear Grumpy's piercing barks. I punch in the garage code and open the door leading into the white kitchen. I remind Olivia to leave her boots in the garage, and I do the same. Olivia's faster than me, and she charges ahead into the great room.

Dopey is running in circles barking, and Sleepy rouses himself sufficiently to howl. I hear muffled yaps, which must be Grumpy, but I don't see the miniature schnauzer or Will. Olivia stays close to my side, obviously surprised by the all the noise. I glare at the dogs; they know me and usually stop barking once I'm inside.

"Will, where are you? Is everything okay?" I shout above the din of howling dogs. I follow the yips coming from down the hall. Then I hear pounding.

Olivia runs past me and stops in front of the basement door, pointing. "Mommy, over here!"

I hurry over and call through the door, "Will, are you in there?"

Will shouts, "I'm down here with Grumpy—I can't get the door open! The lock's jammed."

I try the door handle, but it won't budge. "Hold on, I'm going to find a screwdriver."

I really wish I were a house faerie who could open locked doors with a simple touch. It's a surprisingly useful bit of magic, and if you're a house faerie, it's instinctive. House faeries don't need to be intentional about it at all. Just like Nash's brownie magic, which improves the taste of all the food he prepares—or Phoebe's gatekeeper magic, which helps her welcome guests and discern what food will help them feel more at home—opening locks for a house faerie is a no brainer. They don't even have to think about it because it's part of their natural faerie aura.

Of course, any faerie can use their magic and their intention to open a locked door; it just takes more effort and energy. Gatekeeping faeries like Phoebe are the most powerful of all the faerie types, so it's very easy for them to snap their fingers and open locks. That's also why those nasty little gargoyles listen to my aunt; they don't want to incur her wrath again. Last time, they wound up underneath the café's counter. Next time, they may not be so lucky.

I shake my head at my own non-existent magic and instruct Olivia to wait for me. As I head toward the garage, I toss my puffer coat onto a chair in the kitchen.

My heart squeezes in my chest as I overhear Olivia shout through the door, "Don't worry, Will, we'll rescue you!" She's such an adorable faerie child.

I grab the tool chest from one of the shelves in the garage, lug it back into the house, and set it down next to the basement door. I kneel down and begin sorting through the tools, picking out the smallest screwdriver I can find. Jiggling it inside the keyhole, I try but fail to release the locking mechanism. I sigh, wondering whether it's time to call a human locksmith or ask Phoebe to pop over and direct some of her intentional faerie dust on this stubborn lock.

Then Olivia reaches out her small hand and rests it on the wobbly knob. A ribbon of violet sparkles flies from Olivia's fingers, twirls around her, and settles on the door handle.

I hear a click and suck in my breath.

Sweet moonglow, Olivia can manipulate locks!

But Mom was human, and Dad was a music faerie—apparently we're distantly related to the Pied Piper—but not a single one of our forebears was a house faerie. Then I realize my daughter must have inherited the gift from *her* father. Derek Taylor, my ex, is a very competent house faerie. He's a whiz at cleaning, sewing, and repairing things... such as broken locks.

I hug Olivia tightly, tears forming in my eyes. "Oh sweetie, you're amazing!"

I'm so proud I want to do a happy dance on the spot, but I have to restrain myself because Will is opening the basement door.

Olivia hugs me back, but she doesn't seem to realize *it was her magic that just freed Will*. I'll need to talk to Olivia about it later, and remind her that now she's able to use her house-faerie magic, she'll need to be extra careful around Will and any other non-supers.

Grumpy shoots out the door with a happy bark, and all three dogs run around the great room in ecstatic circles. I'm still on my knees, reeling from Olivia's new magical abilities, when Will emerges. He reaches both hands down, and pulls me up. Gripping my hands in his, Will gives me a slow, sweet kiss on the lips that nearly drives me to my knees again. I'm blushing from my neck to my hair roots. Trust me on this: being a blonde is not as much fun as most people think.

"Thanks for the rescue," he murmurs, gazing at me so intently I feel myself drowning in those bottomless, brown eyes, one of which is still swollen and bruised.

I know my daughter did the rescuing, but I'm not about to point that out to Will. Besides, my mouth is tingling where he kissed me; my face is still flushed, and I'm so overheated I could build a snowman outside without a coat. I take a calming breath.

"Can we go sledding now?" asks Olivia.

I step back from the open doorway and Will's intense gaze. "I think Will needs to eat something first." I lead him into the kitchen, where he reluctantly lets go of my hand and sits at the table. Inside the refrigerator I find a quart of milk, a bag of carrots, a six-pack of beer, and nothing else.

Shaking my head, I peer into the freezer and discover a couple of frozen meals and a pint of ice cream. "Is this what you've been eating for dinner?"

Will looks sheepish. "I never learned to cook, and living on the road and in New York, I've never had to."

I reach into the freezer to grab a meal. "Since this is a rescue operation, I'm going to pop one of these in the microwave, but don't tell Phoebe, or we'll never hear the end of it."

I brew us some fresh coffee and take a seat across from Will, cradling my mug as he tucks into his reheated lasagna. Olivia wanders into the other room to play with the dogs.

I wait until Will is finished eating before I ask him what happened.

"Grumpy happened," he replies and then sips some coffee.

"Huh?"

"After I walked the dogs this morning, Sleepy and Dopey hopped on the sofa for a snooze, but Grumpy ran around the house, barking furiously. Then he led me to the basement door, which I made the mistake of opening. Grumpy scampered down the stairs, growling and yapping, and I followed him. That was my second mistake; I *knew* there was nothing down there, but I went anyway.

"Grumpy sniffed the entire perimeter of the basement and after satisfying himself all was well, trotted back up the stairs to wait for me to let him out. I climbed up after him, thinking about Nash's daily special and seeing you again, but not in that order—"

Will smiles at me, and I stifle a sigh. I'm so far gone at this point I don't see how I'll be able to rescue myself from another broken heart when he leaves.

"—Anyway, when I tried opening the door, the wonky handle wouldn't budge. I'd left my phone and watch on the table, so I couldn't call or text anyone. I tried ramming down the door, but it's solid oak. I was really starting to worry no one would come."

Will runs a hand through his wavy black hair, which

is messier than usual. I want to reach over and push back a stray chunk that's tumbled over his battered right eye. Instead I keep my hands firmly wrapped around my mug.

"We were all worried when you didn't show up at the café this morning," I say. "There's no way one of us wouldn't have checked up on you."

"I'm glad it was you," he tells me. "I was hoping it would be."

I'm still processing that little statement, unsure how to respond without confessing the feelings I'm starting to have for this gorgeous human guy, when Olivia troops into the kitchen with all three dogs. "Can we go sledding now?"

Will and I chuckle, perhaps both a bit relieved at the interruption.

"Sure," I say, "But let's help Will walk the dogs too."

Will rinses out our mugs while I grab the dogs' leashes from a hook next to the back door. The dogs crowd around us, their nails clicking on the tile; Dopey runs too fast and slides into Will's legs. Olivia giggles as I wrestle a red plaid dog jacket onto Grumpy's wriggling body.

"Olivia, where's your hat?" I ask, zipping up my fuchsia puffer coat. I pull on my gray wool cap and fleece-lined gloves. Will returns from the hall closet wearing his new chestnut parka, brown hat, and water-proof gloves. I smile to myself; this man has definitely learned how to outfit himself for northern Wisconsin in December.... with a little help from Malaki, of course.

Olivia runs into the great room and shouts, "I found

it!" She returns with her lime-green beanie jammed onto her blonde curls.

We file outside to the driveway, and I hand the dogs' leashes to Will. "I need to get something out of my car." I open my trunk, toss my purse inside, and remove Olivia's sled.

"Let's head that way," I suggest, pointing at a hill rising gently behind the row of houses on Sam and Estee's street.

I tug the rope handle tied to Olivia's sled and drag it up the hill, Olivia chatting with Will as we ascend. When we reach the top, Olivia discovers one of her friends getting ready to sled down the other side and runs off with her own sled to join her. Will and I walk the dogs along the top of the slope, avoiding the other sledders and snowboarders and watching Olivia with her friend.

"Who suggested the name for the Second Chance Band?" I'm ninety-nine percent convinced it was Will, but I want to hear it from him. I've been obsessing about the band's name since he announced it.

Will removes his shades, frowns at the sunlight glinting off the snow, and pops them back over his bruised face. He leans down to scoop up Grumpy in his arms; the little dog is worn out trying to keep up with the rest of his pack. "I did. I've been thinking about second chances quite a lot lately."

My eyes follow Olivia on her sled, the lime-green hat easy to spot against the white hillside. "I think you're worrying needlessly about rebooting your career. You have too much talent not to get a second chance, and many more chances if you need them."

"Thanks." Will nods slowly. "Actually, I've been thinking about second chances at pretty much everything; my music... my mom's health... my relationships."

I glance up at Will, a healthy dose of skepticism etched into my features. I *want* to believe in second chances, I really do. And I'm *dying* to believe when Will is talking about a new relationship, he's thinking about me, about us. But I can't completely shake off Jake's warnings either, despite the fact my insides turn to putty when Will is nearby.

"What?" he asks. "You don't believe in second chances?"

I shrug. "Sure, for you, and Sophie, and Estee. Some folks seem to attract second chances, good luck, whatever you want to call it."

"But not you."

"Let's just say other folks need to work very hard for those second chances."

"Could it be you're simply not seeing them?" he says.

"Now you sound like Phoebe." I laugh. Using a hand to shield my eyes against the bright sunlight, I search the slope for Olivia, who's trudging back uphill, dragging her sled behind her. "I think Olivia's about finished."

Cheeks pink from exertion and slightly out of breath, Olivia tells me she's been invited back to her friend's house for Christmas cookie decorating and dinner. "Please, Mommy, can I go?" Her friend's mother waves at me from the bottom of the hill.

I wave back. "Sure, I'll take your sled home with me." I call after Olivia's retreating back, "Remember to say 'please' and 'thank you' and help with the dishes!" Olivia waves to acknowledge she's heard me and jogs downhill to rejoin her friend.

Before I can change my mind, I say to Will, "How about we drop off the dogs and then you follow me back to my place for your first cooking lesson?"

"I finally get to learn how to cook! See what I mean about second chances?" Will gives me his high wattage smile, and my heart beats out a wild rhythm inside my chest.

I roll my eyes. "You're not going to be in Riddle Hill long enough to learn to cook, but you'll be able to make at least one meal for yourself, so you won't be reduced to eating frozen dinners for the rest of your life."

"Still qualifies as a second chance in my book."

WILL IS ACTUALLY A PRETTY good sidekick in the kitchen. He follows orders well, doesn't mind chopping vegetables, even onions, and he whistles while he works.

"When you're finished slicing those mushrooms, we're going to sauté them in the frying pan over here. You'll need to keep an eye on them so they don't burn."

Will nods and reaches for a sip of wine. He watches as I drizzle the potato wedges with olive oil, salt, pepper, and oregano. After sliding the potatoes into the oven, I flour and brown the chicken cutlets. I glance over at him and point at the cutting board. "You're falling behind, Mr. Rossi, and it's only your first lesson."

Will winks with his good eye. "Sorry ma'am. Won't happen again." He resumes whistling.

I lower the heat and ask, "What're you whistling? I like the tune."

"Something new I'm working on."

"I noticed your music composition book when I walked the dogs the other day. I might have even taken a sneak peek."

"What did you think?"

I smile. "It's not what I think that counts, although I really like your new songs. When can I hear them?"

"When they're finished. For now, only the dogs get to hear them. I can tell how well I'm doing by how much they howl."

"You sing to the dogs?"

Will nods. "And they howl back. The more they howl, the better they like my music. At least I think that's how it works."

I shake my head, chuckling. "You're a funny man, Will Rossi."

"And here all along, I thought I was a singer. You think maybe I should try stand-up?"

"Definitely not. Music is your jam." I nod at his cutting board. "How are those mushrooms coming along?"

Will carries the board over to the stove and adds the mushrooms to the pan I'd prepped. We cook side-by-side for a while, Will sautéing the mushrooms and onions while I continue browning the chicken, until I motion for him to pour the vegetables into the pan with the chicken. After adding Marsala wine to the mixture and stirring, I lower the heat to simmer.

I carry my wine glass over to the kitchen table and sit

in one of the cane back chairs. "Thank you for spending time with Olivia, and for really listening to her. She looks up to you."

Will sits down across from me. "She's a great kid, and you're doing a wonderful job raising her. Too bad her father lives so far away. I'm sure he enjoys spending time with her."

My eyes well up unexpectedly, and Will looks at me with alarm. "What's wrong?"

I shake my head as one tear, and then another, rolls down my cheeks. Not only is Will the hottest guy to set foot in Riddle Hill, he's also the most thoughtful. Will appreciates Olivia in ways her own father never has. While Derek cares about Olivia, he's never invested the time to really get to know his own daughter.

Will grabs a box of tissues from the counter and hands them to me, his face full of concern. I dab my eyes, try to apologize, and start crying harder. Will brings his chair around next to mine and puts his arm around my shoulders.

I murmur something about needing to wash my face and charge into the powder room, wondering why I reacted so strongly to what Will said about Olivia and her father. I need to get a grip on my runaway emotions.

When I return to the kitchen, I discover that Will has set the table, pulled the potatoes out of the oven, and tossed a salad. He pulls out my chair and insists I sit while he serves the food.

In all the years we were together, I don't recall Derek serving me even once.

Over dinner and a bottle of Sauvignon Blanc, we start

sharing our relationship highs and lows. Will's low point with Roxie was realizing she'd never want children, even though they'd discussed it many times early in their marriage. Will admits he asked for the divorce, not the other way around.

I tell Will about my low point with Derek, which draws his ire. He shakes his head. "I can't imagine a man using his family's food and rent money to buy himself a plane ticket."

"Neither could I, which was why I left."

"That's totally understandable. I'm surprised you lasted as long as you did."

After we put away the leftovers and load the dishwasher, I walk Will to the front door. As we pass through my gray-and-pink living room, he pauses.

I'll confess I'm a bit over the top about Christmas. Pretty much every available surface is decorated for the season, from a Victorian-style Santa and sleigh, to snow globes, a hand-carved nativity, and lots and lots of winged angels.

Will scratches his head; there's one big thing missing at the moment, and I believe he's about to point that out. "Where's your Christmas tree? Hasn't Olivia been asking for one since Thanksgiving?"

"I like to buy our tree the week before Christmas, from the same tree farm my family has used for years. Olivia and I are going tomorrow after school."

"I haven't had a real tree in years." Will sounds so wistful. "I always liked the way they smelled though. When I was little, my dad used to lift me up so I could put the star on top of the tree."

I'm starting to realize Will is homesick, but not for his apartment in New York. I think he misses his childhood home and the family he left behind years earlier when he started touring.

And that image of little Will putting the star on top of the tree?

It's floored me. Will has managed to chisel away every last bit of my armor.

I'm officially armorless, defenseless, and hopeless when it comes to Will Rossi.

He slips on his parka but doesn't zip it up just yet. Instead, Will brings both his hands up to my face, tips my head back, and kisses me until my insides turn molten and my toes curl inside my shoes. Then he tucks me against his chest and murmurs, "Thanks for the cooking lesson… and for breaking me out of accidental confinement." He nuzzles my hair and then releases me.

It's all I can do to remain upright. I've never been kissed like that before—my head is spinning along with my heart.

Will zips up his jacket, retrieves his hat and gloves, and pauses to check his smartwatch. He stares at the screen, looking slightly bewildered.

"Is everything alright?" I ask, concerned something might have happened to his mom.

Will rotates his wrist so I can read the text message… and I burst out laughing. "This is serious, Will. There's a long waiting list to participate in the Riddle Hill Ice Fishing Contest. Consider yourself a member of the inner circle."

"But Jake wants me to meet him down by the harbor tomorrow at *four in the morning*!"

"Just remember to dress in layers. Lots of them!" I call out as he heads to his SUV.

I close the door and wrap my arms around myself, a self-hug to imprint the memory of Will's arms around me.

CHAPTER 21

ICE FISHING

WILL

Tuesday, December 18

I'm definitely not wearing enough layers. I don't think it's humanly possible to dress warmly enough for ice fishing in a frozen tundra in the predawn hours. Are these folks crazy or what? There's only one reason I'm here, and her name is Cassia Spellman. If her brother didn't invite me, and if I weren't concerned about Jake's attitude toward me, I'd be huddled under the blankets back at Sam's place, listening to Sleepy's soft snores.

Instead I'm sitting on a tiny portable stool that threatens to collapse beneath my weight, jiggling a fishing rod above a circular hole Jake drilled into the ice. There's an oil lamp on top of the ice chest beside me that gives off a small glow of light but absolutely no heat. I shiver as the wind sweeps across the frozen bay; I'm tempted to stomp my feet to stay warm, but I know the other fishermen hunching over their own holes in the ice would reprimand me for scaring away the fish.

Jake, who's taller and broader than me, sits nearby on an identical portable stool, bundled inside a beige, ankle-length, down parka with a fur-lined hood. I'm wondering where I could rustle up one of those. Probably at Malaki's. But first, I have to survive my current ice fishing experience without maimed, frostbitten fingers and toes.

Picking up a large thermos, Jake pours coffee into an insulated mug and hands it to me. "Looks like you could use some."

I take a long swallow and wait for my throat to thaw out before answering. "Thanks. Cassia told me to dress in layers, but I guess I didn't layer on enough."

"This kind of cold takes some getting used to, regardless of the number of layers."

We sit in companionable silence, occasionally reeling in a walleye. After topping up the coffee in our insulated mugs, Jake asks, "What's the real reason you're holed up here in Riddle Hill two weeks before Christmas?"

I stare at Jake, who looks ready to lead a dog race across Alaska. I don't like the question, but I've noticed the residents of Riddle Hill are perhaps even more blunt and to-the-point than those from my adopted city of New York. Shrugging, I reply, "Taking care of Sam's dogs. What else would I be doing?"

Jake must hear the defensiveness in my voice because he softens his tone. "It's just that Sam and Estee have a lot of neighbors who would have watched their dogs. What I'd like to understand is why *you* want to spend two weeks tucked away in a little town in northern Wisconsin, about as far away as you can get from New York City?"

I blow out a puff of frosty air and take another sip from my mug. I haven't admitted my real reason to anyone, but before I do come clean, I want to get clear on Jake's motives. "Why do you care what my reason is for spending two weeks in Riddle Hill?"

Jake grunts. "Come on, Will. Let's be frank. You were making out with my sister in front of the entire village. If you knew Cassia as well as I do, you'd realize that's entirely out of character for her. Everyone who cares about Cassia—which is all of Riddle Hill—wants to know why you're here. And why you're so intent on chasing after my sister."

"Let me tackle the second question first." I rub the stubble on my jaw, pausing to get the words right. "I like your sister—a lot. I've felt drawn to her since the moment we met. Sometimes I feel like Cassia has cast a spell over me."

"*A spell?*" Jake practically growls.

I roll my eyes and wince, because my right eye is still bruised and tender, although the swelling is mostly gone. "It's a figure of speech. I'm not accusing Cassia of witchcraft or anything."

Jake harrumphs. "Of course not. That would be silly, as there are no such things as witches... or faeries... or vampires, for that matter."

"Or werewolves," I add, thinking about the big dogs at Howling Shores Pub.

"Yeah," agrees Jake. He scratches his beard and

grunts, "Cassia has asked me to butt out, and because she's my sister, and I respect her judgment, I'm going to do just that. But so help me, if you hurt her, you're going to have to face me."

The way Jake glares at me, I have no doubt he'd give me another shiner to match the one from Rafe. But I'm glad to hear Cassia asked him to mind his own business, which he's clearly struggling to do. "I have no intention of hurting Cassia."

"I'm glad to hear it," he says a bit doubtfully. I guess after the way Cassia's ex treated her, Jake's apprehension is understandable. "Now tell me why you wanted to spend a couple of weeks here."

I don't know if Jake will understand, but I tell him anyway. "Christmas."

"Christmas?" Jake waits for me to elaborate.

"It's my favorite time of the year, and I didn't want to spend it in the city. Don't get me wrong, Christmas in New York can be very special, but I wanted something different this December."

"But aren't you returning to New York on Sunday, when Sam and Estee get back from their honeymoon? Two days *before* Christmas?"

I nod. "True, but by then most of the holiday stuff will be winding down. Besides, there are a couple of movies coming out on Christmas Day that I figure I can go see."

"You must have some family around."

I tell Jake about my parents' cruise and my sister's newborn twins, and Jake scowls, like it's my fault Christmas this year sounds so forlorn. My only hope is that Cassia and I will have some sort of an understanding before I leave town. Because I'm definitely coming back for her... after I pay some bills and figure out how to earn a real living again.

I probably need to diversify, start looking for an alternate income stream, especially since Mack's been slow to come up with any new bookings for me. I could never put Cassia through the same thing she went through with Derek, dragging her and Olivia all over the place while I get my act together. She needs stability, and frankly, so do I.

Jake's brow is furrowed, like I've genuinely touched him somehow. I wasn't planning on playing the sympathy card, but the truth is, Christmas alone in New York is a pretty bleak prospect. "Look, I have a spare bedroom at my place. Why not stick around through the holiday? You can be my plus one for Christmas dinner at Phoebe and Nash's."

Jake's invitation takes me by surprise. I'm not ready to commit yet, because I don't want Cassia to think I'm trying to crowd her or force her affections. And she might not want me showing up for her family's Christmas dinner. "Thanks, Jake, that's very generous of you. Can I get back to you on that?"

"Sure, no problem."

"Do you mind if I ask you a question?"

Jake says warily, "Go ahead."

"Why did you think I was in Riddle Hill?"

Jake pours the rest of the coffee into our mugs. He has the decency to look sheepish. "I've read a lot of stuff about you. Not all of it flattering. I thought you were trying to escape—maybe from creditors, maybe from your ex-wife or ex-manager, maybe from the paparazzi."

"Given all the crazy stories following me around, I'm not surprised," I reply. "Those stories... they're not true. Well not exactly. Some of them have a kernel of truth, like I've been avoiding the tabloids for a few months, or I have nothing to do with Junior, my ex-manager."

Jake reels in one last walleye. "I'm glad to hear your reasons for staying in Riddle Hill are legit. I'm obviously very protective when it comes to my town and my family."

I can't blame Jake, and I tell him so. "You're a very lucky man. You have a special family and a special town."

Jake glances up at the weak December sun rising behind us and starts packing up our supplies. "Thanks. I aim to keep it that way."

Somehow that comes out sounding vaguely menacing, but I choose to ignore the warning. I'm going to be wooing Cassia for the rest of this week and beyond—with or without her big brother's approval.

CHAPTER 22

PERFECT CHRISTMAS TREE

CASSIA

Later Tuesday

"How about this one?" I ask Olivia. "It's nicely filled out all the way around." We're standing in the middle of Balthasar's Tree Farm, surrounded by firs, pines, and spruces, searching for our "perfect" Christmas tree. Or rather, Olivia is doing the searching; Jake and I are her able-bodied assistants, ready to hop to attention when she's found it.

The farm, which is located outside of Riddle Hill and serves both human and supernatural customers, is owned by a gnome. Balthasar has a long white beard, bright blue eyes, and a pointy red cap on his head. He's also six feet tall in his stocking feet. Most gnomes are guardians of the home and garden, which requires size, strength, and solid landscaping knowledge. Notwithstanding all the cute little gnome decorations in the human shops, I have yet to meet a gnome who's under five foot five.

Olivia walks around the tree's perimeter and looks the fir over from tip to base. Shaking her head, she says, "It's got a funny dip in the branches on one side."

Jake leans over and whispers, "She's becoming more like you every day. A perfectionist."

"I am not a perfectionist."

"What's a *prefectinis*?" asks Olivia.

"Someone who likes things just right," replies Jake.

"Oh." Olivia runs ahead to a section of Scots pines. My phone rings, and I pause to answer it while Jake follows my daughter. Bibbidy is confirming the order for Sophie's flowers: white and pink roses, carnations, and anemones with baby's breath and velvety green succulents. I slip the phone back into my handbag and walk in the direction I last spotted Jake and Olivia.

"Cassia!"

I spin around. "Will? What a wonderful surprise! Are you tree shopping for Sam and Estee?"

Will's wearing his new chestnut parka, black jeans, and dark boots. My heart starts racing like a gear in overdrive as he walks toward me. He's so over-the-top handsome the other customers in the tree lot are staring at him, probably convinced he's a movie star.

"Jake mentioned he was helping you cart the tree home, so I offered to bring my SUV. It's got an extra-long roof rack, and he said the Christmas trees have been getting larger each year."

I'm a bit surprised my brother mentioned anything to Will, because Jake's been trying to keep us apart, or at the very least, slow us down to neutral. But then I realize Jake's ulterior motive has nothing to do with me this time; he wants to preserve his new SUV's pristine condition, which means no tree sap or pine needles on the roof.

I chuckle. "It's true. As Olivia's been growing taller, so have the trees." Will's removed his shades because it's getting dark. I'm feeling a little breathless at the way he's peering at me, like he might want to kiss me senseless right here at the farm.

I decide to distract him—and me—by taking his hand. Even though we're wearing gloves, I can still feel the firmness of his grip as he wraps his larger hand around mine. I melt a little bit more inside, and I want this moment with Will, and the next one and the one after that, to slow down and last longer than time will allow. No one, not even Granny Catbeam or Aunt Phoebe, can change time, which is beyond even the strongest faerie magic to manipulate.

We wander about, peering down rows and rows of evergreens, until I spot Olivia in her purple jacket, standing in front of a picture-perfect Balsam fir. Jake is standing beside her, holding the tree's trunk and shaking out its branches, as Olivia jumps up and down.

"I think we've found our tree," I say with a head nod.

Will whistles. "It's a beauty—but will it fit?"

I cock my head to one side and do some quick mental calculations. Nodding, I say, "Looks to be about a foot taller than Jake, which should be fine."

Olivia sees Will and runs over to greet him. Hopping

on one foot in her excitement, she asks, "Can you help us decorate the tree? Please?"

Will glances at me uncertainly. "I'm sure your mother already has tree-decorating plans."

I smile at him. "If you don't mind a bowl of beef stew for dinner, I'd love to have you join us."

I'm suddenly realizing Will is leaving in five days, and I want to enjoy his company in the time we have left. Who knows? Maybe he'll decide to return next summer when the weather is warmer, and he'll stay longer. Wishful thinking, I know, but a gal has to dream.

Will rubs the stubble on his chin as if deep in thought. "Let's see, homemade beef stew and Christmas tree decorating, or frozen egg rolls and singing to the dogs. Hmm... that's a tough choice!"

Jake and Will wrestle the tree onto the SUV's roof, and then up the condo's steps, and finally into its stand in the living room, patiently adjusting the base several times before Olivia and I declare the tree is standing straight. After we eat, Olivia runs back into the living room and opens the first box of ornaments.

She carefully withdraws a hand-blown glass ornament from its layer of bubble wrap and hands it to me. It's a statue of a bride and groom holding hands. As I place it on the tree, I explain to Will that my parents purchased the ornament to celebrate their first Christmas together.

Jake unwraps an antique, red, fire engine ornament, and I laugh, reminding him I predicted his career choice when he was in junior high. Olivia hands Will a guitar ornament, another one of Jake's, to hang on the tree. We unpack and hang about half the ornaments when Jake receives an alert on his phone. He leans over to kiss Olivia goodnight.

"But, Uncle Jake, we haven't finished the tree yet! Do you really have to go?" asks Olivia.

"Afraid so, sweetie, but Will is going to sub for me, so you'll still finish before bedtime."

Will, who's been sitting on the carpet with Olivia unwrapping ornaments, stands up and shakes Jake's hand. He thanks Jake for the ice fishing lesson, and I sense some of the earlier tension between them has lessened. I'm not sure what happened at four a.m., but I'm glad for it.

I walk Jake to the front door, waiting as he grabs his parka from the hall closet. Jake slings his coat over his shoulder as he runs out to his SUV, his cell phone to his ear. I lock the front door and return to the Christmas mess in the living room, a tangle of ornaments on the floor, half-opened boxes, bubble wrap, and paper scattered about, and I notice Olivia has wandered over to the window to watch her uncle drive away.

I place a hand on my daughter's shoulder. "We seem to be missing something."

"What are we missing?" Olivia turns away from the window.

"I think we've lost our Christmas spirit... and I have an idea for how we can get it back."

"How?" asks Olivia.

"We need to sing some Christmas songs, and we happen to have a pretty good singer in our midst," I say.

"Only pretty good?" Will clutches his chest as if in shock.

I smile. "The best."

"Now you're talking." Will grins and sits down at my small upright piano, where Olivia's practice books lean against the music rack. Will plays the introduction to *Rudolph the Red-Nosed Reindeer*, reciting the story of poor Rudolph in his deep baritone. As soon as he reaches the chorus, he waits for Olivia and me to chime in. Will runs through every Christmas song Olivia knows, plus a few she doesn't. While the two of them sing, I wander back to the ornament boxes and finish decorating the tree, except for one final touch.

Olivia jogs over from the piano. "It's the best tree yet!" Pointing to the top, she adds, "But what about the star?"

I hand the box containing the tree topper to Will. "Would you do the honors?"

Will opens the box and pulls out a faded gold star, most of its glitter worn off. Placing the star on the tree's pointed tip, he continues to adjust the star's position until Olivia declares it's "just right."

I kiss Olivia on the top of the head. "Time to say goodnight to Will and then go off to bed."

"Goodnight, Will," says Olivia with a yawn.

Will offers to pick up the paper and bubble wrap while I ensure Olivia washes her face, brushes her teeth, and climbs into bed. I tuck her in with a goodnight kiss and a promise to read her two bedtime stories tomorrow night.

When I return to the living room, Will says, "Thank

you for dinner, for the chance to sing Christmas songs with you and Olivia, and for letting me put that star on top of the tree."

He walks toward me, a tender smile on his lips, and puts his hands around my waist. "You're a special woman, Cassia."

My heart performs backflips as I feel suddenly shy in my own home. I want this man in my life, despite all the reasons why I shouldn't. Will uses his left hand to draw me in and his right to tip up my chin. He leans down for a kiss, but his lips barely brush mine when we both hear Olivia calling out from her bedroom, "Mommy, you forgot my glass of water."

Will leans his forehead against mine and chuckles. "And you're a busy woman." He reaches behind my head, where he releases my hair clip. Then he runs his fingers through my hair, sending tingles up and down my spine. Will kisses me with such longing we don't stop until we hear Olivia repeat her request.

"Mommy, my water please!"

I break away first and call out to Olivia, "I'm coming, sweetie."

His fingers still entangled in my hair, Will whispers, "I've been wanting to undo your ponytail since Sam and Estee's rehearsal."

"What took you so long?" I murmur.

Will chuckles and runs his thumb across my lips, causing me to shiver inside my sweater. "You need to take care of Olivia. I'll let myself out."

After Will leaves, after I bring Olivia her glass of water and kiss her again, after I put away the empty boxes and clear away the remains of dinner, I brew myself some herbal tea and carry my mug into the living room. I sit on the couch in the dark for a long time, staring at the twinkly white lights on my Christmas tree.

Is Will missing me as much as I'm missing him?

And if he is, could we possibly find a way to make this work?

CHAPTER 23

PROFESSIONAL ADVICE

WILL

Wednesday, December 19

I'm sitting in front of the large, plate-glass window at the café, sipping my coffee and watching Phoebe's animated gargoyles, who are back to their usual tricks. They're wriggling their ears and blowing raspberries at me. When I asked Phoebe about the tech behind them, she shrugged and told me there was no tech involved, just magic. I had to laugh.

Phoebe took my order this morning because Cassia's running late. I guess Olivia was up in the middle of the night, all wound up over her upcoming performance in the Children's Pageant. Cassia let her sleep late and should be arriving soon.

I had trouble sleeping myself last night. After I got home from Cassia's, I took a cold shower to cool down. It helped some, but not enough. I'm a raging inferno whenever Cassia is within six feet of me... and forget about it when we actually touch each other.

I'm so into this woman I have to say something—but what can I say—what can I offer her? I'm barely solvent; my reputation is in tatters, and I have zero recording contracts or performances lined up. Meanwhile, Cassia is working two jobs to make ends meet and has a young daughter to look after. I can't possibly improve her life at the moment; in fact, I'm afraid I'd further complicate it.

On the other hand, I'm not leaving Riddle Hill without letting Cassia know how I feel. But I'd rather have something on the back burner, something with income potential, before I say anything at all.

And I have very little time to get something lined up. I'll ring up Mack later this morning and see what's cooking.

Meanwhile, as I'm waiting for breakfast, I flip through a local magazine someone left on one of the tables. A third of the pages contain photos of properties for sale, many of them taken in the summer. I roll my eyes at all the listings by Rob Wolferman. Even that guy's a better bet than I am right now.

I pause at a photo of a barn-like building sitting on a gently sloping hill of grass and wildflowers. The ad includes a description of the property and the contact information for... Rob Wolferman, of course. I toss the magazine aside as Phoebe delivers my breakfast.

I'm savoring Nash's delectable frittata—eggs, chorizo, caramelized red peppers and onions, and queso fresco—when Olivia slips into the seat opposite me. I butter a slice of cinnamon swirl toast, cut it into four smaller squares, and place it on a napkin, which I slide across the booth's tabletop.

"So how's rehearsal been going?"

Olivia picks up one of the toast squares and sighs. "When I practice with Mommy, I can remember my lines and everything. It's kind of fun. But when I'm at school and everyone's looking at me, I get nervous and lose my place." She shakes her head, looking dejected. "I wish they'd let me be one of the angels. They have one song and perform it together."

I recognize the classic symptoms of stage fright. I used to shake before every performance back in Nashville, convinced I'd forgotten the lyrics to my own songs. A decade of concert tours finally cured me of the panic attacks.

Although I haven't given a pep talk to a seven-year-old before, I decide to give it a try. "Do you know what my old manager used to say when I got really nervous before a big concert?"

Olivia shakes her head.

"He'd say, 'Will, old buddy, when you get on stage, just imagine everyone in the audience is sitting out there...' " I pause, realizing I can't repeat what Mack used to say. Olivia chews slowly, waiting for me to continue.

"Your bus is here, Olivia!" Cassia stops by the booth, carrying a light purple backpack and darker purple jacket. "Say thank you to Will for sharing his toast and let's go."

Olivia slips her arms inside her jacket. "Thanks, Will. And don't forget to tell me what your old manager used to say." Cassia hands Olivia's backpack to her, watching as her daughter runs outside and climbs up the steps of the yellow bus.

Turning back to me, she asks, "What was that all about?"

"Oh, just some old story to try and instill a little confidence in Olivia. Sounds like she has stage fright about performing in the pageant."

Cassia looks at me and slowly nods. "I think you may be right." She pauses and adds, "I wonder whether you could watch Olivia rehearse this afternoon and give her some professional pointers... that is, if you don't have other plans today?"

I smile, pleased Cassia is asking for my advice. This is definitely one way I can help Cassia and her daughter. "Of course. Where's the rehearsal?"

"They rehearse at the high school. I could pick you up at three-thirty, if that works?"

"Sure, that works."

"See you later then. And thanks," says Cassia, sounding relieved.

I pay my bill and leave the café whistling a Christmas tune. Zipping up my new parka and pulling on my cap, I walk the six blocks to Sam and Estee's house. As I insert the key in the door, I hear Grumpy's sharp bark and Dopey's lower-pitched woof. Sleepy doesn't even bother. Before I can clip on their leashes, my phone rings.

I see it's Mack and answer immediately. "Hey there, I hope this is good news."

"Still working all the angles, but something will pop soon."

I drop the phone to my chest and take a deep breath.

Sometimes I still can't believe that last year I was playing to sold-out stadiums and now I'm practically begging for work. I put the phone back to my ear in time to hear Mack ask, "How long will you be staying in Wisconsin?"

"My buddy returns from his honeymoon on December twenty-third."

"Any plans after Christmas?"

"I'm flexible. Why?"

"I think there could be something for you in Nashville around New Year's. But don't book your travel just yet. Talk soon." Mack hangs up.

I glance at the phone and shake my head. I'll take whatever I can get, but working the post-holiday club circuit in Nashville sounds pretty depressing.

I shrug and figure work is work. Clapping my hands, I call out to my three charges, "Let's go for a walk, fellas!"

The sounds of galloping paws sliding on the wood floors brings a smile to my face; there's nothing like a pack of rambunctious dogs to cheer up a guy.

CASSIA and I arrive at the school a little before four o'clock. She's wearing a black wool coat with a red scarf around her neck, dark jeans, and leather boots with spiky heels. She looks so beautiful I want to skip the rehearsal and stay in the car, making out with her in the back seat like a couple of high schoolers. But even as I daydream about kissing Cassia, the rational part of my brain recalls we're here to encourage Olivia. I sigh inwardly as Cassia turns off the car and opens her door.

A few adults wave as we enter the mostly empty auditorium, and Cassia explains they're volunteers helping with the pageant. I get the feeling this might be the first time Cassia has brought a man to any of Olivia's events, because I can sense a lot of eyes on us as we walk up the aisle.

I place my hand on the small of her back, and just that merest touch sends a shockwave all the way up my arm. This woman is practically electrifying to me, and I can't get enough.

We find a front-row seat in the main section just as the rehearsal begins. I quickly realize Cassia is every bit as anxious as her daughter because she holds her breath whenever it's Olivia's turn to speak. I'm worried Cassia might start hyperventilating soon if she doesn't relax. I squeeze her hand, lean over, and whisper, "She's doing fine. Holding your breath isn't going to help Olivia."

Cassia dips her head. "I know, but whenever Olivia gets nervous, I get twice as nervous!"

When Olivia reaches her "long speech"—a few lines about the Christmas star—she begins to falter. Her eyes flit anxiously around the auditorium, finally settling on Cassia and me. I give her a thumbs up, and she breaks into a grin, delivering the rest of her lines like a pro.

Cassia glances at me. "How did you...?"

I shrug. "There's nothing like an old-fashioned thumbs up to boost your confidence when it's flagging."

After rehearsal, Olivia runs up to us. She hugs her mother first, and then turning to me, she hesitates before throwing her arms around my waist. I feel my throat tightening as I pat Olivia's blonde head. "You did great, Olivia!"

Olivia steps back and looks at me solemnly. "You need to be sitting right up front with Mommy during the pageant, just like today."

"Oh, Olivia," says Cassia. "Will is leaving when Sam and Estee get back home from their trip."

Olivia shakes her head. "But no one *leaves* before Christmas. That's when everyone *comes home*."

I tousle her hair. "You're going to be amazing, no matter who's in the audience on Christmas Eve." I'm almost tempted to say something right now about Jake's offer of a place to stay, but I want to talk to Cassia about it first.

"But why can't you stay here for Christmas?" Olivia's face scrunches up, like she's thinking. "You can have my bedroom."

"Oh goodness." Cassia looks embarrassed. "Will has his own apartment in New York. Now let's go find your things. I promised Will we'd take him out to dinner."

Olivia's face lights up, and she skips off to find her jacket and backpack. Cassia gives me a sheepish look. "I'm sorry about that. I think there's some hero worship going on with Olivia."

I laugh. "It feels good to have a super-fan again, even if she's seven years old!"

Olivia hands her backpack to Cassia, slips on her jacket, and waves goodbye to her classmates. "Where are we eating dinner?" she asks.

Cassia says, "I'm not sure yet. Let's figure it out in the car. We'll give Will some options and let him decide."

We push open the school's heavy, wooden doors and step outside. The sun has set, and it should be dark, but it's bright as midday. I'm momentarily confused as brilliant, white lights flash in my eyes.

Cassia gasps, and I move in front of her and Olivia to shield them as best I can, but there's very little I can do now they've found me. I call over my shoulder, "We need to move quickly. I'll drive."

Although I've been chased by paparazzi too many times to count, there's something really off about this crew. First, there's a funky smell in the air, sort of like smoldering rubber.

And then there's their faces, which I can't really see because these fellas have so much dark hair that it dangles in their eyes and covers most of their oversized ears and noses.

I shiver, wondering if I'm suffering from the celebrity version of post-traumatic stress disorder. I've not had the best of experiences with paparazzi in the past.

But they move in closer, and Cassia gives a little screech. I put my arms around her and Olivia and shout, "Now!"

The three of us push past them and make a mad dash for Cassia's silver Honda.

CHAPTER 24

GOBLINS WITH CAMERAS

CASSIA

WEDNESDAY EVENING

Will opens the back door for Olivia, who scrambles inside and buckles her seat belt. I hop into the front passenger's seat, holding up Olivia's backpack to hide my face, while Will runs around to the driver's side as paparazzi shout questions at him. Will starts the car and edges out of the parking spot as photographers continue snapping photos.

Although I can't see their faces through all their hair, I can sense their magic, which feels ashy and cloying. I shudder inside my wool coat.

The supernatural paparazzi, who rarely leave New York and LA, have finally discovered where Will Rossi is holed up—and they won't be leaving without a good, juicy story.

I'm positively terrified because now Olivia and I have just become part of the story.

"Mommy, did you see all those goblins with cameras?" asks Olivia. "What are they doing here?"

I can see Will frowning at Olivia's interesting word choice for the paparazzi. But she's spot on. Those *are* goblins chasing us right now, and very aggressive ones at that. I turn toward the backseat and reach out my hand to Olivia, who takes it. Then I whisper, "It's not polite to call them names, even if they're not our friends."

"But Mommy..." Olivia starts to reply. I shake my head slightly, and Olivia catches on, because she says, "Oh... um... why are those yucky men following us?"

The paparazzi have jumped into pickup trucks and are tailing us.

"Because Will is famous," I say, trying to keep my voice steady. It's not fair to blame him. I knew this could happen, with everyone snapping selfies with Will and then Sophie taking photos of us in her bakery. One of those pictures was bound to find its way to the goblin paparazzi.

"They take lots of photos and sell them to newspapers and magazines," says Will. "It's their job."

"But why are there so many of them?"

"Honey," I reply, "we'll answer your questions later. Right now, Will has to concentrate on driving, and I need to help him. Okay?"

Olivia nods and leans her head back against the upholstery. Will takes Highway 42 south. Once we clear the village limits, we're in the country again, with snow-covered trees lining the highway on either side of us. Somewhere off to the right is the frozen bay. I point to a private road, barely visible in the dark. "Take a sharp turn right as you round the bend."

Will doesn't question me, trusting that I have a much better handle on the local landmarks than he does. Since no one is on the highway, except the vehicles behind us, Will cuts his lights as he turns onto the private road, and the paparazzi whiz past us. Flipping on the headlights, he pulls ahead slowly, following the road until it dead ends into a narrow sightseeing spot overlooking the bay, barely wide enough for two cars. He parks the car and waits, his gloved hands gripping the steering wheel.

I shift in my seat, gazing at his profile. "What now?"

Will turns and reaches out to take my hand, but I pull it back. I'm in no mood for coddling or cuddling. I'm completely unnerved, and I need Will to help me navigate through this new and frightening territory. Unfortunately, I can't tell him those are *real goblins with cameras* out there, and they're going be dogging our footsteps from now until he leaves Riddle Hill. It'll be like living under a microscope that's operated by nasty, nosy, ne'er-do-wells... only worse.

"I'm not sure what we can do about them now that they're here." Will runs his hand through his hair.

"You don't seem all that surprised."

"When you've been harassed by them for years, I suppose you eventually become desensitized. But I am surprised to see so many of them in Riddle Hill this close to Christmas—and absolutely appalled they showed up outside the school and took photos of you and Olivia. I feel terrible about this, Cassia."

I shake my head, biting my lower lip to keep it from

trembling. "I'm so afraid Olivia's photo might turn up in some tatty tabloid or online post."

"I'm so sorry this happened. The last thing I want is to hurt you or Olivia."

Olivia pipes up from the backseat. "You didn't hurt me, Will. It was fun, like being in a movie."

I groan and drop my face into my hands.

Will puts a hand on my shoulder. "Are you alright?"

I shrug but say nothing. The silence expands, sitting heavy between us.

"Am I forgiven?" he asks, firmly gripping my shoulder while he waits for me to respond.

I drop my hands and stare out at the ice-covered bay. Moonlight reflects off its rippled surface, the waves frozen in place until the spring thaw. I'm so full of conflicting emotions right now, I don't know how to answer him.

It's not Will's fault he's a celebrity, but the fact is, if he'd come for one weekend and left again after Estee and Sam's wedding, none of this would have happened. But then I wouldn't have fallen for him, for this amazingly sensitive man behind the superstar image... and I wouldn't be so worried now about Olivia's photo showing up in some sleazy post.

"This isn't a matter of forgiveness." I shake my head. "It's not that simple."

Will removes his hand from my shoulder and puts it back on the steering wheel. "I understand this is a lot for you to process," he says gently.

I'm touched by his perceptiveness, and I'm saddened too. He must realize I have to pull back, emotionally and physically—to protect Olivia, if for no other reason. I'm twisting my hands in my lap and force myself to stop.

"I'm sure we've lost the paparazzi for now," I say. "Let's grab some dinner and then head back. It's a school night, and Olivia still has homework."

"Not tonight," Olivia chimes in. "I finished it all before rehearsal. Can we go to Jeanetta's? Please?" Jeanetta's is part motel and part family restaurant, and Olivia's favorite spot for eating out.

"Good idea." I give Will directions as he cautiously pulls back onto the highway. I find myself constantly glancing around, but there's no sign of the paparazzi on the road or in Jeanetta's parking lot. We managed to throw the gossip-hounds off the scent for now.

After we're seated and have ordered, I watch Will toy with his silverware. Finally, he says what's on his mind, keeping his voice low. "In a weird way all this paparazzi attention might give my flagging career a little boost. But I'd never, ever want it to come at your expense. I hope you believe me."

"I believe you," I reply, and I mean it. "Just how shaky is your career?"

"Pretty shaky," says Will.

"But you've been a star for years! How could that change overnight?"

Will stares into his mug of hot cider, a cinnamon stick floating on top, which Olivia insisted he order. "Roxie was the powerhouse of our duo. Sure, I wrote the music we performed, but she's the one who drew the crowds at our concerts and sold our songs. She's already embarking on the next phase of her career, performing duets with a lot of very good singers, who happen to bring along their own original music. It's a win-win for everyone. Well almost everyone." He takes a sip of the cider and when he looks up, his smile doesn't quite make it to his eyes.

I hear the self-doubt in Will's voice, so unlike his normal exuberance. "But you're the one all the girls had a crush on. Do you remember your *There's Always Hope* tour? My friends and I went to Chicago for the concert, and all three of us bought the same t-shirt, the one where you were looking a bit lost and vulnerable. It was the only shirt without Roxie's image. I can tell you that t-shirt sold out faster than all the rest."

Will sits up straighter and grins at me, his brown eyes regaining some of their twinkle. "You were actually at a Roxie and Rossi concert and bought that t-shirt? Do you still have it?"

Olivia says, "Mommy still has the t-shirt. Sometimes she sleeps in it."

I exclaim, "Olivia, it's not polite to discuss sleepwear. I'm sure Will's not interested."

A smirk dances across Will's lips. "Quite the contrary, I'm very interested."

Before Olivia can reveal anything else, I say, "Let's get back to your career. What are you doing about it?"

Will slumps against his chair. "I hired my old manager back in Nashville. He thinks he may've found some work for me after the holidays."

"Well that's good, isn't it?"

Will nods but without much enthusiasm. "It'll be good to be working again. It's just that—"

"Daddy!" Olivia shouts, hopping out of her seat. She dashes over to the only man in the restaurant with bleached hair and a California tan in the dead of winter.

"*Derek?*" I gape at him. "What are you doing here?"

Derek saunters over to the table, Olivia's hand in his. "Can't a man visit his family for Christmas?"

I feel my face turning to stone like one of my aunt's gargoyles. Between goblin paparazzi descending on Riddle Hill and my ex showing up unexpectedly, I'm struggling to stay calm. I take a deep breath, and then another. I've spent the past few years in therapy so I can deal with Derek without triggering my stress symptoms.

"We're not a family, Derek. And you didn't call to let me know you wanted to see Olivia." My mouth turns down at the corners.

Derek shrugs, "I got a break in filming." He pauses and adds for Will's benefit, "I play Brad on *Doctors and Nurses*. It's a small role but the lead writer wants to develop my character. Anyway, I decided to come home for a few days, booked a room at Jeanetta's, and here we are." Derek winks at Olivia. "I thought I'd hand-deliver Olivia's Christmas gifts."

Olivia beams at her father, and I bite my tongue. My therapist would be proud; so far, my ears and eyebrows are not going all faerie on me.

The waitress walks over and hands Derek a menu. He orders a burger, no bun, no fries, with a side of cottage cheese. I wonder what Phoebe would do with that food order and figure she'd probably let it ride. She's not a fan of Derek either.

While Derek eats, Olivia tells her father about school,

the pageant, and the "prazzi" as she calls them. Derek scowls at me. "What were you thinking, letting Olivia be photographed like that?"

I know Derek is intentionally provoking me; even so I'm piping mad. Before I completely lose my temper with him, Will interjects, "The fault's all mine. The paparazzi are after me, and unfortunately, Cassia and Olivia just happened to get in some of the shots."

Derek nods. "Thanks for owning up, man. I did see a photo of you and Cassia online."

I realize he must have seen one of the photos Sophie posted to SuperSuite. Now everything is starting to fall into place. Derek isn't here because of Christmas. He normally sends Olivia her Christmas gifts because he doesn't like winter; he never did. Derek is probably hoping to catch some free publicity by hanging around Will Rossi for a few days. I'm not about to call him out in front of Olivia, whom he loves in his own self-centered way.

The waitress brings the check, and Will reaches for it. Derek thanks him and leans over to kiss Olivia. "I'll pick you up after school tomorrow, Liv."

"Her bus drops her off at the café, so meet us there," I say.

A shadow passes over Derek's chiseled features. He probably doesn't want to run into Phoebe and Nash. Nodding, he walks out whistling a Christmas tune.

During the drive back to Riddle Hill, Olivia chats happily about Derek's visit, speculating about her Christmas gifts that I'm certain he hasn't purchased yet.

Derek's sudden appearance reminds me of how much I invested emotionally in my first marriage.

I recall the promise I made to myself when I moved back to Riddle Hill with Olivia: I'd never allow myself to get carried away again.

I need to remind myself how different Will and I are... and all the reasons why we could never make it work.

I need to go back to leading with my head and not my heart. I brush a tear from my cheek and stare out the window all the way back to Riddle Hill.

I NO SOONER SIT DOWN ON the sofa, balancing a cup of chamomile tea on my knee, when my phone vibrates. I turned off the ringer to avoid waking Olivia, who was too wound up to go to bed. Between the pageant rehearsal, being chased by goblins, dinner out at her favorite restaurant with Will, and her father showing up, Olivia couldn't settle down. I drew a bubble bath for her and brushed her hair for a while. Eventually, Olivia stifled a few yawns, and I let her curl up on the opposite side of the sofa, so long as she stopped asking questions and tried to sleep.

I answer the phone as quietly as possible. "What are you whispering for?" Phoebe asks.

I walk into the kitchen and sit down at the table. "Olivia's fallen asleep on the sofa. Too much excitement for her to go to bed."

"I'm not surprised! I heard a couple of goblins

showed up in front of the school tonight, chasing after Will and you with their cameras."

"More like a drove of goblins, seven or eight, at least," I say. "I know they have to make a living, but I don't like them. Their magic feels all wrong to me, like wisps of smoke and soot, instead of trails of faerie sparkles." Although goblins can't help their unfortunate appearance—with their long, narrow noses, sharp chins, big ears, and thick, long facial hair—I shudder anyway. I'm certain there must be some very nice goblins somewhere, whom I haven't yet had the pleasure of meeting, although Aunt Phoebe seems just as put off by them.

"Eight goblins? That must have scared Olivia."

"It scared me, but not Olivia. She thought it was fun, just like being in a movie."

"Oh boy," says Phoebe. "She sounds just like Derek."

"Who also showed up tonight."

Phoebe almost shouts into the phone. "*Derek's in Door County in December?* Whatever for?" I tell her about our dinner conversation, and my theory on Derek's sudden appearance.

"Look, as hard as it might be, try to get some rest," advises Phoebe. "I have a feeling this whole paparazzi thing isn't going to blow over anytime soon. Especially with Derek in the mix."

I say goodnight and hang up, worried my aunt's intuition will prove right once again.

And worried about Will... and me... and saying goodbye. Even thinking about it makes my chest ache with longing.

And then my tears, which I've held in check all evening, start streaming.

CHAPTER 25
CAMERA ANGLES

WILL

Thursday, December 20

I debate whether to show up at the café at my normal time for Phoebe's breakfast recommendation or wait until later. I don't want to disrupt Olivia's morning routines in case the paparazzi tag along, but on the other hand there's no point in hiding from them anymore either.

I take the dogs for their early morning walk; it's still dark outside, and we have the road to ourselves. Then I use Sam's treadmill, shower, and dress warmly for the six-block walk to the café. I notice a couple trucks parked down the road that weren't there when I walked the dogs earlier. I head toward town, stepping around the icy patches in the road and wondering whether the photographers will follow me by car or on foot. Hearing the crunch of tires on snow behind me, I have my answer.

I guess the paparazzi don't like the snow any more

than Derek Taylor, with his fake tan and dyed-blond hair. I took an immediate dislike to the guy when we first met, which only deepened when I saw how he tried pushing all of Cassia's buttons. He's a scoundrel alright. But he's also Olivia's father, and she's the sweetest kid I know. As much as I can't stand him, I can only hope he's not as selfish as he appears.

The gargoyles roll their eyes when I enter the café. If they could speak, they'd probably mutter something like, "Here's the chump who ruined his life, his career, and his relationship with Cassia."

There's no sign of paparazzi inside the restaurant, which I suspect is Phoebe's doing. Olivia is sitting at the counter having breakfast. She starts to climb off her stool when she spots me, but Cassia whispers something, and Olivia merely waves her hand and turns back around.

I didn't think I could feel any lower, but that small rejection nearly does me in.

Cassia is protecting her daughter's privacy by keeping her out of sight from those paparazzi, which means keeping her away from me. I get it... and she's right... but it still hurts.

Phoebe comes over to pour my coffee and tart cherry juice. She recommends a light breakfast, soft-boiled eggs, and lightly buttered toast, which sounds about right since I have zero appetite. But I can tell she's practically bursting at the seams to tell me off, so I invite her to sit down.

"What's on your mind?" I ask, determined to rip off all the bandages at once. What's a little more pain at this point?

Phoebe puts the juice carafe and coffee pot on the table and sits across from me. She nods out the front window. "There are two trucks filled with paparazzi sitting outside my café, Mr. Rossi, and I don't like it one bit. Even worse, there's another couple of photographers staking out Cassia's condo, which I like even less. Her brother had to drive her and Olivia to the café this morning."

I wince and run both my hands through my hair. What a disaster! Why are they so focused on Cassia? It makes no sense. Sophie snapped a few photos of us standing together... so what?

"I'm so sorry about this. I had no idea something like this could happen."

"Really?" Phoebe asks, one eyebrow arched higher than humanly possible. This is one formidable woman and not someone I'd ever want to cross. "That's hardly credible, Mr. Rossi, given you've been hiding out in your New York apartment for months."

Now she's calling me Mr. Rossi. This is going from bad to worse.

I gaze at the counter, seeking some sort of reassurance from Cassia, praying she isn't completely through with me. Cassia glances up and our eyes lock, but then her lower lip trembles. She turns away, but not before I see her swipe her cheeks. She's been crying.

I blink away the dampness in my own eyes and stare out the window at the two trucks parked across the street. I sense Phoebe glaring at me, so I turn back to face her. "I've been at the mercy of the tabloids for a long time, so it's not unexpected that some paparazzi would track me down here. But what I don't understand is why they're targeting Cassia. And why there are so many of them."

"You haven't said or done anything to encourage them?"

"Of course not!" Now I'm getting hot under the collar, and that's not just a figure of speech. I'm downright indignant. "I'd never do something to harm Cassia!"

Phoebe leans back, folds her arms across her chest, and cocks her head to one side, clearly assessing my sincerity. And then something very strange happens.

Across the restaurant, the gargoyles mimic Phoebe's gestures. Five little stone creatures cross their arms and tilt their heads at me. I can't afford to be distracted by this weird synchronicity, so I tuck it away in the back of my mind, where I've stored all the other freakish stuff I've witnessed since arriving in Sam's peculiar little town.

Phoebe Spellman gives me a curt nod, rises from her seat, and picks up the coffee pot and juice carafe. "I'm going to give you the benefit of the doubt for now. But if I find out you've involved my niece or great-niece in some cheap publicity stunt, you'll regret ever setting foot in Riddle Hill."

There's no way I'm going to tussle with Phoebe Spellman. She's scarier than anything I thought I saw at Howling Shores Pub.

"Yes, ma'am," I reply meekly. One thing you learn when you group up in Tennessee is when to keep your mouth shut and take your lumps like a man.

"Meanwhile," says Phoebe, pointing out the window, "do something about those trucks."

"What do you have in mind?"

"I don't know, bring them coffee, let them take some photos, and answer a few questions. Maybe they'll move on once they're satisfied."

I shake my head. "I don't think they're leaving anytime soon." The truth is, I've never dealt with the media by myself. Roxie and Junior were always on hand to redirect and deflect.

But Phoebe is glaring at me again, and now so are the gargoyles.

I throw my hands up in defeat. "Fine, you win. I'll carry out enough coffee and pastries for two trucks of hungry paparazzi, and we'll see what happens."

Phoebe nods. "I'll place your order."

AFTER OLIVIA BOARDS her bus and I finish my boiled eggs and toast, Phoebe brings me a cardboard tray of to-go coffees and two bags of pastries. I thank her, and she says, "Oh, don't thank me. I've added it to your bill."

She sniffs and returns to Cassia, who's standing behind the counter looking so lovely and forlorn that I want to rush over, apologize for this mess I've somehow created, and tell her my true feelings.

Instead, I square my shoulders, zip up my parka, and march out the door armed with hot coffee and good intentions.

The paparazzi roll down the frosted windows of their

trucks and start clicking away on their cameras as I cross the street. A few of them hop out, probably so they can shove a lens in my face for a closeup.

They're looking neater today, definitely more cleaned up. Their hair is combed back from their faces, and they appear to have normal-sized ears and noses, so I don't know what I was seeing last night. But they still smell like they took a dip in rancid cooking oil. I want to hold my nose, but I can't afford to anger them, so I become a six-foot-tall mouth breather.

"Morning, gentlemen." I smile broadly. One of the guys takes the tray of coffee off my hands, and someone else takes the bags of pastries.

"Thanks," says the fellow who's passing out the coffee. He's younger than the rest, possibly an understudy for the more senior photographer next to him. "Hey, Will, how do you feel about Roxie's announcement?"

"Which one?" I wonder if maybe I've missed something important during the past week. I'm not scouring social media the way I do when I'm in New York.

"She's just signed a book and movie contract to tell her life story. She'll be starring as herself in the movie," replies the kid, while his buddies take some more close-ups. "The producers will be looking for a no-name singer to play you." This kid's meaner than a hungry grizzly.

I attempt to restrain myself from rolling my eyes on camera, but there probably are a few photos of me looking perplexed. I smile. "Roxie is a talented woman. I wish her well."

"How about a few photos of you with your new girl?"

shouts someone else. By now they've all piled out of their vehicles and surrounded me, snapping photos and jostling me in an intimidating sort of way.

I'm starting to sweat inside my heavy parka. "She's not my new girl, fellas."

"Sure looked like you were together last night, the way you had your arms wrapped around her and her cute little daughter."

"Just leave Cassia and Olivia out of this," I growl and then immediately regret mentioning their names.

"That would be Cassia Spellman and Olivia Taylor?" prompts the mean kid.

"How'd you two meet all the way up here? It's practically the North Pole," grunts an old geezer with yellow teeth. Then he mutters something about pretty faeries dating dumb rockstars and what's the world coming to. He's obviously two cans short of a full case.

"Was Cassia Spellman the real reason behind your break-up with Roxie?"

"What? Not at all." I'm rapidly losing control of the situation.

There are so many paparazzi in the street now that cars are swerving to avoid us. But no one honks. The drivers slow down to take a look, a few even waving at us. Not like New York; the horns would be blasting from the eastside all the way to midtown.

"The way we heard it," says the guy with yellow teeth, "you were the one who asked Roxie for the divorce."

"What? Who told you that?" I ask, finally realizing

I'm in way over my head. Just then a squad car pulls up and a huge bear of a police officer steps out.

"You're tying up traffic and creating a hazard," the officer barks at the paparazzi. "Move it along or I'll be giving out tickets like Christmas candy." He looks over at me and says, "I believe the mayor would like a word with you, Mr. Rossi. He's in his office at the fire station."

"Yes sir, officer." I can't remember the last time I've been so happy to see a cop. I want to throw my arms around him right there on Main Street. I skirt around the photographers, sprint the three blocks to the fire station, and dash into the blue lobby with relief.

Jake immediately emerges from his office down the hall—he's obviously been waiting for me—and nods brusquely. "Will, come inside and have a seat."

Jake ushers me into his office and closes the door. Wondering whether I'm about to get an old-fashioned tongue-lashing, I perch on the edge of the chair across from Jake's dark oak desk. He sits down, opens the browser on his laptop, and turns the screen around so it's facing me.

I gape at a photo of me, my arms around Cassia and Olivia, running from the school last night. The caption reads, *Is she behind the break-up of Roxie and Rossi?*

Jake stabs his finger at the photo and asks angrily, "Can you tell me what's going on here?"

I shake my head, feeling slightly nauseous. "I don't know. It's almost like someone is feeding them a story."

"Are you using my sister and niece to help advance your career?" Jake glares at me.

"No! And I resent this line of questioning, first from

Phoebe and now from you. And I'll tell you the same thing I told her: I'd never do anything to hurt Cassia or Olivia." Shaking my head, I add, "There's something very fishy here, and I'm afraid I just made it ten times worse."

"What do you mean?" Jake huffs, leaning forward in his chair.

I tell him about my latest run-in with the paparazzi on Main Street, which I admit to mishandling terribly. Jake shakes his head, his mouth set in a firm line. "I don't see how they could have known Cassia's and Olivia's surnames if you didn't tell them."

"I can't understand it myself, but I swear, the first time I mentioned their names—completely by accident and because I'm a walking media disaster—was this morning." I pause, considering the events of last night. "Although Cassia did seem pretty upset when her ex showed up at the restaurant last night. Is it possible he could have called one of his pals in the media and said something?"

Jake bolts out of his chair. "Derek's in town? No way!"

Jake calls Phoebe and paces around the small office as the two of them discuss the paparazzi-plus-Derek situation, while I listen to the one-sided conversation.

My attention wanders until it settles on a poster tacked up behind Jake's head, listing all of the activities for the Riddle Hill Holly Festival, beginning with the annual snowball fight, weather permitting, and culminating in the Children's Pageant on Christmas Eve. Probably another reason Jake is so anxious to send both the paparazzi and Derek packing. The man wants his town, and his family, back to normal.

Jake glances over at me and says before he hangs up, "He's sitting right here. Yep, I'll tell him."

I sit up straight. "Am I being run out of Riddle Hill on a rail, Mr. Mayor?"

Jake cracks a half-smile. "Not exactly, but you're on the right path. We'd like you to give the dogs a long walk and then go for a ride. Explore Door County. Here, I'll circle a few areas of interest."

Jake marks up a map and hands it to me. I trace the route with my finger. "It'll take me all day to drive around visiting these 'areas of interest.' And it'll keep the paparazzi busy, bored, and away from Cassia and Olivia."

Jake nods. "They'll go home when they realize there's no story. And so will Derek."

I remember the happy look on Olivia's face when she saw her dad. "But won't that disappoint Olivia? She clearly loves her father."

Jake sighs. "Derek's been disappointing Olivia all her life, and he's going to keep on disappointing her. He can't help himself. There's nothing we can do about it, except shower her with extra love. And I can't begin to tell you how badly he's hurt Cassia. Everyone's better off when Derek's in California."

I stand up and offer my hand to Jake, which he shakes. "I'll do anything I can to make this right."

Jake compresses his lips, frowning. "One more thing. Please stay away from the café, and from Cassia and Olivia, until this blows over. Phoebe will deliver anything you need."

"Fine," I say. "I get it."

I walk outside into the bright winter sunshine, retrieve my shades from inside my parka, and slip them on. I spent the past several months in stealth mode in New York, hiding out from everyone—friends, fans, and photographers alike—and I can do it again.

But I feel like I've just been kicked in the gut.

Having breakfast at the café is one of the high points of my day, because I get to see Cassia. The other high point is anything else that involves seeing, nuzzling, or kissing Cassia. But now she can't look at me without crying.

I'll avoid the café for now, like I promised Jake.

But there's nothing he can say or do that'll keep me from seeing Cassia again. I'm going to beg her for one more chance to demonstrate my feelings for her—and to prove I'm nothing like Derek Taylor.

CHAPTER 26

LOVE TRIANGLE

CASSIA

THURSDAY AFTERNOON

As I refill the dessert carousel at the end of the countertop, I shake my head at the gargoyles beneath it. They were misbehaving earlier with Will, and now they're being just as snarky with me; they're pretending to be snapping photos of me with their three-fingered hands. Totally rude.

Phoebe answers her phone and then takes the call in her office next to the kitchen. I figure the call has something to do with Will, the paparazzi, and the sudden appearance of Derek, and I'm dying to listen in but force myself to continue working.

I'm clearing a table when I notice Phoebe's returned to the front. I drop off the dirty dishes for scrubbing and join her at the counter. "Fill me in before my curiosity kills me," I whisper.

Phoebe hands me her phone. I take one look at her

open browser, and my stomach sinks to my knees. It's an online post with a photo of Will, his arms around me and Olivia, dashing from the school to my car. Will appears determined, his jaw set. Olivia seems surprised, and I look positively terrified, my mouth agape and my eyes widened.

But it's the caption that makes me queasy, *Is she behind the break-up of Roxie and Rossi,* with an arrow pointing at my head. "How can they make up such lies?"

"I have no idea. But they get away with it most of the time." Phoebe purses her lips. "Under the circumstances, Will is going to avoid you until this blows over. Jake is sending him on a 'tour of Door County' for the day, in the hopes that'll draw the paparazzi off. We want those nasty goblins to see there's no story here so they leave."

"I hope it works... but I think it'll take more than a simple diversion to send them packing."

Despite the obnoxious photo and caption, and my tearful resolution to distance myself from Will, I'm disappointed he so readily agrees to avoid me. I don't know what to think, who to believe, and how to manage this paparazzi mess on my own. Can I trust Will? How much of this could he have prevented? And why has Derek turned up all of a sudden? My head keeps spinning, but I don't have any answers.

After my shift, I remove my apron, smooth my burgundy sweater over my jeans, and slip on my puffer coat. I glance out the picture window and don't see anyone pointing a camera back at the restaurant. I call out to Phoebe and Nash, "I'm heading over to the inn to see Mona. We need to go over a few details for Sophie's wedding. I'll be back in time to meet Olivia's bus. Derek said he would be picking her up."

Nash says, "Hang on a minute, Cassia. I'll walk over with you."

I glance at my uncle. "It's a couple of blocks, in broad daylight, in Riddle Hill. I'll be fine."

Nash zips his jacket over his chef-sized bulk. "I don't want anyone confronting you while you're alone."

I don't object to his overprotectiveness. Nash has been a hoverer ever since I lost my parents. And Jake is no better. Fortunately, Sophie and Phoebe were around to counterbalance all that male hovering, although even Phoebe is hovering today.

Nash insists we exit through the kitchen door at the rear of the café. When we arrive a few minutes later at the inn without any paparazzi in pursuit, I kiss Nash on the cheek and tell him I'll see him later.

I find Mona in the inn's Victorian-style lobby, sitting behind the antique mahogany desk used for checking in guests. I pull up an extra chair, and we run through the final details for my cousin's wedding.

We double-check the food, beverages, decorations, and floral arrangements, and confirm we're in good shape for the wedding ceremony and reception. However, we're both concerned about the goblin paparazzi and decide to add an extra layer of security, especially since Will is performing on Saturday night. Every wedding guest and their kid brother knows about it by now. Mona speaks with her contact at the police station, who agrees to rustle up some off-duty cops willing to work security at the inn.

I breathe a sigh of relief, feeling better already about the extra backup for Saturday. "Well, I think we're as ready as we can be." I close my tablet and stow it in my purse.

Mona teases me. "Just so long as you can stay out of the limelight. We don't need any more goblins snapping photos of you making googly eyes at Will Rossi!"

"Ha-ha. Very funny." I roll my eyes. As I slip on my coat for the short walk to the café, Mona puts out her hand, waving me back to the front desk. "I think you better see this before you go."

Mona turns her laptop around so I can see the latest post. At least Olivia isn't in this photo, which shows Will's arm around me inside Sophie's bakery, spliced next to Derek looking directly at the camera, chiseled chin jutted forward in dismay. Mona reads the caption out loud, "Rossi Love Triangle? Girlfriend's Ex is Derek Taylor of Doctors and Nurses." She looks at me. "Something shifty is going on here."

I sit back down, my legs wilting beneath me. My phone rings, and I pick up when I see it's Jake. "Did you see the latest photo?" I can hear the barely controlled anger in Jake's voice.

"Derek is meeting me at the café in about twenty minutes to pick up Olivia. I'm going to get to the bottom of this," I say with more conviction than I feel.

"I may pop over myself, for a little moral support."

I grimace. "I don't think that's such a good idea, since the two of you can't stand each other."

"I'm still coming over. This whole thing has gotten way out of hand," Jake grumbles.

As I hang up, my phone pings with three texts from Sophie, all apologizing for posting the bakery photos, with lots of sad faces and exclamation points.

Mona says, "Cheer up. They'll move on to another story soon enough, and this will be all forgotten."

"But in the meantime, it's like starring in a reality TV show. I don't know how Will stands it." I get up for the second time to leave. Jogging back to the café, I zigzag through the alley to avoid seeing anyone.

When I open the back door, I hear raised voices in the now-closed restaurant. Nash and Will are asking Derek to explain the latest online photo, while Phoebe is reminding them Olivia will be arriving soon and to keep their voices down. Everyone's milling around in front of the counter, and the gargoyles are hopping up and down, making vulgar gestures with their hands.

I didn't expect to see Will here in the café confronting my ex; I'm so surprised I'm temporarily speechless. My heart starts thumping hard, and my breath comes in short little rasps, because Will isn't avoiding me at all. Instead he's taking on Derek!

Now I just wish the paparazzi—and Derek and the gargoyles—would all disappear so I could have an actual conversation with Will. There's only one positive in all this commotion; I've been able to manage the extra stress without going all faerie.

"Aren't you supposed to be driving around to draw the paparazzi away?" Phoebe asks Will.

Will nods without taking his eyes off Derek. "I was halfway across the county when I saw the latest photo.

It's clear to me why Derek is here, and it's not to see his daughter."

Jake enters through the back door and rolls his eyes, probably because Will didn't stick with the plan. Then Olivia's yellow bus pulls to a stop in front of the café. The door opens to let her exit. Derek nods at the room as if it's his stage, adjusts his bright blue scarf—the same shade as his eyes—and walks outside.

I follow Derek and mouth, "Stay put!" to everyone else. Not that I expect anyone to listen. My family is the loving, interfering sort. They all grab their jackets and pile out the door after me, including Will.

Olivia bounds down the steps of the bus and hugs me, then Derek. That's when she notices Will, Jake, Phoebe, and Nash, standing in front of the café, watching us. Olivia asks me in a small voice, "Is everything okay, Mommy?"

I'm about to reassure her when a photographer steps around from the right side of the café, and another one comes around the left corner, snapping photos of Olivia, Derek, me, and Will, who's moved over to stand next to me. A truck pulls up and double-parks, spilling four more goblins onto the sidewalk, taking photos and shouting questions at Will and me.

A small crowd of onlookers gathers on the sidewalk on either side of us and across the street, in front of Sophie's bakery, to watch the real-life celebrity drama unfolding in front of them.

Will puts his hands up to block two of the photographers. "You've taken enough photos, and we're not answering any more questions."

Jake steps in front of the new arrivals, blocking several more. "You heard Mr. Rossi. It's time for you to leave."

Derek spreads his hands and smiles winsomely at the cameras. "Come on now, fellas, there's no cause for rudeness."

Jake spins on his heels, stalks over to Derek, and stops abruptly in front of him. Patting the lapels of Derek's camel hair coat, he whispers so softly only Derek and I hear him say, "Time for you to go too."

Will clears his throat and addresses Derek. "Didn't you come to pick up Olivia so the two of you could go shopping for her Christmas gifts and then out to dinner? I think you mentioned Sturgeon Bay?"

Derek's eyes flicker over at Will, and he works his jaw into a smile. Derek turns to Olivia and says, "Olivia, honey, I think it's time for us to head to Sturgeon Bay."

As Olivia slips her hand inside Derek's and they walk toward his parked car, I call out, "It's a school night, Derek. Please have her home by eight-thirty." Derek waves his hand to acknowledge he's heard me. He'll still drop Olivia off late, but hopefully before nine o'clock.

A squad car pulls up alongside the double-parked truck in the street. The same huge officer who showed up earlier this morning gets out of his car and slams the door shut. Marvin is not only Jake's friend, he's also a member of his pack. He approaches the cluster of goblin paparazzi and barks, "You're disturbing the peace and creating a traffic hazard. Now clear out."

An old cameraman shouts, "We'll move the truck, but the First Amendment says we can take photos if we want." The rest of the paparazzi mumble something similar, and my heart sinks, because Marvin grunts but doesn't argue the point—which means we're going to be stuck with these awful goblins for a while.

Several paparazzi head to the truck, but the rest of them keep taking photos.

"Come on, let's go back inside," mutters Nash, ushering us into the café. The paparazzi attempt to follow, but Nash and Jake—one big, angry, kitchen faerie and an even bigger, angrier werewolf—block the goblins from entering.

"Back off," Jake growls. "This is private property, and you're not invited."

The oldest goblin shrugs. "Fine. But like I said to the copper over there, we have our rights too." He turns away and the others fall in behind him.

I'm shaking so hard my teeth are chattering. Will reaches out, engulfing one of my trembling hands in his. "Take deep breaths, Cassia. You're safe, and they're gone for now."

"But they'll be back!" I cry as tears spring into my eyes. "They'll never leave us alone!"

CHAPTER 27
CAFÉ CONFESSIONS

WILL

LATER THURSDAY

I pull Cassia into my arms as she sobs into my shoulder, trembling and frightened. I want to soothe this beautiful woman whose life has been invaded by the nastiest paparazzi I've ever encountered. And while I'm angry at them, most of my wrath is directed at Derek Taylor, who's involved somehow. He obviously used his ex-wife and young daughter to advance his own agenda, which I find unconscionable.

Jake must agree because he says, "It's no coincidence Derek showed up here at the same time the paparazzi descended on us. He must've tipped off a friend or two in the tabloids."

Nash runs a hand over his bald head and sighs. "We may be stuck with those darned gob... er... paparazzi for now, but with a little encouragement, Derek will be on his way."

Cassia lifts her head from my shoulder. "Oh no, Uncle Nash. Not again."

Nash shrugs. "It's fine, honey."

Cassia cries harder, and my heart breaks to see her this way. Phoebe steps up, places an arm around Cassia, and gently guides her away from me and toward the back of the restaurant. I'm torn between wanting to stay close by Cassia's side and needing to understand Nash's comments.

As Phoebe and Cassia pass by the stone gargoyles, they bow their heads as if in solidarity with Cassia. It's the weirdest thing; I can't quite explain it, but they *seem almost alive* to me.

I frown at the gargoyles but turn back to Nash and Jake for an explanation. "What does Cassia not want you to do?"

"She doesn't want me to give Derek any more 'encouragement,'" replies Nash. "However, I find Derek is much more agreeable when I accompany my suggestions with hard, cold cash."

"In other words," explains Jake, "Nash has to bribe Derek into behaving like a decent adult."

Nash says, "I really don't mind, since it helps Cassia and Olivia in the end."

All I want is to enfold Cassia in my arms and keep her safe from such pain and disappointment. I commit right then to never causing her that kind of heartache.

Jake checks his phone. "I've got to get back to the station. Ping me if anything pops up."

After he leaves, Phoebe rejoins us. "Cassia will be out shortly. She's feeling better. I think perhaps Nash and I should head home now, and the two of you can stay holed up here for a while longer."

Nash nods. "Excellent suggestion. In fact, why don't you and Cassia fix yourselves something to eat and wait out the paparazzi—or at the very least, make them wait until you're ready to face those goblins again."

"Goblins?" I scratch the stubble on my chin, confused by Nash's word choice. "What a coincidence. That's what Olivia calls them too."

Phoebe and Nash exchange a glance before she replies, "It's not such a coincidence, when you consider we're a fairly isolated community. Even our vocabulary is rather provincial."

I shrug. "I think it's a rather colorful description. Brings up all sorts of images in my mind."

Phoebe and Nash smile, wish me a goodnight, and leave through the rear door. I sit down in my favorite booth, but with the shade drawn I'm unable to see outside. I check my phone and find emails and messages from my family and friends, who ask if I'm alright and who's the pretty woman in the online posts. Sam sounds more worried about Cassia than me, which is fair.

And then there's Mack, who congratulates me on raising my online profile, claiming it'll be easier for him to book some new gigs for me. I'm repulsed by Mack's attitude, but I can't deal with him at the moment. At least I've set some things in motion that'll make me less dependent on him in the future. But for now, I still need Mack and his connections.

Cassia is back, and she slips into the seat across from me. She's washed the tears from her face and applied fresh lipstick, but I can see right through the brave smile she's attempting to give me. She's been hurt again by her ex-husband, and she's probably wondering whether she can trust me.

I reach across the table, grasp Cassia's hands in mine, and bring them up to my lips for a kiss. "I'm so sorry. I never meant for you and Olivia to be chased by paparazzi because of me. If I'd known this would happen, I wouldn't have volunteered to watch Sam and Estee's dogs, and—"

"Oh, Will," Cassia interrupts me just as I'm about to tell her how I feel. Her mouth is trembling slightly.

I lean across the table to kiss her perfect, pink lips, slipping one hand behind her neck to draw her closer. I want to take her into my arms again, but there's a table between us. And it's clear Cassia has something to say, which is a good thing. I want her to feel free to speak her mind.

I sit back down, and Cassia takes a deep breath before continuing. "I'm sorry too, and I'm so ashamed by Derek's behavior. He's the one who fed the rumor mill, even supplying Olivia's name to the press. If not for Derek, I don't think we'd be plagued by so many paparazzi, and such nasty ones at that."

"I have to agree they're a pretty awful bunch. And have you noticed their odor?" I grimace. "Like cooking oil that's gone bad."

"I didn't realize you could smell them too," says Cassia.

"Can't everyone?" I ask. "They stink so badly I have to hold my breath around them."

Cassia brings a hand to her mouth and snorts. I arch an eyebrow at her, which brings on some giggles. I start to chuckle and before long, we're both laughing out loud.

As I gaze at this stunning woman sitting across from me, her green eyes sparkling with laughter after shedding so many tears, my heart squeezes in my chest. I have to tell her how I feel right now, before I lose my nerve.

I reach across the table once more and grip her hands firmly, willing her to believe me. "If I'd not agreed to watch Sam's dogs, I never would've met you, which would've been a devastating loss." I pause for emphasis. "As it stands now, my life without you is quite… unthinkable."

Cassia tilts her head, gazing at me from beneath her bangs. "Before you came to Riddle Hill, my life was sweet at times, and always safe, predictable. But now—"

She stops, and I'm sinking toward despondency, certain she's going to tell me to get lost, nicely but firmly. "But now?" I prompt, wincing slightly.

"Now I'm sitting in a closed café with the famous—or perhaps infamous?—Will Rossi, who says he likes me. There are horrid paparazzi outside, waiting to pounce on us when we leave, who won't give us a moment's peace until after Christmas. Then there's my precious daughter, who thinks you've hung the moon. And my aunt Phoebe, who's taken your measure and thinks you're pretty special too, convinced you're nothing like Derek."

"What about you, Cassia? How do you feel?"

Cassia shakes her head, and I'm ready to slip beneath the table. "I would think it's obvious by now. I don't roll around in the snow with just any guy, making out with half the town looking on."

"Well I'm glad to hear that," I smirk.

Cassia glances down at our intertwined hands for a moment and then back up at me. A ghost of a smile dances across her mouth, but her eyes are serious as she gazes into mine. "The truth is I think I've lost my head over you... and definitely my heart... and I'm afraid, so afraid of what that means."

I slip out of the booth, tugging Cassia with me until we're standing a hand's width apart. I open my arms wide, and she steps into them, reaching around my waist. We stay locked in that embrace for a minute, perhaps longer, and then I gently lean back, tip up her chin, and lightly kiss her brow, her nose, her cheeks, and finally her lips.

I've never been this happy. Nothing I've done, or achieved, or owned compares to this perfect moment.

Cassia tries to stop my flow of kisses by placing her finger on my lips, but I nibble it. She purses her mouth disapprovingly, but her eyes are twinkling. "We can't stay in here forever, smooching in front of the gargoyles and my ancestors."

"Ancestors?" I ask.

She smiles and extends her hand, waving it around the café. "These are my forebears on the walls."

I notice a gentleman in a navy uniform, with a patch over one eye and a hook for a hand. I'd swear he's just winked at me with his one good eye. "Wow, they're so lifelike. Who painted them?"

Cassia clears her throat. "Oh, various artists through

the years." She takes my hand and leads me toward the back of the restaurant.

"Where are we going?"

"We need to eat."

"You mean I'll finally get to see behind the curtain, where Nash performs culinary magic to create his daily masterpieces?"

Cassia stops walking, her eyes widening. "What magic?"

I burst out laughing. "You should see yourself. You look like I just revealed some deep, dark secret."

She chuckles. "Sometimes I can't tell when you're teasing."

As I follow her into the kitchen, I notice the gargoyles are puckering their lips and blowing us kisses. One of these days I'm going to get Phoebe to tell me the truth about what makes them tick.

CHAPTER 28

QUESADILLAS AND KISSES

CASSIA

Thursday Evening

I put Will to work chopping vegetables while I prep the frying pan and oven. But he keeps pausing in his task to wander over behind me, wrap his arms around me, and draw me back against his chest. My pulse rockets each time Will touches me, kisses me, even looks at me with the same longing I feel for him. I'm a surfer catching wave after wave, balancing on the edge of the crest, but never crashing. This night is pure magic—in the human sense of the word.

And here's the best part: I truly believe I can trust Will. He's proven he's here for me and Olivia.

I lightly slap Will's hands as he reaches around my waist for the fourth time. I turn down the heat under the pan and spin around to face him. "Do I need to finish the veggies for you, Mr. Rossi? Because you're definitely falling down on the job. I don't think you'll last the night."

Will gives me a wicked, little grin. "Oh I can assure you, Miss Spellman, your veggies are safe with me. And I always last the night."

I snort and give him a little push. "Then please deliver them now, Mr. Rossi." He starts to move in for another kiss, but I put my hand on his chest. "I'm speaking of the veggies, sir, not your kisses. My frying pan is ready."

Will arches his eyebrow and smirks. "You don't know how long I've waited to hear those words from your lips."

We both burst out laughing. Eventually, between kisses, giggles, and more kisses, we manage to pull together veggie quesadillas, with tortilla chips, refried beans, guacamole, and plenty of salsa on the side.

I withdraw a crisp Riesling from one of Nash's coolers, which Will opens and pours out for us. It takes us several trips, but we carry our plates of food, the toppings, wine, and sparkling water to the counter out front. As I climb onto the stool next to Will, I give my aunt's gargoyles a hard stare... and those little freaks salute me. Whether they decide to behave or not, at least I won't have to look at them while I'm sitting down.

Will wipes his mouth on a napkin and takes another sip of wine. "I believe you've inherited your family's remarkable talent when it comes to food. That was delicious."

"Thanks... I'm glad you enjoyed it. Although compared to those frozen dinners you've been consuming, I'd think even a boiled egg would taste fantastic."

"True enough." Will grins, and then he pauses and plays with his napkin. "How would you feel if I crashed your Christmas celebrations with your family? Jake invited me to stay at his place over the holiday, but I didn't want to accept without asking you first."

"*Jake invited you?*" I ask, flabbergasted by my brother's thoughtfulness. When Will nods, I say, "That would be wonderful! I'd love for you to stay through Christmas!"

I reach out, grasp Will's hand, and rub the calluses on his fingers, earned through years of guitar playing. He pulls me off the stool and spins me toward himself. My pulse soars as my heart does a happy dance inside my chest. Will cups my face in his hands and kisses me so deeply, so thoroughly, that I'm dizzy. I hold onto his waist so I don't topple backward.

We finally stop, and Will brushes back my hair, which he's managed to unclip at some point. "I need to get you home soon, before Olivia arrives. And you're working tomorrow."

"And I do need my beauty sleep."

"No, you don't, Cassia. You're beautiful just the way you are." Will gives me the sweetest grin and then starts carrying the dishes into the back.

We clean up the kitchen, return to the front, and sort out our coats, hats, and scarves discarded earlier in the evening. I lead us to the back door, but Will puts his hand on the door handle before we step outside. "Do you have your keys ready?"

I hold up the restaurant's keys. "I'm ready to lock up and make a mad dash for the car."

Will nods. "Why don't I drop you off at your condo, and then I'll drive your car back to Sam's. Jake can help me deliver your car later."

"That seems like a lot of work for a short ride home."

"Until we know the paparazzi have moved on, I don't like the idea of you encountering them alone."

I worry my lower lip between my teeth and then nod. "You're right. I don't want to deal with them by myself."

Will flings open the door and steps through first. He tries shielding me as I lock up the door, but it's no use. Cameras are flashing; goblins are shouting questions, and the odor in the alley behind the restaurant turns my stomach.

My hand shakes as I fumble with the key, but I manage to lock up. "Okay," I whisper. "Now!" And we're off, pushing past the paparazzi, who hound us until we've slammed the car doors; then they scurry off, probably into their vehicles.

Will starts my Honda, and we're off, driving as fast as the road conditions allow. Although I live less than two miles from the café, the streets are twisty and hilly, and it's dark. Will parks and dashes up the front stoop with me, as two photographers who must have been parked next door run over, snapping yet more photos. One of the men shouts, "Hey, Will, how about kissing the faerie lady?"

I'm mortified! Don't these goblins observe any of the normal conventions? They know Will is a non-super. Fortunately, Will mishears them, because he replies, "You want me to kiss the fair lady, huh?"

"Yeah! That's right! Go on now, lad."

Will flashes his celebrity grin at me, and I shake my head slightly, but he's already leaning in. He scoops me in his arms, bends me backward with dramatic flair, and plants a kiss on my lips worthy of every classic Hollywood romance ever filmed.

The goblins hoot and holler and take their pictures. Will releases me with a wink and watches as I open my door. "Goodnight, Cassia," he whispers, giving me one last, sweet kiss on the lips.

"Goodnight," I murmur, still reeling from Will, his kisses, and the fact he's staying in Riddle Hill to celebrate Christmas with me and my family—I couldn't ask for a better gift.

It'll be the perfect Christmas.

Brownlee–Barker Wedding

Phoebe Spellman and Nash Brownlee
invite you to share in their joy at the marriage
of their daughter

Sophie Spellman Brownlee
to
L. Theodore "Teddy" Barker

Saturday, December 22
At six o'clock in the evening

Mooncrest Inn
Door County, Wisconsin

Reception to follow

SAGE MAGE SUPPER CLUB

WILL

Friday, December 21

I'm sitting in my SUV in front of the chapel's blue door, waiting for Cassia. Sophie, Teddy, Phoebe, and Nash left for the restaurant about ten minutes ago, along with Olivia and the rest of the bridal party. The rehearsal dinner is at the Sage Mage Supper Club, the same spot where we had Sam and Estee's dinner two weeks ago.

I can hardly believe everything that's happened since then. And it's all good stuff for a change—well most of it. I could live without these stinking paparazzi shoving cameras at me and Cassia at every turn. She's been struggling, close to tears once or twice, especially when they snapped photos at Olivia's bus stop this morning.

But Jake and I paid a visit to the wrinkly geezer with the yellow teeth, who seems to be in charge, and threatened legal action if any more photos of Olivia appear online. He complied, telling us he's "here for the Rossi-

New Girlfriend angle, and that's it. The kid's a small side show, and so long as we have good shots of her fair mama and singing Willy here, we're good."

Jake had to drag me away; I was about to sock the ugly old man.

Cassia comes out of the chapel and pulls the heavy wooden door closed behind her. She's carrying a few items that must have been left behind: a black scarf, a blue mitten, and a wide-brimmed fedora.

I get out of my SUV and open the passenger door for her. The wind is something fierce, whipping up the inn's painted wooden sign, and sending a Christmas wreath tumbling down the street. The paparazzi remain in their vehicles, staying cozy and snapping pictures at us from across the road.

As I climb back behind the wheel, I point at the stray clothing in Cassia's hand. "Looks like you've had a rough night."

Cassia smiles. "Rehearsals can make or break the real thing, as you know. Though come to think of it, you missed most of Sam and Estee's rehearsal, didn't you?"

"True, but I've made up for that lapse by scheduling an extra rehearsal for the Second Chance Band tomorrow. We'll be on fire—no pun intended—for Sophie's wedding."

I start the SUV and pull away from the curb. "How did things go with Olivia and Derek last night?"

Cassia gives me a brief run-down. "Olivia came home very chipper, carrying her gifts for under the tree. Derek actually apologized, which is a rare occurrence. Whether it's his guilty conscience or Nash's 'encouragement' that prompted him, I'll never know. He's back in California by now, where he'll happily stay put until spring at least."

She glances behind us. "I guess they're following us to the restaurant."

"Yeah," I huff. "I was hoping they'd call it a night, after the wild goose chase I took them on today, but no such luck."

"What's it going to take for them to leave, do you think?"

I shrug. "No idea. They're stuck fast for now, so we're just going to have to do our best to ignore them."

Cassia sighs, glancing over at me. "I don't know how you've done this for so long."

"You mean the paparazzi?"

"And the limelight," she says. "It's all so... exhausting."

I pass a slow-moving car before answering. "At first it's totally amazing, like you can't believe it's really happening to you. Then after a while, it begins to take a toll. But it's also part of the cost of fame—you can't be a celebrity without fans, and you can't have fans without giving them what they want—photos, news, and gossip. And those fellas in the trucks behind us are getting all three at the moment."

Cassia tilts her head, like she's not sure she's following me. "So they're getting photos and gossip, whether or not it's true. But what's the news?"

I wait until I've parked the car, and then I turn to face her. I take one of her hands, peel off her glove, and slowly kiss her palm until she trembles. "According to news sources, Will Rossi's in love with his very own 'fair lady.' That's their nickname for you, and I like it."

Cassia leans across the seat and gives me a sweet kiss on the lips. She runs her fingers delicately over my mostly healed eye. "And your 'fair lady' feels the same way about you."

I smile down at her, my heart so full it's overflowing, when bright lights suddenly flash in our faces. Those relentless paparazzi startle us both, snapping photos through the windshield. I can see the apprehension and anxiety creeping back into Cassia's jade-green eyes.

"Not again," I groan. "Ready to run on the count of three?"

Cassia puts on her game face—a brave smile that doesn't quite reach her eyes—and nods. I wait until she's slung her purse over her shoulder, and she's slipped her glove back on her hand. Then I murmur, "One... two... three!"

We open our doors and are surrounded by cameramen with bad breath. I dash around to Cassia's side, grab her hand, and we push through them together. Old yellow-teeth shouts at us, "Hey, Will, care to comment on the rumor you're buying up land out here in the boonies?"

I roll my eyes and grip Cassia's hand harder.

Then two massive guys and two equally muscular gals run interference for us as we dash into the lobby; I suspect they're off-duty firefighters hired by Nash. Those paparazzi won't be crashing the rehearsal dinner with that security detail out front.

I glance up at the knight sitting on top of his steed in

the lobby and shake my head. "He sets quite an example for the rest of us fellas. It's hard to measure up."

Cassia smiles up at me. "I don't need a knight in shining armor."

"No?"

"No," she says. "I need you. I need Will Rossi, the talented, handsome, singer-songwriter from Nashville who's writing his next chapter."

I grin and pull her into my arms, but Phoebe, who must have been waiting for us, stops me cold. "That's enough smooching my niece, Mr. Rossi," she says, although her tone is friendly. "The party's about to begin but we're missing the maid of honor!"

"Coming!" Cassia laughs. I start to follow, but my phone pings.

I tell Cassia to go on without me and then take the call. "Hey, Mack, what's up?"

"You're back in business, Will! Your old friend Mack's got you a sweet gig." As Mack describes it, my heart starts to sink. I'm not familiar with the Nashville "hot spot" where he's booked me. But I thank him anyway and hurry down the corridor where I saw Phoebe and Cassia heading.

The stone flooring echoes underfoot, and the paneled passageway is dark and gloomy. I have no idea which private dining room we're in, and there's no one around to ask. Rather than barging in on someone else's party, I pause outside each thick wooden door, listening.

The first room is silent, so probably unoccupied. I hear the low rumble of all-male voices in the second, so I pass by. But in the third, I hear barking, growling, and snarling. I have a sudden flashback to Howling Shores Pub, with all those monstrous sledding dogs; I break into a cold sweat and race past it. I want to shout Cassia's name, like Sly Stallone at the end of *Rocky*, hollering, "Adrian! Adrian!"

Maybe Cassia senses I'm feeling lost at the moment, because she opens door number four and pops her head out. "There you are! Perfect timing; we're just about to eat."

I practically sprint toward her, so grateful for this woman in my life I want to break into the *Hallelujah* chorus (it's the right season for it), but I restrain the impulse. Besides, I've just finished composing a new Christmas song that I plan to dedicate to Cassia during Sophie's reception. I'm hoping my music and lyrics can convey the depth of my feelings for her and leave no doubt about my intentions.

I give Cassia a peck on the cheek as she loops her arm through mine, leading me to the spot next to hers. I exhale, knowing I'm safe from whatever weirdness is happening down the hall. We're in a different room than last time, but the decorating is just as Old World, with stone floors, black iron chandeliers, and faded tapestries on the walls.

Cassia asks, "Everything alright?"

"Of course," I murmur, although I'm still feeling unsettled, and the snarling sounds outside of door number three aren't the only reason.

I've never heard of the Nashville club where Mack booked me, and I know nearly all of them (or at least I used to). But the music scene has changed since I left

Tennessee, and I need to rely on Mack for guidance. "That was my manager on the phone. He's lined up a six-week engagement for me at a Nashville nightclub."

"Congratulations! You must be excited." Cassia peers closely at me. "Um... you don't seem too thrilled."

I shrug, frowning. "You're right, I'm not exactly over-joyed about this. Don't get me wrong. I'm grateful for the gig, but I feel like I'm taking a big step backward in my career."

"Then why do it?"

I butter a roll as I try to explain my reasoning. "Because it's still work in my profession, and some work is better than none. My manager strongly hinted that opportunities for me to perform are few and far between, at least right now."

"When do you start?"

"My first performance is on New Year's Eve," I reply. "But I'll need to get down there a day or two earlier."

"That's plenty of time," says Cassia.

"Plenty of time for what?"

"To enjoy a real Riddle Hill Christmas." The servers remove the salad plates and replace them with the main course, veal scaloppine with saffron and roasted red potatoes, steamed asparagus, and cranberry chutney.

I glance at her with mock seriousness. "I might need to find a local tour guide, someone who can make sure I'm not missing out on anything Riddle Hill has to offer for the holidays. Do you know anyone?"

"I think that can be arranged."

I rub my hands together. "Great, when does my tour begin?"

"I hope you dressed warmly." Cassia chuckles mischievously.

I peer at her uncertainly. "Why? We're not going ice fishing again, are we? Because I'm definitely under dressed if I'll be hunching over a hole on the frozen bay."

Cassia shakes her head. "No more ice fishing, this week anyway. We're going to the Riddle Hill Sing-Along."

"And that's an outdoor activity?"

"It's Christmas caroling. Of course it's outside."

"Whatever happened to singing inside in the winter, where the heat's on and you don't need to dress in four layers?"

"You're in northern Wisconsin, where we actually like winter."

I raise my hands, palms up. "When it comes to my Riddle Hill full-immersion experience, you're in charge."

"Good, I'm glad that's settled."

After dinner, I drive Cassia and Olivia to the tall Christmas tree in the town square, where a crowd of carolers—and those stupid paparazzi—have gathered, eager to begin. Jake hops on top of a wooden crate and waits for the chattering to settle down. Searching among the crowd of faces, Jake points at me and shouts, "We have one of the best musicians in the country joining us for Christmas this year. Let's give it up for Will Rossi!"

The carolers whistle and applaud, and Jake invites me to lead the singing. Feeling slightly bewildered, I walk up front with Cassia and Olivia. The photographers start pushing toward us, but the Riddle Hill crowd takes no guff. They shove the cameramen back, and suddenly there's a lot of jostling on the sidewalk and street. I'm worried about a fistfight breaking out in front of the children, but then I spot old yellow-tooth, the mean kid, and a few of their colleagues huddling all the way in the back.

"Whew," says Cassia, and I squeeze her hand.

Jake nods toward the back of the crowd and whispers, "Don't worry about the paparazzi; we have a lot of friends here tonight." He hands me a pitch pipe and says, "Just blow into the pipe to get us started. They know the songs by heart."

"But what's the first song? I want to get the pitch right."

"*We Wish You a Merry Christmas.*"

I hum the tune to myself, blow into the pitch pipe, and the carolers burst into song. Olivia slips her hand into Cassia's and mine, walking between the two of us, like a real family. I feel a lump form in my throat, which I clear away so I can keep singing. But the pressure in the back of my throat lingers on, a reminder of all that's missing in my life.

After we finish caroling, we head back to village hall, where I parked my vehicle.

"For a newbie at sing-alongs, you did surprisingly well," says Cassia, teasing me.

"I guess my vocal lessons finally paid off."

"Hmm… I think we've found our lead singer for Christmas Day. We're a family who enjoys singing together—Phoebe at the piano, Jake on guitar—you can bring your own guitar, of course."

"Of course." I give her my most winsome grin.

"But I thought Will has to go back to New York."

Olivia looks up at me and asks, "Are you really staying here for Christmas?"

When I nod, Olivia's face lights up. "Then you can come see me in the Children's Pageant!"

"Wouldn't miss it for the world. I've already asked your mom to get me a special seat, so when you look down the center aisle, you'll see me giving you a thumbs up."

Olivia throws her arms around my waist to hug me, and that lump in the back of my throat returns. I'm incredibly thankful for my gorgeous new girlfriend and her young daughter, and I'm feeling mighty protective too.

I want to be here for Cassia and help her raise Olivia. I want this to be the beginning of something special for us all, which means I need this gig in Nashville.

But I'm not happy about leaving all this behind, even temporarily.

CHAPTER 30
SOPHIE AND TEDDY'S WEDDING

CASSIA

SATURDAY, DECEMBER 22

I help Sophie fasten the sparkly crystal beads around her neck. We both step back to look in the mirror affixed to the closet door inside the chapel's cramped office, which serves as a staging area for brides. My cousin is wearing a floor-length, satin-and-lace, ivory gown with a plunging *V*-neckline and a twenty-foot train that's fit for a faerie princess. "You look gorgeous, Soph," I tell her. "Poor Teddy is going to swoon when he sees you."

My moss-green gown has a sweetheart neckline, slender shoulder straps, fitted lace bodice, and a full, tea-length skirt. I feel a little bit like Tinker Bell, my middle-name sake. I check my updo in the mirror; the stylist tucked my hair behind my ears, and I didn't try to stop her. I figured if Derek and the goblin paparazzi didn't trigger my faerie stress symptoms, neither would my cousin's wedding.

Sophie grins at my reflection. "If you don't capture Will Rossi's heart in that dress then the man is made of stone!"

I shake my head, laughing. "You're as bad as your mother with the matchmaking."

There's a knock on the door, which I cautiously open. Nash pops his bald head inside, compliments our dresses, and then adds, "The natives are getting restless."

"Tell the natives we're about to begin." I shoo my uncle back out the door.

Then I turn to Sophie, my cake-baking, stay-up-late-gossiping best friend and cousin. "I predict a long, happy marriage for you and Teddy. You love each other too much for any other outcome!"

Sophie hugs me gingerly, so as not to mess up our hair, make-up, or dresses. "Thank you for everything you've done to help me get ready for today, and well, for everything else, too."

My eyes begin to well, so I sniffle, straighten my spine, and point at the door. "We better get out there before we both start crying."

Sophie nods. "Just one thing. Make sure you're in position when it comes time for me to toss my bouquet, because I'm determined you catch it. You hear me?"

"Yes, ma'am." I laugh. It might be fun to actually catch the bouquet for a change, given all that Will and I have been talking about these past few days.

I open the door and invite Nash to step inside with Sophie, while I signal to Teddy and Jake that we're ready to begin. Teddy escorts his mother down the aisle, followed by Jake, who guides Phoebe to her seat.

Then the vampire string quartet I hired begins to play Pachelbel's Canon in D. Olivia and Davey, Teddy's nephew, walk slowly down the aisle together. Olivia strews silk rose petals from a basket, while Davey carries both wedding rings attached to a small pillow. He stumbles at the halfway point, but Olivia pauses long enough in her flower-tossing duties to catch him and right the pillow. I bite my lip to keep from chuckling out loud.

Next, I send each bridesmaid and groomsman down the aisle in pairs, until it's my turn to walk with Teddy's brother-in-law to the front of the chapel. I turn around and face the pews filled with friends and family, easily spotting Will in the third row, seated among the Friends of Spellman-Brownlee.

My new boyfriend looks incredibly dashing in his black suit, and when he winks at me, my stomach flutters like the wings of a hundred hummingbirds taking flight. I take several deep breaths to steady my racing heart.

Sophie enters the back of the chapel on Nash's arm, and the guests stand and turn around to face her, their eyes following the bride as she proceeds up the aisle. I love this part of the ceremony, always pausing in my wedding planner duties long enough to catch the groom's reaction as the bride walks toward him. Teddy looks nothing less than enthralled, just as I expect. Sophie hands me her bouquet to hold as the minister begins the ceremony.

We're almost finished, and I hear sniffles from the front of the chapel. The sniffles grow louder, turning into hiccupping sobs. Heads are turning to figure out the source of the noise. Phoebe leans past Nash's bulk to stare across the aisle at Teddy's mother, her face buried in a handkerchief. The tips of Teddy's ears turn bright red.

I stare into the two bouquets I'm holding to keep from giggling out loud. The minister clears his throat and picks up his pace. Before long Sophie and Teddy are exchanging vows and rings, and then sharing their first kiss as husband and wife.

After we wrap up the formal photos in the chapel, a tiny sigh of relief escapes my lips. With Mona and her staff handling the reception dinner, and Jake and Will in charge of entertainment, I feel like I might be able to relax. In fact, this might turn out to be the easiest wedding I've managed all month.

As I enter the inn's side lobby, which is filled with guests chatting and servers circulating with appetizers and drinks, Will slips alongside me with two glasses of white wine. "I know you're technically working, but I hope you're allowed a little refreshment," he says with a wink.

I accept the glass with a chuckle. "As maid of honor, cousin, and best friend of the bride, I think I'm covered."

Will makes no pretense of checking me out in my fancy dress. I sip my wine, trying to steady my pounding heart.

"Your cousin makes a lovely bride," he says with a twinkle in his eye. "But I couldn't take my eyes off you tonight. You're beautiful, Cassia."

I resist the urge to tug a chunk of hair down over my

ears, remembering my updo. "Thanks... " I smile up at him. "You're looking pretty sharp yourself."

Actually, he looks like he just stepped away from a modeling job to get something to drink; I half-expect him to be called back to work. I won't be able to look into those liquid-brown eyes of his much longer without melting into a puddle on the floor.

Mona's assistant comes up to me and whispers, "Everything's under control, except for the groom's mother, who's in the ladies' room having a good cry... and she's getting kind of furry, if you know what I mean."

I know Sophie is worried about her mother-in-law, who wolfs out when she has too much alcohol or gets too emotional—such as at her son's wedding, where she's already been enjoying the champagne and sobbing her heart out.

"Oh, I guess I'd better check on her."

But Will stops me and asks what's the matter. I tell him about Teddy's mom but leave out the part about her getting furry. He nods and turns back to Mona's assistant. "I believe Teddy's sister is standing over there. Would you mind asking her to see to her mother?" He flashes his special grin at the young woman, who nods eagerly and leaves to do his bidding.

I shake my head, laughing. "Where did you learn that skill?"

"What skill?"

"The useful knack of misdirection? Thank you for saving me from playing nursemaid to Teddy's mother for the evening."

Will's eyes crinkle in amusement. "That's because I'm saving you for myself this evening."

With mock seriousness I ask, "Shouldn't you be setting up with the band, Mr. Rossi? I believe you're performing soon."

"We set up before the ceremony, so I'm free for at least another twenty minutes. Care to go for a stroll?" Will winks at me again, and my heart stampedes inside my chest.

He takes my hand and guides me through the ballroom, passing Christmas trees with sparkling burgundy and moss-green ornaments, and tables festooned with white poinsettias, and sprigs of holly, mistletoe, and small, gold-tipped pinecones.

He leads me into the inn's main lobby, in front of the fireplace where I found him two weeks earlier and escorted him back to Estee and Sam's reception. We sit down on the small sofa facing the fire.

"Hmm, this feels good. I could curl up here right now," I say, putting my wine glass on the low table nearby.

Will sets his glass next to mine and takes my right hand, threading my fingers through his. "I could stay here all night, with you right here beside me." Sliding closer on the sofa until our knees touch, Will turns to face me. With his free hand he traces a pattern along my bare arm, sending a surge of tingles down my spine.

I tilt my head up and lean forward, yearning for Will's kiss. He obliges, gently at first, and then he groans as he deepens the kiss. My pulse quickens in my throat, my heart soaring in a dance of pure joy. I want to sink deeper into Will's arms and skip dinner entirely... until an outburst of giggling causes us both to break away.

I take a deep breath, waiting for my heartrate to return to normal.

Will recovers his voice first. Raising his eyebrows, he whispers, "I think we have company."

I murmur, "Over there, behind the drapes."

Will springs up from the sofa and crosses the room. When he pulls aside the heavy drapes that cover the inn's front windows, Olivia and Davey burst into another round of giggles.

I come up beside Will, my hands on my hips. "Olivia Merryweather Taylor, what on earth are you doing hiding behind those drapes? Aunt Phoebe must be looking all over for you."

Olivia says, "Davey wanted to explore the inn, so I came with him to make sure he didn't get lost."

Davey adds, "Olivia knows all about the inn." Olivia smiles sweetly at Davey, and I resist the urge to roll my eyes.

Phoebe dashes into the lobby, worry lines creasing her forehead, until she spots the two children. "Olivia, Davey, come with me please, and don't go wandering off again!" Phoebe shoos them back into the ballroom, where the guests are beginning to filter in for dinner and the musical entertainment.

I turn to Will reluctantly. "Looks like it's time for us to rejoin the party." In this moment, I want nothing more than to pick up where we left off, snuggling on the sofa with him. I'm one hundred percent ready to risk my heart again.

"I'll come find you later," promises Will. He cups my face in his hands and bends down for one brief but tender kiss. Then he strides toward the ballroom where the band will be performing shortly.

I'm quickly absorbed in my duties, as both maid of honor and wedding planner, running interference for everyone with a question or problem, including Teddy's mother, Mona and her assistant, and even Rob Wolferman, whom Sophie invited when she thought Rob and I might become a couple. Instead, Rob taps me on the shoulder after my maid-of-honor speech and launches into one of his real-estate stories.

This time, though, I pause long enough to actually listen, since Rob is talking about Goldmeadow, a lovely piece of property with a barn-like building where concerts are held all summer long. I adore the old place, which is owned by an elderly werewolf couple.

"What do you mean, you have no idea who's buying it?" I ask.

"A limited liability company is purchasing Goldmeadow," explains Rob.

"And you don't know who's behind the LLC?"

He shrugs. "Nope, everything's been worked out by lawyers. All I know is the contract was signed today."

I stammer, "I can't believe it. I've gone to concerts there every summer since I was a kid and planned to continue the tradition with Olivia."

Rob pats my arm. "I hate to be the bearer of bad news. Well, I see one of my clients sitting over there. Merry Christmas, Cassia."

"Merry Christmas," I say half-heartedly.

There's a drumroll, and everyone stops talking as Jake steps up to the microphone. He instructs the ladies in the room to line up for the bouquet toss. I position myself behind Sophie's right shoulder, exactly where she told me to stand.

The bouquet sails over Sophie's shoulder and heads straight for my outstretched hands. But suddenly Teddy's mother swoops in to snatch the bouquet just as it's grazing my fingertips, waving it over her head like a wide receiver celebrating a touchdown. Sophie turns around to look at her new mother-in-law with a stiff smile.

I gape at Mrs. Barker, who's whooping over her victorious bouquet snatch. For some reason I can't explain, I feel ridiculously let down, deflated even, and I struggle to shake off my mood.

I console myself with listening to Will and the Second Chance Band, which sounds pretty amazing for a group of firefighting werewolves and one very hot human. When the band finally takes a break, I notice Will frowning at his phone. He hops off the dais and heads toward the lobby, probably to return a call. I hope everything's alright, especially with his mom.

He returns to the ballroom just as the band is wrapping up their break. I can tell by the set of his shoulders something's wrong. He pulls Jake aside to tell him something, and Jake nods. I want to rush over and help Will through whatever he's dealing with, but the band takes up their instruments again.

Then Sophie gives me a panicked look, and I quickly realize why; Teddy's mother needs to be escorted to the restroom again before she starts howling. I can spot a bushy tail peeking out from beneath her gown, and her nose is growing into a snout. I hurry over and whisper in her ears, which are now large and furry, "You're shifting again, Mrs. Barker! Let's go find the lounge where you can wolf out in peace."

Teddy's mom gives me a friendly yip and scampers alongside me, until we near the dessert table. I guess she loves chocolate as much as champagne and bridal bouquets, because Mrs. Barker snatches up a whole chocolate cream pie, buries her face in it, and chows down. I hear Will's voice falter, and Jake sings louder to cover the misstep.

Holy moonbeams! Will must have seen Mrs. Barker in all her fuzzy glory.

"Oh, Mother!" cries Bella Barker, Teddy's sister. "You're making a scene again!" Bella firmly grasps her mother's arm and drags her out of the ballroom. I can hear Mrs. Barker whining all the way to the restrooms on the other side of the lobby.

I head toward the dais, determined to enjoy the rest of the night. The band's almost finished for the evening, and I don't want to miss a single song. Will has obviously recovered from the shock of seeing Mrs. Barker's wolf-form gulping down a full pie, because his voice is as amazing as ever.

Sophie and Teddy spot me swaying to the music and pull me onto the dance floor. The three of us dance together, and then more friends join us, and before long we're all laughing and singing along with Will, Jake, and the rest of the band.

I feel like it's the perfect ending to Sophie's wedding weekend.

I gaze up at Will, and the smile on my lips freezes in place. My heart turns to ice inside my chest. Will glances away, crooning to a bunch of older ladies and men dancing nearby. But I saw the look he gave me—a combination of fear, sadness, and downright desperation—and I don't think I can blame it on Mrs. Barker's bushy tail.

No, something else has upset Will.

Who was on the phone just now? And what did they say that's left Will so bereft?

CHAPTER 31

THE RIDDLE IN RIDDLE HILL

WILL

SATURDAY, VERY LATE

Cassia can tell something's wrong, and she's one hundred percent correct. What's worse, I have only myself to blame for my predicament.

I spoke with Mack a short while ago, after receiving three texts and a voicemail urging me to get in touch. I almost didn't return his call because I figured it was bad news. And I was right.

"Finally, you call me back!" Mack shouted into the phone. I could hear him chomping on the end of an unlit cigar, still trying to kick his smoking habit. There was loud music in the background; he was probably observing an act. "Look, there's been a change of plan. You need to get down here tomorrow."

"What? Tomorrow? But the gig doesn't start until New Year's Eve."

"That's why I've been calling," hollered Mack. I had to hold the phone away from my ear. "The other act canceled. Flu or something, and the club needs you to perform on Christmas Eve."

I wasn't about to let someone else's problem ruin my Christmas with Cassia. I gripped the phone more tightly and said, "Mack, I appreciate that you're looking out for me, but I have plans for Christmas. Important plans that—"

Mack stopped me cold. "Look, Will," he yelled. "I've got to be straight with you. You don't have any other options at the moment, and if you don't commit right now to showing up for Christmas Eve, you can kiss the entire gig goodbye."

I felt like I just swallowed a belly full of lead. I cleared my throat but nothing came out. Mack waited a few more beats and then shouted, "So what's your answer? I need to let the club manager know right now."

I pinched the bridge of my nose, debating whether to say no, but realizing I was stuck. I really, really need this job. I'll have to put my Christmas plans with Cassia on the back burner. "Fine, message received," I mumbled. "I'll be there."

A jumble of thoughts tripped through my head after that call. Cassia is just starting to trust me. But how can she believe I'm the real deal when I have to leave tomorrow, after telling her I'd be here for Christmas?

When I shuffled back to the ballroom to play our last set, I told Jake to skip the new number I'd written. It's about small towns, second chances, and finding true love —and Christmas—in the most unexpected places. I planned to surprise Cassia tonight by dedicating the song to her, but there's no point now. I'm pretty sure she's going to break up with me when I deliver my news.

Then, to make matters even worse, Mrs. Barker starts acting up again as soon as we resume playing. *And this time, I see a furry tail sticking out of her dress.*

There's no way Jake can explain that away—especially after the woman sticks her face in a pie and gobbles the whole thing down—just like a real wolf!

Okay, so I'm totally freaked out, but I'm also a professional. I've performed with fevers, rashes, even a broken leg (I sat on a chair). I manage to get through the last set of songs, my eyes wandering over to my sweet Cassia, who's having a grand old time.

At one point, our eyes meet, and I have to look away. I know how this night is going to end, and it's not going to be good. I consider calling Mack back and turning down the job, but I can't afford to lose the only gig in the works.

After we finish our last song, I pose for a lot of photos and selfies, forcing myself to smile. Then I take my time packing up my red guitar, dreading the conversation I'll be having shortly with Cassia. I shake hands with Jake and the other band members, thanking them for the opportunity to perform. Jake claps his hand on my back and tells me he'll have a room ready for me tomorrow night, after Sam and Estee get back to town.

I won't be anywhere near Riddle Hill by then, but I don't tell him that, not yet anyway. First, I need to speak with Cassia, who's gazing at me uncertainly.

I walk up to her, my guitar case in hand. "Can we talk somewhere private?"

Cassia nods, a small frown line forming between her brows. "Sure, there's a room on the other side of the lobby we can use."

She leads the way, past the inn's twelve-foot Christmas tree and cheery fire, down another hallway and into a wood-paneled library that smells of old books, leather, and something else, something nasty and moldering. I figure it's mouse droppings and try to ignore it. Cassia wrinkles her nose in the most adorable way, and it takes every ounce of willpower I possess not to pull her into my arms.

We sit opposite each other, in stiff wingback chairs covered in a nubby, maroon fabric. The room is dimly lit, which suits me just fine. I don't want her to see my face when I fall apart. I keep running my hands through my hair, my stomach clenched in knots, as I try to find the right words.

Instead, I blurt out, "Something's come up with that job in Nashville. I'm sorry, but I have no choice. I have to leave in the morning, but I'll be back as soon as my gig is over."

There, it's out in the open. Not exactly an eloquent performance, but it's the truth.

Cassia seems confused, and her frown lines deepen. "What do you mean? What's come up?"

I explain about my call with Mack, and his not-so-subtle threat that I'll lose the entire gig, which is now seven weeks long, if I don't turn up in Nashville by tomorrow night. "My first performance is on Christmas Eve."

Cassia sniffles and clears her throat a few times, and I'm already feeling like the biggest heel ever. The timing of this couldn't be worse. "I thought it was supposed to start on New Year's Eve."

I reach across the gap between our chairs, but she pulls back her hands, twisting them in her lap. "I thought so too," I say gently. "But the other performer got sick or something, and the club needs me now."

"The *club* needs you now?" she asks in a small voice. Her eyes are starting to well, and so are mine. "What about me? About us?"

"Oh Cassia," I drop my head in my hands. "I'm sorry about this, but I really have to go; I can't afford to lose this job. But I'm coming back, and I'll stay longer next time. We'll celebrate Valentine's Day together, I promise!"

Cassia holds up her hand. "Don't make promises you can't keep. Just. Don't."

I sputter, "That's not fair. I keep my promises."

"I guess you won't be needing that ticket to the Children's Pageant anymore."

I smack my forehead with the heel of my hand. I *had* promised Olivia, and now I'm breaking that promise. "I'm really sorry to miss the pageant. Let me explain it to Olivia, tell her how much I was looking forward to seeing her perform."

Cassia rolls her lips together and stands up. Her voice starts to quiver as she whispers, "Don't bother, I know you're busy. I'll tell Olivia."

Rising from my seat, I say, "But I really want to tell her myself. Please." I reach out for her again.

Cassia ignores my outstretched hand. "Olivia is used to being disappointed. She'll be fine."

"Are we talking about Olivia's disappointment or yours?"

Cassia opens her mouth to respond but nothing comes out, except for a small mewing noise. She clamps her mouth shut and then brings both hands up to her ears. I don't know why Cassia is holding the sides of her head, and I'm concerned she might have a migraine or something. I rush toward her, but I'm stopped in my tracks by cameras popping off in my face.

The paparazzi have found a way past the inn's security detail! They're grinning gleefully as they shove their lenses in Cassia's face. Now she's sobbing, trying to run away, and I go berserk.

At least, that's what Jake tells me afterward, when I find myself staring up at him. I'm lying flat on my back on the library's Persian rug. "Cassia?" I mumble. "Is she?"

"She's fine," says Jake. "Sort of. She's pretty upset and said you tackled two of the paparazzi, knocked their heads together, and smashed their cameras. The third guy managed to put you in a choke hold, but he squeezed too hard and you passed out. He says he didn't mean to make you faint, and I tend to believe him."

"Ouch." I rub the back of my head. "Where's Cassia? We need to talk."

Jake gives me a hand up off the floor and guides me over to one of the wingback chairs. I nearly trip on a broken camera lens as I take my seat. Jake picks the other chair off the floor and sits down in it. "My sister doesn't want to talk to you right now. She says you're off to Nashville in the morning."

I groan, partly due to the pain in the back of my head, but mostly due to how much I've messed up things with Cassia. I explain the entire situation to Jake, including the fact I'm coming back to Riddle Hill.

"Did you tell Cassia you'll be back by Valentine's Day?" Jake asks.

"Of course, but I think she stopped listening to me by then. Not that I blame her. But the truth is I'm in love with Cassia. I can't imagine my life without her—I'll even relocate to your weird little town for her—and that's saying a lot, after tonight."

Jake sighs heavily. "Mrs. Barker?"

"Yeah, and your aunt's gargoyles, and those dogs-slash-wolves at Howling Shores Pub, and Doc Demetrius's fangs, and Rafe's fur-covered fist as he punched my lights out. And a bunch of other stuff too. Your town is like some secret government project, isn't it?"

"Huh?"

"You know, it's like another Roswell or something, where the CIA experiments on humans to create a super species. Although I still don't see how Cassia fits in, nor Olivia."

Jake starts to laugh, and I feel my temper rising. He must realize I'm in no mood for joviality, because he quickly sobers. "There is something different, and special and secret, about Riddle Hill. But before I tell you the truth, you have to swear you'll never tell another human soul."

I lean forward. "I swear, but please don't make me drink that horrible cocktail that Malaki uses to seal his vows."

"Malaki uses tart cherry juice mixed with salt and hot pepper sauce," says Jake, who removes a small knife from his jacket pocket and slashes the pad on his thumb. "This is much more serious."

He reaches over to do the same to my thumb, but I yank my hand back. "We need to perform a blood oath?" When Jake nods, I tell him, "Even though I want to know the truth, you're freaking me out. Plus, I need all ten fingers, nimble and uninjured, to play my guitar. Here—" I roll up my pants leg and pull down my sock "—cut my leg instead."

Jake rolls his eyes. "Fine." He makes a small slash, presses his bleeding thumb against the cut on my shin, and says, "We're now connected, blood to blood, man to man, species to species, in a bond never to be broken this side of the grave. Do you understand?"

"Yes, I understand." But do I really? My anxiety is ratcheting up another few notches. Just how weird *is* this place?

Jake pulls two bandages out of his pocket, hands me one for my leg, and slaps the other one over his thumb. He waits until I've secured the bandage and has my full attention.

Then he intones, "By the authority vested in me, Jake Grayclaw Spellman, Mayor of Riddle Hill, and affirmed just now by the elder council—that would be Doc

Demetrius, Catbeam Spellman, and Trixie Wolferman, all of whom were present tonight and observed Mrs. Barker's meltdown in front of a human eyewitness—and in consideration of the fact you are in love with my sister and wish to reside in our town, I will now reveal to you the truth about our village.

"Riddle Hill was founded by faeries in the eighteenth century to provide a safe haven for supernaturals fearing persecution after the Salem Witch Trials. Non-supers are welcome to live here so long as they demonstrate they can be trusted with our secret. And just so you know, most states have at least one town or village designated for paranormal species. California has five."

I wait for the rest of Jake's revelation, but he says nothing more. "That's it? No CIA, no secret government facility, no alien spaceships?"

Jake shakes his head. "Nope. Sorry to disappoint you, but supernaturals are just what we sound like; we're part of the natural order, same as you, but with special gifts. Some, like me and Teddy, are werewolves, and we've been gifted with strength. Others, like Malaki and Doc Demetrius, are vampires, but they don't drink blood—"

"They drink tart cherry juice instead!"

"Exactly."

"And Cassia and Olivia?" I ask, my voice faltering.

"They're faeries. Or to be more precise, Olivia is definitely a house faerie like her father, Derek, and Cassia is half faerie. She and I had the same human mother, but different supernatural fathers."

I gulp. The woman I love is half faerie! Her brother's a werewolf, her daughter's a house faerie—I guess there must be different kinds of faeries—and this whole town is nuts.

Then I realize my best friend lives here too. "And Sam? What's he?"

Jake blows out a puff of air. "Normally, I'd say you need to direct that question to Sam, but he's texted me a few times, telling me it's time for you to learn the truth about us." He hesitates and then looks me squarely in the eye. "Sam is a faerie, and Estee is a vampire."

I grip the arms of my chair. "And those gargoyles in your aunt's café, they're real, aren't they?"

"Yep, they're real. And those paparazzi you just tackled? They're actually goblins." Jake stands up. "Look, I know you have a lot to think about, and you're leaving for Nashville in the morning. Feel free to call me if you have any questions later. And if you decide you can't stomach living here in Riddle Hill with a bunch of supernaturals, at least come back one more time and tell Cassia why. I won't say anything to her until you take the first step."

I stand up, grip my guitar case, and mumble, "Understood."

We shake hands, and then I force myself to nod pleasantly at everyone I encounter as I'm leaving the inn. Once outside, I run all the way to my SUV, fighting back tears because the woman I love isn't who I think she is.

Cassia Spellman has the face of an angel, but she's only half human.

I sit inside the SUV, my chest heaving as everything I thought I knew comes crashing down around me. I've anchored my dreams on a future with Cassia, but now I'm sinking fast beneath a tidal wave of doubt.

It's probably just as well I'll be heading to Tennessee in the morning, if for no other reason than to take my mind off Cassia.

But my battered heart tells me that might be my hardest gig yet.

CHAPTER 32
DEPARTURES

CASSIA

Sunday, December 23

It's well past midnight, which means it's technically Sunday. I've been in the small restroom reserved for hotel staff for the past twenty minutes, maybe longer, sobbing and hiccupping. Mona has brought me water, pulled the pins out of my hair because my updo is a complete mess, and supplied me with a fresh box of tissues.

She's also the one who heard the commotion in the library and ran to get Jake, who arrived just as Will collapsed on the rug. I was hysterical by then, screaming Will's name and convinced the young, pouty goblin had killed him. The goblin looked equally horrified, probably afraid of the same thing.

Thank heavens for Jake, because he checked on Will, who was already coming to, and then he called security to round up the goblins. I seriously doubt I'll be seeing their foul faces anytime soon.

But the one face I want to see, despite the fact he's crushed my heart, is the only face I won't be seeing. Will is leaving for Nashville in the morning. Despite all his sweet talk and promises, Will is putting his career ahead of me and Olivia.

I dab my eyes again as Mona returns. "I just spoke with Jake. The goblins have left and so has Will. It's safe for you to come out now."

I let out a long, hollow breath, rinse my face in the sink, and pat it dry with a paper towel. Then I apply extra makeup to hide my splotchy skin, dab on fresh lipstick, and run a comb through my long tangles, ensuring my pointy ears are well camouflaged. I have to adjust my long bangs to hide my tipped-up eyebrows.

I'm not worried about any humans seeing me at this point; I don't want to let on to my family and friends that my faerie symptoms have broken out. They'll know something's very wrong, and I refuse to upset Sophie on her wedding day.

I'm just glad Phoebe and Nash have already left, and they brought Olivia home with them. They'll find out soon enough about Will, the goblins, and my broken heart.

Mona removes an ivory shawl from around her shoulders and drapes it across my back. "To hide your wings," she explains.

I turn to look at her. "But I don't have wings," I say. "Just baby wing stumps."

Mona snorts, pulls off the scarf, and turns me sideways so I can see my profile in the mirror. "Those are wings, Cassia!"

I touch the mirror, tracing the outline of my faerie wings, which are shockingly bright pink with touches of white and silver in the outer feathers. "I don't believe this! On the worst night of my life, my wings finally decide to manifest."

Mona repositions the scarf across my shoulders. "Remember to hold your wings tightly furled against your back." Then she whispers at my reflection, "You're a very brave woman. You're going to be just fine."

I turn around to face her. "Me, brave? You're the one who's spent the past decade sailing around the world!"

Mona shakes her head, her long, dark, curls bouncing. "I spent a decade running from love. But here you are, in love for the second time around."

"Not exactly," I stammer. "I've *loved and lost* twice now."

"I don't think you've lost Will at all," says Mona. "I've seen how that man looks at you, and he's definitely coming back for you."

"He's not coming back," I whisper as I leave the restroom.

I hold myself together long enough to say goodnight to everyone who's still in the ballroom, mostly the bridal party and a few of the elders, including Granny Catbeam. No one notices I've pulled out my updo, although Sophie does give me a look I choose to ignore. Fresh tears stream down my face as I drive home.

I unzip my maid-of-honor dress and let it drop in a green heap on my bedroom floor. I pull a flannel nightgown over my head and hear the fabric tearing as my new wings poke through the back.

Aargh.

My tops and dresses, which I purchase in town, are designed for faeries, although tonight is the first time I've needed the hidden openings in the back. However, I always use non-super nightgowns because they're half the cost. I couldn't see the point of splurging for my non-existent wings.

I stumble into the bathroom... I've got to get myself under control, but how?

I examine myself in the mirror: red eyes, runny nose, a pair of faerie ears and eyebrows, and a rather large pair of wings. I slowly wash the layers of makeup off my face, brush out my snarled mass of hair, and sniffle a lot. I swallow two ibuprofens for my throbbing head and shuffle into the kitchen. Taking a half-pint of peppermint fudge ice cream from the freezer, I grab a spoon and shuffle back to the living room, where I eat my ice cream while watching *White Christmas*.

But I forgot the movie focuses on performers—singers and dancers—falling in and out of love during Christmas. I finish my ice cream and turn off the movie prematurely, when misunderstandings and hurt feelings abound, when I can still identify with the characters. I'm tired of happy endings, where everything is wrapped up in a neat bow by the end of the story. Life just doesn't work like that.

Except for Phoebe and Nash, still in love with each other after thirty-three years of marriage. And then there's Sophie and Teddy, Marie and Beau, Estee and

Sam, and all the other couples I've helped get to the altar. My wedding planning business is predicated on the idea of happy couples tying the knot. I exhale a long, mournful breath and decide I'm not ready to throw in the towel on happy endings just yet.

The problem is those happy endings don't seem to be evenly distributed, and they skip over some people entirely.

I STIFLE a yawn as I pour coffee for one of the café's regulars. I had so little sleep that I'm practically sleepwalking on the job. I'm glad Olivia stayed over at Phoebe's house, where several out-of-town cousins are also spending the night. Olivia will have plenty of loving, attentive company until I can pick her up this afternoon.

A movement outside catches my eye; a black SUV slows down in front of the café's window, and my heart turns over. For a moment I think it might be Will, that maybe he's changed his mind about leaving, but then the vehicle speeds past. I shake my head. Sometime around three a.m. I promised myself I'd stop crying over Will. He's made his choice, his music career over me. There's nothing more to cry about.

As I carry the coffeepot to the warming plate behind the counter, the gargoyles all sigh in unison; they're being exceptionally nice to me today. Phoebe emerges from the kitchen, takes one look at my face, and blurts out, "What happened?"

I'm grateful Jake didn't tell anyone else about Will

and the goblins. I'm not ready discuss Will's departure just yet. The pain is still too fresh.

I shake my head. "I'm just tired."

"I've seen you tired, and this—" Phoebe waves her hand at me, "—isn't 'tired.' This is miserable. So out with it. What's going on?"

I focus on making a fresh pot of coffee so I won't see Phoebe's reaction, which I know will be sympathetic. I can't handle sympathy right now, because even a small dose will cause me to burst into tears all over again. My wings are gone, my ears and eyebrows are back to normal, and I don't want a relapse.

"Will's manager called him last night and told him he had to leave for Nashville right away," I say, "something to do with another act canceling at the club. His first performance is tomorrow night, on Christmas Eve. He's probably already left for the airport."

"Oh, I'm sorry, honey," says my aunt, and I can feel my eyes start to well up. "I know you were really looking forward to spending Christmas with Will. Did he say when he'd be back?"

I glance at my aunt and frown. Phoebe doesn't seem to understand what's really happening. Will left town, left me, so he can chase after his dream. He put his music above everything and everyone else. "It doesn't matter when he'll be back because I'm not waiting around for him. We're through, even before we really got started." I stammer, my voice catching in my throat.

Now it's Phoebe's turn to frown. "But why? It's clear he likes you and you like him. What's stopping you?"

"His music, which is more important to him than

anything else," I mumble, edging close to another bout of tears.

Phoebe stares at me. "Wait a minute. Please don't tell me you're comparing Will to Derek. The two men couldn't be farther apart—in temperament and in their feelings for you—than if they came from two different planets."

I bite my bottom lip and peer out the front window. The winter sky is beginning to brighten; the sun's almost over the horizon. "Will said one thing and is doing another. He's putting his music above everything else. And he's disappointing Olivia, who expects to see him at the Children's Pageant tomorrow. I'd say that sounds an awful lot like Derek."

"From what I understand, Will needs this job, needs to turn his career around, and his agent seems to think this is his best opportunity to do just that. His departure before Christmas has nothing to do with how he feels about you."

"His departure has everything to do with how he feels about me. It tells me what his priorities are." I cross my arms, miffed that my clear-thinking aunt can't understand my point of view.

"Could it be you're letting past hurts cloud your judgment?" asks Phoebe gently.

I ponder Phoebe's words for the rest of the morning, wondering whether I've judged Will too harshly. I decide it doesn't matter at this point, since Will is heading to Nashville, and I'm staying in Riddle Hill. Our lives intersected for a short while, and now they've diverged again. I have to put the past two weeks—as thrilling and heartrending as they've been—in the rearview mirror, same as Will.

Besides, Will knows nothing about my faerie heritage or Riddle Hill's unusual population, and that kind of secret is pretty hard to conceal after a while. Eventually, the elder council would have to agree to tell Will the truth.

He'd probably run off to New York in a flash at that point. And I couldn't blame him; it's a lot for the average human to handle.

My phone buzzes, and I glance at the screen. Phoebe must have clued in Sophie, because she's just sent this text: "Come see me at the bakery. Now!"

I write her back, "Don't want to talk about it."

I wish my well-intentioned, interfering cousin was already heading to her Costa Rican honeymoon, but Sophie can't afford to close the bakery during one of its busiest seasons. She and Teddy will be leaving the day after Christmas.

"You have to talk about it," texts Sophie.

I roll my eyes at my phone. "Fine," I type.

I start to tell Phoebe, but she just waves her hand. "Go on."

I toss my coat over my Sit for a Spell apron and walk across the street to the bakery. There's a long line of customers, so I sit down by the window and wait for my cousin. Sophie calls over one of her part-timers to man the counter for a while and pulls out a chair across from me.

"I'm so, so sorry. I know you're hurting right now," she says, squeezing my hand. I sniffle and nod. "And the best thing is to talk about it. Don't bottle it up inside. Tell me everything, what he said, what you said. I'm here for you."

I rub my forehead, exhale a shaky breath, and tell Sophie what happened, including the goblins showing up and fighting with Will. I don't mention my faerie wings manifesting, because that's something I should be celebrating, but how can I be happy about my wings when I'm so sad about everything else? When I'm finished, I swipe my damp cheeks and wait for the sympathetic pep talk I'm sure will come.

"Poor Cassia," says Sophie. "You've had an awful night—and frightening, with those paparazzi showing up and fighting Will—but it's not all bleak."

"What do you mean? Will *promised* he'd spend Christmas with me and Olivia, but he's already gone, on his way to Nashville to reboot his career."

Sophie sighs. "You're the smartest person I know, but you're completely wrong about Will. Guys like him come along *once in a lifetime*. If he said he's coming back, then he will. I think you should take Will at his word."

I don't understand why Sophie is taking Will's side in this. "Can't you see he's just another entertainer, here today and gone tomorrow? I've been there, done that, and I'm not doing it again."

"Oh, I see," says Sophie. "Will has to pass a special litmus test because he's a performer. If he were an electrician and had to go out of town before Christmas for his job, I guarantee you wouldn't overreact like this."

"I'm not overreacting." I'm blinking rapidly to stem another bout of tears.

"The man tells you he wants to spend Valentine's Day with you, and you send him packing. If that's not overreacting, I don't know what is." Sophie pats my shoulder as she stands up. "I'm sorry to be so darned honest, but you asked."

"Actually, I didn't ask. You volunteered," I point out. "But I appreciate it just the same, even though none of this matters."

"Of course it matters."

I put on my coat. "I guarantee Will's going to be so busy in Nashville he'll forget all about me."

"And I guarantee you're flat-out wrong," insists Sophie.

CHAPTER 33

TRUE BLUE CHRISTMAS

WILL

Sunday, December 23

Sam and Estee's plane landed an hour ago, and they'll be back home before lunch. I walk the dogs for the last time, freshen up their water bowls, and head out to my SUV. I've packed light—I won't be needing my fancy new clothes from Malaki's shop down in Nashville—so Sam's going to store my stuff for now.

It's still dark when I drive past the Sit for a Spell Café on my way out of town. I slow down a fraction, hoping for one last glimpse of Cassia. I glance through the café's plate-glass windows, holding my breath. There she is, pouring coffee for an old man in a ball cap, hunched over his Sunday paper. The café's lighting reflects off her blonde hair, creating a halo effect, which seems fitting given the season.

Instead of slamming on the brakes and running into the café to try talking with her, I press my foot on the accelerator. Cassia isn't the type of woman to be moved by more talking. She needs to see the actions behind the words, and unfortunately, the only move left to me now is to leave town so I can start earning a living again.

I have to kick-start my flagging career, and the music industry is ridiculously fickle; I'm walking proof of that. If I turn down this opportunity, I might not get another. At least Nashville is familiar territory, although I've never heard of the club where Mack is meeting me later tonight. Then again, I've been living in New York for the past couple of years and no longer keep up with the Nashville music scene.

I head south on Highway 42, the only car on the road this early on a Sunday. I have a long drive to O'Hare airport, plenty of time to think about Cassia and how much I've messed up everything.

And then there's what Jake told me about Riddle Hill —and about Cassia. I tossed and turned all night thinking about it. And you know what? I don't care that Cassia is half faerie and has a werewolf for a brother.

It doesn't change how I feel about her.

I FOLD myself into the sub-compact car I'm renting at the Nashville airport. This tiny vehicle isn't designed for a guy with my long frame, and I have to hunch over the steering wheel to fit inside. I was so upset when I made the airline reservations that I forgot to reserve an SUV, my vehicle of choice when I travel.

I punch the address Mack gave me into the maps app

on my phone and wait for the directions to pop up. As I follow the exit signs out of the airport, my thoughts wander back to Riddle Hill. Cassia will be dropping off the donated food and Christmas gifts for the homeless families right about now; maybe Jake will be helping her, or perhaps Phoebe and Nash.

Is she thinking about me as much as I'm thinking about her?

During my drive to O'Hare, on the flight down to Nashville, and now navigating through the city streets toward a gig I don't even want, all I can think about is the woman I left behind.

I spot a diner and pull into the parking lot. I skipped breakfast, had a bagel at the airport while running for my plane, and I'm hollowed out. I have to eat something before showing up at the club, but no amount of food will fill the hole I'm feeling inside.

This is a modest restaurant that seems to have a fairly loyal following, which brings to mind the Sit for a Spell Café, Nash's incredible cooking, Phoebe's crazy gargoyles, and the most beautiful server I've ever met. I pull open the door, determined to stop thinking about Riddle Hill and Cassia for the time being. I can't afford any distractions before my first solo performance.

But thinking about loving and losing Cassia Spellman isn't just a distraction—it's a major obstruction that I can't see my way around.

CHAPTER 34

DELIVERIES

CASSIA

Later Sunday

"That's the last box," I confirm, glancing at my clipboard for the McClain family. Sam and Estee, back from their honeymoon, volunteered to help deliver food and Christmas gifts to the families displaced by the fire. Sam has to rearrange the boxes a few times before he's able to close his trunk.

"I'm going to grab some coffee to go," says Sam, heading back inside the community center, which has served as a temporary warehouse for storing and sorting the donations. The Sit for a Spell Café has provided refreshments—coffee and pastries—to fortify the volunteers working this afternoon.

I turn to Estee, standing on the sidewalk beside me. "Thanks so much for delivering these to the McClains." One of the drivers I'd originally lined up had to work a second shift unexpectedly. Jake and Rob are making an extra delivery run for me, and I planned to make the last delivery myself. However, Sam and Estee heard about the fire and wanted to help.

"Of course." Estee nods. "It's the least we could do. We feel blessed in so many ways. We have our home, our three crazy dogs, and each other. When we heard about the fire, we had to help out."

"I feel the same way. Even when I'm having a not-so-great day, I still have Olivia, my family, and my home. It's just so easy to take things for granted, until one day you wake up and they're gone." Thinking of Will, I sputter and cough.

Estee glances at me. "Are you okay? You look kind of pale."

I wave my hand. "I'm fine. It's been a hectic month and to be honest, as much as I love Christmas, I'll be kind of glad when it's over."

What I don't tell her is that I lost my Christmas spirit with Will's departure. I feel like I have to pretend to be full of good cheer, when all I want is to crawl under my covers and stay there until New Year's.

But Phoebe would never let me wallow in my own misery; she'd pepper me with so much folksy wisdom that I'd have to keep going, just to stem the tide of her free advice. Besides, crawling under the covers isn't fair to Olivia, who loves Christmas and can hardly wait for December twenty-fifth to roll around.

My heart sinks even further when I think of Olivia. I went straight from my shift at the café to the community center to organize the deliveries. I still need to pick up

Olivia at my aunt's house, bring her home, and explain that Will won't be around for Christmas after all.

Estee hesitates and then plows ahead with what's on her mind. "I saw those photos of you and Will online."

"Oh," I say, shaking my head. "We had a wild few days here in Riddle Hill. I'm glad the paparazzi left town."

"What about Will?"

I squint at Estee, whom I've known since fifth grade. Even if it meant detention after school, Estee always spoke her mind and still does.

"What about him?" I ask cautiously.

"I probably shouldn't say anything because Sam and Will are best friends. But they texted a lot during our honeymoon, some stuff about the dogs and the house, but most of the stuff was about you."

"About me?"

Estee nods. "Sam says Will is crazy about you, and that he hasn't been this upbeat in a long time." Lowering her voice, she adds, "Will's had a pretty rough time of it with Roxie and then his mother's illness."

My head reels; I just can't reconcile what Estee is saying with the fact Will has left Riddle Hill and left me. I quickly fill in Estee, who listens without interrupting. When I finish, Estee replies, "I'm sure Will felt like he had no choice but to leave for this gig. But if he said he'd be back, then he will."

Sam rejoins us, carrying a cardboard tray with three coffees. Handing one to me, he says, "You look like you could use some." Sam offers me cream and sugar packets from one of his pockets.

I smile at him. "Thanks, Sam, for the coffee and for volunteering."

As Sam climbs into the driver's side, Estee gives me a quick hug before opening her car door. "Have a little faith. 'Tis the season!"

I step away from the curb and wave at them as they drive off. Sipping my coffee, I return to the community center to thank the volunteers and head home. Estee's parting words stir something inside me, something I want to think more about later. But first, I need to talk to Olivia.

SOON AFTER WE ARRIVE HOME, Olivia announces, "I need some wrapping paper please."

I meant what I said to Estee; I wish Christmas was over already. But I smile at my daughter's sweetness. "I thought we finished wrapping all the Christmas gifts."

Olivia shakes her head. "We forgot to wrap Will's."

Olivia and I had created a scrapbook for Will, capturing various moments during his time in Riddle Hill. Olivia had even insisted we include "the 'goblin-prazzi' part." She places the scrapbook on the kitchen table and waits for me to retrieve the wrapping paper and ribbon.

"Let's sit down first." I take Olivia's hand, guiding her into the living room. I sit on the sofa and pat the seat cushion next to me. I can't let Olivia continue to believe we'll be seeing Will for Christmas.

I clear my throat. "Remember when we thought Will had to leave before Christmas?"

"Yep." Olivia nods.

"Will found out last night that he had to leave early after all, *before* Christmas, because of his new job."

Olivia sticks her bottom lip out and thinks about it. "Is it a singing job?"

"Yes, he'll be singing in the town where he grew up."

"Okay," Olivia stands up and tugs my hand. "Let's go wrap his gift."

I'm surprised; Olivia is taking Will's departure better than I expected—far better than me. "But, honey, Will's already left Riddle Hill. He's not going to be here for Christmas. He wanted you to know he's really sorry to miss the Children's Pageant tomorrow."

"I still want to wrap his Christmas gift, so we can surprise him when he comes back."

"I'm not sure when he's coming back," I murmur, deciding it's simpler to wrap the gift than prolong the discussion.

As we finish tying the ribbon on the package, the doorbell rings. I drop the extra paper and ribbon on the kitchen table and go to open the door. A large, familiar-looking man wearing a red suit with white fur trim is standing on my front stoop.

"Santa... Jake?"

Jake booms in his deep voice, "Ho, Ho, Ho, Merry Christmas! Grab your coats and come join me for a ride!"

"Is it a sleigh ride?" squeals Olivia, who's run up behind me.

"Santa's heard you were a good girl this year and

wants to take you for a special ride." Jake waves his hand behind him, where two dappled gray horses pulling a white carriage wait in the street. "But we need to hurry, since Santa has other stops to make."

Olivia's eyes widen. She flings open the hall closet, dragging out her coat and boots. "Hurry up, Mommy! Santa is waiting."

I look at my brother and mouth, "Thank you!" Grabbing my coat and hat, I follow Olivia out the front door. Jake helps us climb into the carriage, which is lit on all sides with tiny white lights and draped with red bows and green holly. Red ribbons adorn the horses' manes, and sleigh bells run along their leather leads, jingling whenever they move.

Jake picks up the leads. He expertly guides the horses down the road, toward Riddle Hill Park and the harbor, as a light snow begins swirling in the sky above us. Nearly every house sports Christmas lights and decorations, brightening our route. Neighbors smile and wave when they spot Jake in a Santa suit, shouting "Merry Christmas!" as our carriage passes them.

Olivia asks a few questions about the horses and then settles under the heavy woolen blanket on the seat, content to watch and wave at the passersby.

Jake glances over at me and asks softly, "Do you want to talk about it?"

I frown slightly. "Not really."

"I understand... but let me just say this. I was pretty hard on Will when he first arrived and kept aiming his puppy dog eyes in your direction. But as I've gotten to know him better, I've learned to respect him... quite a bit, in fact. Will deserves another chance, and so do you."

I shrug. "Maybe. But Will is busy relaunching his career, which could take him all over the country, and I'm not doing that again. Besides, he's the one who left me, remember?"

"When his gig is over, he'll be back, I'm sure of it. But you'll need to let him know he's welcome back."

I blow out a puff of air. "We'll see."

Changing the subject, I say, "I thought it was interesting that Mona ran to you last night, and not the security guards, or anyone else for that matter. Care to comment?"

Jake raises his fake white eyebrows at me. "I've liked Mona Lisa DeMaris since we were kids. But she's never given me any encouragement. Besides, she's only here until her dad is well enough to run the inn again on his own."

"Oh well..." I humph. "I thought maybe you and Mona might be good for each other."

"Well you never know what the future holds, now do you?" replies my cryptic brother. Perhaps there *is* a spark between Jake and Mona after all. If I can do anything to fan the flame between those two lonely hearts, I definitely will. Maybe Phoebe and Sophie can help me.

After Olivia goes to bed, still chatting about her carriage ride, I open my purse and retrieve my phone, which I intentionally stashed away for the day, with the sound turned off.

No messages from Will. Not that I'd expected him to call, but I can't help myself. I've gotten used to having

Will Rossi in my life; now I'll have to adjust to having him gone.

I consider texting to see if he arrived safely in Nashville but decide it's too soon. After all, if Will is really interested in what—and who—he left behind in Riddle Hill, he'll be the one to reach out first.

Right?

CHAPTER 35
CHILDREN'S PAGEANT

CASSIA

MONDAY, DECEMBER 24

I feel my phone vibrating in my back jeans pocket as I drop off three more lunch orders for Nash to prepare in the kitchen. Packed with the normal Monday crowd, plus last-minute shoppers and kids home from college, the café's customers are keeping me so busy I only have time to think of Will whenever I pass his old booth. Then a small pang stabs my chest, and I take a deep breath and move on.

Since I dash past that booth at least every five minutes, I'm doing a lot of sighing; one of my customers even asks if I have asthma. I want to tell her no, just a broken heart, but I shake my head and keep going.

I hesitate before pulling out my phone to look at the missed call, hoping it might be Will. Disappointed again, I carry the phone into Phoebe's small office and call Sophie back.

"How many times have I bailed you out of a hot mess for one of your weddings?" asks Sophie.

"Not fair!" I grumble good-naturedly. "I get to guilt you into doing favors for me, not the other way around."

"I know it's Christmas Eve, but I'm desperate. Can you give me a hand at the bakery after your shift? Two of my part-timers had to travel out of town for Christmas, and my third helper is expecting her third child. She needs to get off her feet, like now."

I run through my afternoon schedule; if I help Sophie, someone else will need to deliver Olivia and her costume to the high-school auditorium one hour before curtain time for the Children's Pageant. I figure I can probably ask one of the parents to take Olivia, who at the moment is home baking Christmas cookies with her favorite babysitter, a fourteen-year-old with a killer recipe for chocolate-gingerbread men. "Let me find someone to drive Olivia, and I'll see you in about an hour."

"You're a lifesaver!"

"It takes one to know one, Soph—and I mean that in the best way possible." I call one of the pageant organizers to arrange a ride for Olivia.

When I return to the front, I discover the gargoyles are performing the can-can to the general amusement of the entire dining room. Even I have to laugh.

Phoebe scoots past me to place two more lunch orders. "Everything okay?"

"When I'm finished here, I'm going to run over to the bakery to give Sophie an extra hand."

"Oh." Phoebe draws out the "oh" sound, pursing her lips.

I look at my aunt, surprised by her tone. "What's that supposed to mean?"

Phoebe shakes her head. "It's nothing. Nash wants your grandmother's double-fudge chocolate cake for Christmas dessert. I thought you might be able to bake it this afternoon and bring it tomorrow. But you're not going to have any more time than I will, so don't worry about it; I'll think of something."

I cock my head to the side, trying to unwind my aunt's sentence. Nash rarely asks anyone for anything, and I definitely want to help. Besides, I've never tried that recipe before, which has become part family legacy and part myth. Granny Catbeam, Aunt Phoebe, and Sophie each made that cake for their future husbands.

The funny thing is that Phoebe only recently gave me the recipe. It never occurred to me to ask her sooner... which is why I never made the double-fudge chocolate cake for Derek.

"I'll have time tomorrow morning, after Olivia opens her presents and before we come over to your house. It'll be fun. Olivia and I will learn that recipe together." I sound more upbeat than I feel. I'll be baking a dessert the Spellman women have made for their true loves for generations, and I have no one special in my life to share it with. How sad is that?

"Great idea... and thanks!" Phoebe gives my arm a quick squeeze before the two of us scurry back to our tables.

I arrive at the Rhyme 'N Riddle Bakeshop to a throng

of customers becoming slightly impatient with the slow-moving line. Tossing my puffer coat onto a hook, I grab a frilly black apron with the bakery's name stitched in green letters across the breast pocket, and begin serving customers. Several hours later, with the bakery cases nearly bare and the last customer wishing us a good Christmas on their way out, we lock the door.

Sophie flips the sign in the window to Closed, leans back against the door, and heaves a relieved sigh. "Thanks. I couldn't have done it without you. Actually, I couldn't have done half the stuff in my life without you alongside me."

I smile, remembering one Christmas many years ago. Phoebe and Nash invited the same elderly faerie to Christmas dinner every year, because otherwise she'd spend the holiday with only her cats for company. Sophie and I had promised each other we'd never let either of us spend Christmas alone. So far, we've kept that promise.

"Right back at you, Soph."

Sophie hesitates before asking, "How are you doing?"

My eyes cloud over, and my voice wavers. "I can't get him out of my head."

"You haven't called him yet?"

I shake my head. "I've been kind of hoping he'd be the first to call. But I'll call him tonight if I haven't heard from him. Olivia and I want to wish him good luck with his new gig."

"That's a great idea. I'm sure Will is missing you as much as you're missing him. Performing on Christmas Eve doesn't sound like too much fun to me."

I nod, glance at the clock on the wall behind Sophie's head, and squeal. "Olivia's performance is in thirty minutes! I was going to run home to change, but I better just run!" I remove my apron, smooth my cranberry turtleneck sweater over my black jeans, and grab my coat from the hook.

Sophie waves me out the door. "Teddy and I will meet you over there."

I slip on my coat as I jog to the car. I'd reserved a row of seats near the middle of the main section for the Spellman-Brownlee clan: Phoebe, Nash, Jake, Sophie, Teddy, and me. I gave my extra ticket—Will's ticket—to Mona, because she hasn't seen the pageant in ten years. Besides, I didn't want to leave an empty seat in the row. I don't need any more reminders that Will is gone.

I have barely enough time to park and run backstage to give Olivia a big hug before someone flicks the lights to indicate the show is beginning momentarily. One of the pageant volunteers walks onstage, reminding the audience to take their seats and silence their phones.

I find my seat and sit down between Jake and Sophie. The curtain rises on a stable where the animals, including Olivia as the Talking Donkey, tell the Christmas story. They're assisted by a chorus of angels and shepherds praising the newborn king, who loves *everyone*, even quirky supernaturals.

Olivia delivers her lines like she's born for the stage, which I sincerely hope is not the case. On the other hand, if Olivia really wants that someday, I'll help her get there.

When the performance ends, the audience erupts into a standing ovation as all the children gather to take a bow. The pageant director walks to the front of the stage, the curtain closing behind her. She waits for the applause to subside before thanking the volunteers, the children, and the community for their support. Then she adds, "And now, we have a very special treat for you, so please take your seats."

As we sit back down, Sophie whispers, "What's going on? This isn't the type of a show with an encore, is it?"

I glance around the auditorium and whisper, "Everyone else seems just as puzzled."

The director smiles broadly. "Ladies and gentlemen, please join me in welcoming Will Rossi, who will be performing an original Christmas song for the very first time, right here in Riddle Hill!" The crowd breaks into wild cheering and applause as the director slips behind the curtain.

"Will?" I whisper, my hand clutching the front of my sweater. The director has made a terrible mistake. Will is in Nashville, getting ready to perform at a club in a few more hours.

The curtain opens, and the best-looking man in Riddle Hill is sitting on a stool in front of a microphone, a red, twelve-string guitar resting in his lap. He looks so at home up there, in his green plaid shirt, blue jeans, and cowboy boots... like he's where he belongs. All of the pageant children, still in their costumes, sit on the floor scattered around his stool. Olivia has managed to scoot right beside him.

Sophie grabs my hand. "Will's here, honey. He came back."

I nod, still in shock, "But why?"

Sophie smiles. "Isn't it obvious?"

I shake my head, unable to answer.

Will speaks into the mic, his Nashville twang melting my resistant heart. "My song is called 'Second Chance Christmas,' and I'd like to dedicate it to Cassia Spellman." He strums the opening chords to the melody that I remember from his composition book, the tune that got inside my head and wouldn't let go.

I bring my hand to my mouth, not sure whether to laugh out loud or cry happy tears. Jake pokes me in the side. "Go on, get up there."

Mona chimes in, "Go backstage so you can be there when Will is finished singing."

Phoebe leans across Teddy and Sophie and says in a stage whisper that can be heard two rows back, "This is your second chance, Cassia, now go get it."

I take a steadying breath, squeeze past Jake and Mona, and slip out of the row. I head up the side aisle until I reach one of the doors leading backstage.

As I walk, I'm listening to Will's lyrics about second chances at various stages in life, after an illness, a bumpy career, and heartbreak. He sings about believing you'll never love again, and then finding your second-chance-at-happiness love where you never thought to look.

One of my friends from previous pageants guides me to left stage. I watch Will finish his song to loud applause and shouts of: "Encore!"

Olivia spots me and whispers to Will, who glances over at me with a boyish smile. He beckons to me, and I hesitate, suddenly shy. Olivia runs over to the wings and takes my hand. When I step onstage, the crowd erupts in another round of applause. I want to turn right around, but Olivia's small hand in mine calms my jangly nerves.

We stand next to Will, who's giving me his signature grin. I chuckle at him, and he winks. Then he turns to the children clustered around us and asks, "Can you help me out with the next number?"

Will begins singing, *Have Yourself a Merry Little Christmas*, and calls out to the audience, "Come on now, everybody join in." I sing alongside Will as Olivia holds my hand and carols with gusto.

When we reach the end of the song, we all shout in unison, "Merry Christmas!" The curtain closes to one final burst of applause. Pageant volunteers begin guiding the children backstage, where their parents are picking them up.

Jake steps onstage and calls over to Olivia. "Say, little donkey, how about you come back to Aunt Phoebe's house with me?" Olivia throws her arms around me and Will, and then skips across the stage, slipping her hand into Jake's.

Will stands up, places his guitar flat across the top of the stool, and waits. I realize it's up to me to make the next step.

"You came back," I say softly, my voice quivering with emotion.

"I told you I'd be back by Valentine's Day."

"You're a bit early." I smile up at him.

Will grins. "Is that a problem?"

I shake my head. "Not at all. I'm just curious, I guess. I thought you needed this job."

"I thought so too, until I saw the club Mack had

booked me into. I fired him on the spot. It wasn't any place I'd ever be comfortable taking you to, or my mother, for that matter. I realized I'd been a fool, leaving you behind in Riddle Hill while I chased after something I didn't even want."

I have one more question. "I know how worried you've been about rebooting your career. What are you going to do now?" Will he be staying in Riddle Hill or leaving again for the next gig in some other town?

Will draws himself up straighter. "You're looking at the proud new owner of Goldmeadow. I'll have a lot of work to do to get it ready for the concert season next summer. I'm going to need help from the most organized person I've ever known."

"*You* bought Goldmeadow? I thought it was some company!"

"It was my LLC, which I'd set up a couple of months ago in case I came across any real estate I wanted to purchase. It provides me with anonymity," says Will. "Not even your friend Rob knew I'd bought the place."

I remember something... something important. "Rob told me Goldmeadow was sold when I saw him at Sophie's wedding, which means you planned on coming back all along, didn't you?"

"Yep, which as I recall, I did try telling you." Will pauses and adds with a mischievous glint in his eyes, "Of course, I did have a moment of sheer panic when I real-ized I'd bought property in a supernatural village."

My mouth drops open. "You know about Riddle Hill?"

"Yes, ma'am." Will's eyes twinkle with amusement.

"Turns out my best friend, Sam, is a faerie; I sure didn't see that coming. I know Jake, Teddy, and Rob are were-wolves, and Doc Demetrius, Malaki, and Estee are vampires—which explains all the tart cherry juice—and the rest of your family are faeries."

"Who told you?"

"Jake. The elders gave him permission to tell me after Mrs. Barker's display of fur at the wedding." Will chuckles. "After word got out I knew about Riddle Hill's unique qualities—and that I'd purchased Goldmeadow and was courting you—the floodgates opened. I think I heard from half the town. "

"Oh!" I clap my hands over my ears, which have suddenly gone faerie-pointy.

My heart's fluttering and my face is tingly, but oddly enough, my tongue isn't sticking to the roof of my mouth. I hear a flap of wings bursting through the hidden slits in my sweater, and Will's eyes grow wide. Suddenly, shiny sparkles of magic are swirling all around me and Will, embracing us in a bright, pink, twinkly glow.

"Oh," I repeat. "Pink magic!"

Will pushes my hair back from my ears and smiles. "Ooh... I like your faerie ears." He runs a finger over my brow. "And your cute, tipped-up eyebrows. I can see the Tinker Bell resemblance."

I roll my eyes. "Aunt Phoebe?"

He nods. "She said you need to believe again for your faerie magic to shine through."

"But I've always believed in magic."

Will shakes his head gently. "You believed in

everyone else's magic, and in their happy, faerie-tale endings, but not your own."

My eyes well with happy tears; I don't trust myself to say anything.

Will gazes at me and whispers, "Well, Miss Cassia, I'm happy to stand here all night on this stage with you, but I think they'll be wanting to close the doors pretty soon. It *is* Christmas Eve."

I laugh as Will wraps his arms around me. "I'm glad you came back," I murmur. Pure joy bubbles up inside me, making me feel almost giddy, like Olivia on Christmas morning. I stand on my tiptoes, put my arms around Will's neck, and kiss my gorgeous boyfriend squarely on the lips.

Will draws me closer to prolong the kiss. "And why is that?" he asks playfully.

"I'm baking Granny Spellman's famous double-fudge chocolate cake for Christmas—you wouldn't want to miss it."

"Hmm." Will nuzzles my hair. "Christmas in Riddle Hill with the Spellman-Brownlee clan, double-fudge chocolate cake and all. Count me in."

EPILOGUE – RAINBOW CONFETTI

WILL

Thursday, February 14

I'm standing up front in the little chapel at Mooncrest Inn, wearing my black designer suit from Malaki's, my polished leather boots, and a *pink tie*. Yep, bright pink —because that's what Cassia wants.

When it comes to wedding planning, and keeping me organized, and most other things too, my beautiful bride knows best.

"She's almost ready," whispers Nash, taking his seat with Phoebe in the first pew on the left. My parents are coming up behind them, and they sit across the aisle on the right side of the room. My mom beams at me, and I grin back.

I'm more nervous than I expect, but then again, I'm marrying a faerie, settling down in a supernatural village, and renovating Goldmeadow for the summer concert season. A lot is changing—and for a change, all of it is really, really good.

The quartet (my human relatives don't know they're vampires, but I do) begins playing the processional. It's an all-string version of my new single, *Second Chance Christmas*, which Cassia asked me to arrange for her Valentine's Day wedding.

Olivia is all smiles as she walks down the aisle, tossing silk rose petals from her basket. She's excited for me to become her stepdad, but I'm the one who's truly lucky. I have a lot to learn when it comes to parenting a faerie child, and Olivia is very patient with me.

Here comes my sister, Maggie, escorted by Jake, followed by Estee and Sam, and then Sophie and Teddy. The ladies are wearing various shades of pink and purple, which I've learned is Olivia's favorite color.

Now everyone's rising and turning toward the back of the chapel to see the bride, who's gazing up the aisle at me.

Cassia's honey-blonde hair falls in soft layers around her shoulders, just the way I like it. She's wearing a short, pleated, bright pink dress with a scoop neckline, dangly earrings that twinkle as she walks toward me, and glass beads around her slender neck.

Is it possible for a guy to swoon for love? I don't know, but I'm feeling a little faint at the moment and pretty choked up.

I take a deep breath to steady myself, and then I give Cassia my most winsome grin. When she smiles back, my heart explodes in a starburst of happiness. I'm beginning to have a better appreciation for faerie tales about the magic of true love.

Cassia hands her bouquet of pink and white roses to Sophie, and we face the minister together. He's a short, rotund gnome with a pointy white beard who's both jolly and efficient.

I want to remember every detail of this ceremony, but it flies past. Before I know it, we're exchanging our vows and wedding bands, and then the minister pronounces us husband and wife.

Now comes the part I've been waiting for, the best part of the ceremony. "You may kiss the bride," says the gnome with a wink.

I take Cassia in my arms and kiss her slowly, completely, leaving no doubt in her mind—or in the minds of every super and non-super crammed into this small chapel—that I'm madly in love with this woman. When I finally straighten, Cassia reaches her arms around my neck and pulls me close for one more long, sweetly satisfying kiss. Our family and friends burst into applause and even a few whistles and cheers.

"Well, my lovely Miss Cassia," I murmur. "Our fans are waiting for us to kick off this party. Let's lead the way."

As we link arms, my bride giggles. When I raise my eyebrows, she explains, "Brilliant sparkles are spinning all around us. Every faerie in the room is showering us with a dusting of magic. It's sort of like magical rainbow confetti."

We both laugh, and I lean down again to kiss Cassia

Tinker Bell Spellman—the half-faerie girl of Riddle Hill who's captured my whole heart.

CATBEAM SPELLMAN'S SECRET RECIPE

DANGEROUS DOUBLE-FUDGE CHOCOLATE CAKE

IF YOU'RE IN LOVE AND TRULY WANT TO SEAL THE DEAL, THEN bake this cake with intentionality and serve it to your sweetheart. It wouldn't hurt to throw a pinch of salt over each shoulder while you're at it. But if you have any doubts whatsoever about your heart's desire, then do the sensible thing and wait.

Cake ingredients and instructions:

2 cups sugar

½ cup margarine

¾ cup cocoa

2 eggs

2 cups flour plus pinch of salt

2 teaspoons baking powder

2 teaspoons baking soda

1 cup milk

1 cup brewed coffee (boiling or very hot)

Preheat oven to 350 degrees. Cream sugar and shortening. Add cocoa and eggs and mix well. Add all other ingredients in the order given and blend well. The batter will be very thin. Bake in a tube pan for about an hour or until the cake springs back when lightly touched. Let it cool thoroughly before frosting.

Fudge frosting ingredients and instructions:

2 squares (2 ounces) unsweetened chocolate

1 can sweetened condensed milk

1 tablespoon water

1 teaspoon vanilla

Heat water in double boiler. Break chocolate into small pieces and place it with the sweetened condensed milk into the top of the double boiler. Heat the chocolate and condensed milk for about five minutes, stirring constantly until chocolate is melted and mixture is thickened. Add water and vanilla. Remove from heat and allow mixture to cool completely before frosting the cake.

Slice and serve the first piece of the cake to your true love. And, my dear faerie child, remember all things are sweeter if served with a smile!

AUTHOR'S NOTE

Thanks so much for reading *Half a Faerie*! I hope you enjoyed this sweet, closed-door paranormal romance about Cassia Spellman, the half-faerie single mom, and Will Rossi, the out-of-work rock star in need of a second chance. I've been carrying this story around in my head for a decade, and I'm so happy it's now in print. Please consider taking a moment and leaving a review, even a sentence or two. Reader reviews help other readers discover new books—and they are vitally important for indie authors like me.

If you're new to the Faeries of Door County series, each novel is a standalone story focused on a different main character from the Spellman family. Chronologically speaking, *Rhyme, Riddle, and Romance* occurs the summer before the events in *Half a Faerie* and *Return to Mooncrest Inn*, however, the books can be read and enjoyed in any order.

Producing a book is a collaborative process, and this one is no exception. Many people helped to shape this story, including friends, family, and my husband Steve, who read and commented on early drafts, Martha Reineke of MK Editing who provided invaluable feedback, Diogo Leite of Book Design Company who designed the cover and character art, and my amazing

ARC team of readers and reviewers. I adore you all—
thank you!

Lastly and most importantly, I give thanks to my
Heavenly Father, the Author of the greatest story ever
told. All other love stories pale in comparison to His.

Toni Cabell
John 1:1

BOOKS BY TONI CABELL

If you're looking for sweet, slow-burn romance with swoony kisses, second chances, and funny, heartwarming characters, don't miss the complete **Faeries of Door County** series. Winner of Best Paranormal Romance, each novel is a standalone story set in the same cozy small town:

- *Rhyme, Riddle, and Romance*
- *Half a Faerie*
- *Return to Mooncrest Inn*

A fast-paced adventure full of magic, romance, humor, sword fighting, dangerous creatures, and the power of light versus darkness, **Serving Magic** is a YA Epic Fantasy series with Steampunk and Regency vibes. Winner of The Wishing Shelf Book Awards and recognized by Indies Today as a Top 5 YA Fantasy series by an indie author:

- *Lady Apprentice, Book 1*
- *Lady Mage, Book 2*
- *Lady Liege, Book 3*
- *Lady Spy, Book 4*
- *Lady Reaper, Book 5*

In the arid hills of Toresz, there's one thing more dangerous than divining for water... falling in love with the enemy. **Water Witch** is YA Romantasy duology packed with action, danger, intrigue, royal politics, and romance. Winner of The Wishing Shelf Book Awards:

- *The Lightness of Water, Book 1*
- *The Way of Water, Book 2*

Find all Toni's available books and upcoming new releases on tonicabell.com and Amazon. All her novels are also available in audiobook format on Audible and Apple Books.

About the Author

Toni Cabell is a closed-door fantasy romance author whose books reflect her Christian values, which means you'll find no swearing, no excess violence, and no spice. Here's what you *will* find...

- Clean fantasy | magical worlds
- Wholesome romance | just kisses
- Deep friendships | quirky families
- Sassy and strong gals | swoony and protective guys
- (YA books) Swords and battles | no gory descriptions

Her novels have won Silver and Bronze Medals in The Wishing Shelf Book Awards, two Gold Medals in the Global Book Awards, multiple B.R.A.G. Medallions, and awards for writing Clean YA Fantasy from Incipere Awards.

Toni lives with her handsome husband in a small village along the shores of Lake Michigan, where she's able to walk to the bookstore, library, coffee shop, and bakery (although not always in that order). She's happy to report her adult children reside nearby and provide her with a steady supply of affection, amusement, and just the right smattering of chaos.

Toni loves to stay in touch with her readers. Please sign up for her newsletter at tonicabell.com, where you can download two free novellas:

Toni posts regularly about her indie author journey, life lessons, what inspires her, and her books on Instagram and Facebook. Also consider joining her Reader Group on Facebook, @onceuponaswoon, where she hangs out with some of her closed-door author friends and readers like you.

www.ingramcontent.com/pod-product-compliance
Lightning Source LLC
Chambersburg PA
CBHW022011310726
48972CB00006B/1602